IMPERIOUS
PUBLISHING

Praise for The Ten Year Date

"Henderson's writing is captivating and fluid with erotic undertones. ***The Ten Year Date*** is the bible for women who have dated one man for far too long. Well written and worth reading."

-Black Issues Book Review

"The Ten Year Date will make you think, act, and restructure your relationship.

A must read for every woman who has dated one man without a commitment."

-Bebe Moore Campbell, Author

"With ***Sunshine Has Rain,*** Author Sherrance Henderson inspired us with a tail of triumph over despair now she brings Channa back to us. In a tantalizing tail of non committal boyfriends, brothers on the down low, drama loving sisters, voodoo spells, secrecy and more lies. Readers will be taken on a hard knock journey with Channa that gets emotional, bold and vulgar while remaining a riveting page turner."

-Bruce Banter- Cultural Critic and Book Reviewer Playahata.com

"Several letters shy of R-A-U-N-C-H-Y, this R-A-C-Y erotica-spirituouso proves Channa's ability to overcome shortsightedness, carnality and her overwhelming circumstances with Faith, Spirit and the WORD."

-Michael Llraé Clark, BlackPlanet.com

"Sexy, Powerful, and Lustfully Devious...an explosively dynamic tale of control, deceit, and passion. A page turning delight."

-Dewar Empire Films
www.DewarEmpireFilms.com

"Sherrance Henderson keeps it real with this graphically detailed book. Everyone who has either had their heart abused, emotions torn by sex and their head toyed with by lies can reflect and relate with this book."

-Don Diva Magazine

"***The Ten Year Date*** by Sherrance Henderson is a wake up call for sistahs all over the world to take responsibly for their beautiful black wombs. It is a gripping ride through the twisted reality of black sexuality; a fresh voice with a sensual melody."

-Jessica Holter, Founder, The Punany Poets
www.jessicaholter.com

"***THE TEN YEAR DATE***: Sex, Secrets, and Lies by Sherrance Henderson is a sexy, steamy romantic tale filled with angst, tension and suspense."

-Alice Holman
RAWSISTAZ.com

"Powerful story that will make a woman evaluate what she believes is important to her when it comes to relationships. It forces you to realize that all that glitters is not gold."

-Alissa R. Terrell...Member of S.I.S.T.E.R Book Club, Troy Michigan
Membership by invite only

"Interesting page turner.....will keep you on the edge of your seat wanting more!"

-Kenyatta Ingram, SistaGirl Founder/President, Chesapeake, Virginia
Sistagirlbookclub.com

"Wonderfully written, honest, powerful, provocative, and a real page turner. Definitely a great book club choice."

-Keesha Parker, Sisters of Unity Book Club, Church Falls Virginia
Sistersofunity.com

"An excellent read. Many women have experienced the cheating brothas, the employed but whorish brothas, and the he just looks too good to be attracted to another brotha- brotha, but it happens. Not to mention the, I-will-do-anything- to- get- him- brothas, but, I warn you ladies to be careful of what you ask for because, you just might get it. ***The Ten Year Date*** is intriguing, enlightening, scary and real to the core. A worth while read and should be read by both women and men who date men; especially those in a long term relationship with a man that won't commit."

-Terra Nealy, Woman2Woman
Book Club of DeLand, Florida
www.woman2woman.4t.com

"Wow! I am speechless. I think, I was more nervous than Channa waiting for the results. This was a very powerful story that is a wonderful resource for HIV Awareness. The story was so real and believable. There are brothers in our community that live this life so carelessly and only thinking about themselves and there are so many sistas that were not as lucky at Channa. The characters were well developed in this story which played a major part in being believable. I will definitely recommend this bond to my club as a monthly selection. Thanks for enlightening message of HIV within our community and its strong presence amongst us today."

-Shonta Bass, President, a.k.a FLYYGAAL
GAAL BOOK CLUB of ATLANTA
www.gaalbookclub.citymaker.com

Praise for Sunshine Has Rain

"A story of redemption...very human and relatable."
-Black Issues Book Review Magazine

"You'll admire Channa's intellect, be intrigued by her sense of humor, touched by her courage, and cry because of her strength. No matter where you are in life right now, ***Sunshine Has Rain*** should be read by any and everyone."

-Kareema Cockrell
Sister2Siter Magazine

"***Sunshine Has Rain*** is a tale of inspiration, grit to glory, and reminder that life is not always what we wish it to be. An excellent life lesson tale that should be read by everyone.
-Bruce Banner
Playahata.com

"***Sunshine Has Rain*** is powerful, and will enthrall readers with a captivating tale of life's triumphs and tragedies. An excellent story! A novel one just has to include in their collections of Must Read materials."
-J. Zamgba Browne, Senior Reporter
The New York Amsterdam News

"In ***Sunshine Has Rain,*** Channa's journey begins in a one-dimensional world where she is fed only by her physical desires. However, the story comes full circle showing Channa's redemption and development into a three-dimensional being that recognizes that she has a mind, body and spirit to nourish. What an evolution! What a testimony! What a great read!"
-Michael Llraé Clark
BlackPlanet.com

"Moving and heart wrenching, the author of ***Sunshine Has Rain*** proves that she is an unpretentious storyteller with a candid ability to capture life's ever-changing lanes on which we all must travel."

-Black Diaspora Magazine

"As Ms. Henderson delved deeper into her storyline, I found myself totally engrossed in this very realistic portrayal of one woman's realization that in this thing called life, we must go through the storm in order to fully enjoy the sunshine."

-Renee Williams
RAWSISTAZ.com

"Page tuner for all readers not just ones with Spinal Cord Injuries. ***Sunshine Has Rain*** is a well written novel and a thought provoking story."

-Lori A. Woods, Orbit Magazine
***United Spina*l**

*"**Sunshine Has Rain*** is a cautionary tale for the 21st century woman. Through Channa's heroine, the author Sherrance Henderson takes the reader on a heartfelt and triumphant journey from superficiality and self-centeredness to a spiritual awakening."

-Cynthia Franklin, Editor-in-Chief
KIP Business Report

*"**Sunshine Has Rain*** is excellent introduction to the world of fictional writing for first time author Henderson. You will laugh, get mad, cry, and value all the things which are not material. ***Sunshine Has Rain,*** will teach you that life is precious, so enjoy it! Highly recommend read."

-Blue Notes from Blue World Travel
Largest African American Cruise Line in the world serving over 100,000 Black Travelers yearly.

"Sherrance Henderson writes the way she talks: engaging, witty, down-to-earth, and rich in wisdom. This is not just another books on self-realization and relationships. ***Sunshine Has Rain*** is magnetic in its drawing power, provocative in its style, and encouraging in its earthiness. I have devoured this book and anxiously await the next!!!"

-Tiffany G. Shepard
Actor/Model/Vocalist

"***Sunshine Has Rain*** is an outstanding inspiring motivating read!

My beliefs have been confirmed; it's who you are on the inside and our relationship with our Heavenly Father that gets us through the rain, so we may appreciate the sunshine even more the second time around."

-Tracy Howard, Author
Poetic Diary

"Excellent read that you won't want to put down. Well written page tuner."

-Sistahs Who Read African-American Writers a.k.a SoRaw

Sex, Secrets, & Lies

SHERRANCE HENDERSON

a.k.a Queenbee of Fiction™

Acknowledgments

My life isn't always Sunshine, and isn't always filled with Rain. Sometimes, there needs to be a couple of storms for me to appreciate the glory of Sunshine and the pain of Rain. In 2007, I am enjoying the Sunshine, but I hold tightly to the gray thoughts of my Rain. I guess that is life. Sometimes life has Sunshine, and sometimes life has Rain.

I thank God for saying "yes" to my first novel, ***Sunshine Has Rain***. I gave my heart and soul to my readers. I put my heart and soul into creating it for my readers' enjoyment. Life doesn't stop when changes enter the door; I just had to learn how to change when true "change" came. *Feel me?*

Milton A. Dewar, thank you for being the best companion a woman could ask for. When tears dropped like rain, when I felt discouraged, when I couldn't find my Sunshine, you would always say, "Don't cry baby, don't look down. Hey, somebody loves you." Thank you.

To my mother, grandmother, brother, and Auntie G., thank you for always doing all that you could to help me succeed in this world of publishing. Whatever I do, it seems like you guys are always are my biggest cheerleaders. Thank you, thank you, and thank you all again. Auntie Max, thanks for spreading the word about my novels to each and every person you meet. Thanks for never letting bad blood come between us.

T. Adams, Esq., thanks for letting the wolves out when we needed to kill the dogs. M. Clark, what are friends for? You showed me the meaning of friendship in all that you do. Bro Leroy, you always help me in time of need. Thank you. Eric at A and B Books, thanks for paying a sister on time. Nakia, how could I get everything done at the speed of light without you? Thanks, lady. Six degrees of separation. Hey, ask Allison Oxner. She'll tell you the story. Thanks, Ally for being

Ms. Hollywood, showing me your strength, and offering me wisdom. Voice Over Crew, thanks for the radio commercial. Folks who came to my home and read the very rough samples of the galley; Scott Lucas, Jeanette Mitchell, Arshapalla Brown, Jeneisha Reeves, Jeretta C. Holland, Jessica Silver, Shae James, Lois Lane (not Superman's woman, but a real live Lois Lane), Tea Bradwell, Andre Leura Dimech, Karen Brown, Andre Hogan (can there ever be a HU party without "us"?), Janice Sheffield, and Sophia Jackson-Jenkins. Thank you guys.

Without the fruits of life with hard pits in the middle, would I have any stories to tell? Without lemons, would I have any sweet-tart drinks to make on a hot sunny day? Without dreams as big as the Empire State Building and as deep as Victory Lake, would there be a story to tell? No. Enjoy the tale, but don't go too deep and forget.

Imperious

Publishing by Imperious, 174 Washington Street, Suite 3, Jersey City, New Jersey 07302.

First (1st.) edition.

Library of Congress Date filling 8/2005 and 12/2006
 Published by Imperious Publishing.Printed in Canada.

ISBN-13: 978-0-9758624-2-1

1. Channa Renée Jones, Arnelle, Deja, Kevin Dean Walker, Tyron, Tyshawn, RN Comfort, Richard Greene, Great- Granddaughter of Marie Laveau- Fiction.
2. New York Knick, Tango, Montclair, New Jersey, Starbucks, GMHC, Ruby Foo, Newark Health Service Agency, Newark Medical, Morgan Pharmaceutical, Columbia University, Howard, Houston Restaurant- are used as works of Fiction, or as fictional places or things.

The Ten Year Date is an Romantic Drama. It is a tale of a woman's will to have her date of ten years to commit. Channa learns the craft of Voodoo from the great-granddaughter of Marie Laveau in New Orleans. Kevin Dean Walker does commit but with a price bigger than Channa is willing to pay.

Book cover designed by Candace K. Cottrell
Author's graphic by Will Armstrong
Edited: G. Poteat and Candace K. Cottrell
Readers 1. TJ Fishburne 2. Andréa Hogan
3. Nakia A. Britt

The Ten Date is a part of a trilogy of novels by Sherrance Henderson.

Please read . . .

Sunshine Has Rain - First
1st.

Ten Year Date - Second
2nd.

Girlfriends, How Many of Us Have Them - Third
3rd.

= The full story of Channa Renée Jones

Girlfriends, How Many of Us Have Them
is due to be released in 2008.

Good sex is the root of lust,

Which is the birth to weakness.

This will conquer one's soul, and

Make one do actions that could never be told.

Secrets are actions which are done in the dark,

In the mist of one or two agreeable lovers, who knows the lie.

Lies are things not to be discovered.

But all things in the dark must come to light.

The Ten Year Date is a journey that must be experienced by Channa.

She

Would never let go of Kevin

&

He

Would never stop being Channa's date.

Until the secret is discovered.

This book is dedicated to every woman who has dated a man far too long without a commitment. Let this novel be a lesson. You don't need to live the experience, to learn the lesson!

Prologue

Have you ever had a lover who was so good that you forgave his trifling ass for anything? I'm talking about a Magnum-Extra Large, F-I-N-E brotha who knew how to use his python and his tongue like a pro. This brother, Mr. Pro, had a dick that left a memory mark in my love canal that reminded me that he came, conquered, and yes, he controlled. When he was conquering, he always had his way to control my thoughts, actions, and heart. His disappearing acts, his evasiveness, and his lies were all understood as long as he was hittin' it. As long as he returned to my bed, my thirst was quenched. The craving for his touch was then satisfied, but only for a moment. This masculine animal always knew just what to say and when to say it. With lust in his eyes, he would make my body a four-course meal that was well served. Saying my full given name in a Barry White voice that made me so wet, he gave me no recourse but to just reach across the table and ride that winning Kentucky Derby horse to the finish line.

Go, baby, go!!!!! Yeah!!! Go, ba-by, go. Yeah.

I'm telling you, having a man like that on speed dial will keep the pep in your step. Am I right? He knew how to make me feel like Beyonce on one of my Shen-eneh from *Martin,* days. It didn't seem to matter if I splashed Jean Naté® or Chanel N° 5, his kissing, hugging, and singing sweet music in my ears made me feel like a baby doll. He was a magician. He had a charm to make me feel special when he was there, and magic to make me remember when he was gone. Hmm, I was ready to do anything—an-nee-thannggg, honey—to have his pimpin' ass on lock. I wanted to be able to go home to *that*, wake up with *that*, have *that* in the shower. He was a better at getting me perky than a cup of black coffee—*mmm!* And, girl, I knew he was always good to the last drop!

Child, it was a beautiful thing, him swinnnnn-gggging that thing! Whoa!

And at the same time, no one else could give me such a headache from sheer tension. When he would undress me slowly, making me feel exposed and vulnerable, it gave me a stress and pressure headache. Kissing me on the correct part of my neck was on the money. *Ooh, damn, that's my spot!* He knew how to brush his thick thumb over my soft nipple, making it hard like a diamond. When he'd whisper, "*Girl, you're the hottest chick around,*" he was excited and I knew it, and nobody could've told me differently. I had to be ready for him to lay me down and start the action. His soft, plush lips gently kissing at the trail to his treasure. Stopping at my belly button like he was giving me a courtesy call. "*Baby. I'm almost there, baby, I'm almost there.*" He'd find the fuzzy mound and start to dig—deeper, d-ee-ee-per. His burning tongue navigated the raging waters, it swirling around causing a typhoon, a tsunami! Just when I was about to get there, my head thrown back, and my mouth open…he stops. He peeks up from between my legs and says, *not yet*.

It could have been enough to make me lose my ever-loving mind, but I didn't mind. I loved it. I was on the edge, looking at the land of my realized dreams, ready to step off and fall into everything I ever wanted, but he stopped me, teasing me with the memory of how much fun the ride had been so far.

Of course, the tongue action was just a tempting appetizer. Just a little dim sum, when I just want to get some. He knew where I wanted to go but wouldn't let me get there. Girl, he made love like an R. Kelly song; so many parts, and I watched out for the remix. He wanted to slip inside me, pound it down. He made sure to remind me how badly I wanted it—everything my "it" was, with every swift thrust, and with every slow withdrawal.

He watched me and liked me watching him. This man took pride in making me want it all. In and out. I felt it growing. Out and in. It was too much to take. I forced my legs open wider, wanting him deeper. Leaning up, I reached for his firm, round butt wanting to just grab hold of him and push him in far enough to disappear. Girl, if he got any deeper he'll be knocking out my molars! And then, he stopped. There I was, confused. There he was, smirking and speaking softly. "Not yet, my sweet pet. Not yet."

Anyone can see the pattern. He liked taking me to one step short of a promised land just to say, "OK, let's turn around and go home." But if that journey wasn't so damn good, I could have been able to "stop him."

That was my life, building up to ecstasy and having my man pull out before I could cum. Sometimes, the love-play was worth it, but most of the time it caused sadness. Some guys just know how to keep me coming back for more. Other times, it felt like someone pulled out my heart without anesthesia. I thought that everything was going right in my world, only to have the wind knocked out of my sails, revealing his charade for which I'd fallen.

In 1994 my life was perfect; anyone who knew me would agree. My family was loving and supportive. My transition from college graduate to a corporate career woman went smoothly, and I was well compensated. My student loans and bills were paid on time, I tithed faithfully ten percent of my income, and I volunteered with the Newark Health Service Agency to help with teen birth control issues and HIV testing. I wore designer clothing that flattered every curve, making heads turn wherever I went. I drove the flyest car on the market and had a nice home of my own. I was *all that* and I knew it. *Well, I thought I was all that.* Most importantly, I was also successful in love. I was engaged to Andre, a brilliant, sexy, sophisticated man who was the absolute love of my life. He took me on unforgettable vacations, he bought front row seats to the US Open, and he loved me passionately with kindness and understanding. I was living the life I always dreamed of living. Life was going to the beat of my tempo, and I loved the song it sang. I had my health, my independence, my family, and a FINE man that loved me.

But I couldn't have been more wrong about Andre, and even more wrong about my Mr. Pro, Kevin Dean Walker.

A broken heart is a very real injury. You can feel the pain on the left side of your chest. It is not gas. It aches like a cavity in a tooth that has tasted too many days of Now and Laters. You need more than a little clear strip of a Band Aid to heal the wound, but you have to be very careful. Even the best medicine comes with a warning label. When taken at the right dosage, you're guaranteed to feel better, but feel-good drugs wear off. And most are only prescribed for a short time. When you are coming down from the ultimate high, you can't help wanting to get another hit. My addiction couldn't fit into a medicine bottle, but I surely hid it on the back shelf, saving it for recreational use. I grew dependent on the relief of my drug of choice. I didn't care who I hurt in the process. Like every addict, I had to hit rock bottom to end the vicious cycle of getting my heart broken.

Chapter 21

It was a dazzling, sun-drenched spring afternoon when I left work early to drive to my mother's house in the Clinton Hill section of Brooklyn. Overcome with excitement, I was suddenly sensitive to my surroundings and took in the beauty of the drive. I noticed the trees had tiny, bright green leaves as well as flowers budding in every color of the rainbow. What seemed like God's gift just for me was the overabundance of red flowers. Those were my favorite. Red geraniums were hanging out of window boxes, red roses were creeping up trellises along the sides of rooftop gardens, and red Gerber daisies were displayed outside of florist shop. My smile grew wider as my mind collected the images and I made a mental bouquet. When I reached the edge of town, I was alone with my thoughts. My attention turning to the R. Kelly's song blasting on the car radio, I joined the chorus:

I don't see nuthin' wroooonnng,
Wit' a li'l bump n' grind....

Obviously, it made me think of my man, Andre. I sang this song at the top of my lungs with no rhythm in sight. I had to laugh at myself. You'd think I was on stage for Amateur Night at the Apollo. As R. Kelly carried on, I couldn't help but think of last night with Andre. *No, no, no, there wasn't nuthin' wrong with OUR bump n' grind.* He'd surprised me with rose petals in my bath again and joined me in the steamy water. After ending up on the bedroom floor wrinkled and satisfied, we spoke with whispers of anticipation.

"I could do that forever," I told him, leaning my head on his ripped abs.

"And forever is what I'm giving you, baby," Andre said, still out of breath from exertion.

"I'm so glad I'm going to spend my life with you. I love you so much. It hurts sometimes, just how much. I love that you're all mine and that I'm all yours."

"Me too."

Andre dozed off on the last word. I smiled, taking pride in a job well done.

R. Kelly was done with his song and I was on my mother's street. Auntie June, Grandma, and Cousin Treasure were all gathered to discuss my wedding plans. I had visualized my wedding a hundred times. The church dressed with a million roses, tasteful bridesmaid dresses, full of family and friends, and most important—a beautiful bride and groom. There was so much to do—much more than I ever could have done on my own, but I didn't need a wedding planner; I had five of the classiest and stylish women working on my behalf night and day. Everyone was willing to pitch in, and I knew my wedding day would be just as elegant and magical as Princess Diana's.

I drove with high speed to my mother's house and quickly parked the car. I ran to the door and rang the doorbell over and over. Ding...Ding...DINGDINGDINGDING! I laughed at my annoying way of alerting everyone inside to my arrival.

"Girl, what is wrong with you ringing my doorbell like that?! Come here!"

My mother swung the door open, seemingly aggravated by my childlike behavior, but she quickly dismissed any signs of irritation with a bear hug and a laugh.

"Sorry, Ma." I bounced in the door. "I just can't wait to get this party started. Is everyone here?"

"We're all in the dining room. Let me hang your sweater up, and you go ahead in there."

I handed my mother my thin, cream-colored, waist length sweater and waltzed into the dining room. Auntie June, Grandma, and Treasure were huddled at the massive oak table covered with dozens of bridal magazines, all of which pictured beautiful, smiling brides surrounded by hundreds of flowers. Every corner of the room was packed with something related to the wedding, from the pure white flowers in a bucket next to the door, to the hundreds of brightly colored honeymoon brochures on my mother's oak buffet, to a huge plastic box filled with white, chocolate, and carrot cakes interlaced with small cups of pastel-colored frostings and fillings smack in the center of the table. The wedding had never seemed so real to me as it did then with the smell of lilies in my nose, and the color white filling my eyes. I began to picture myself on the cover of one of those magazines, and I knew that those women couldn't hold a candle to how I would look on my wedding day. Treasure pointed to the shopping bag she'd brought over, which was full of different samples of material for the bridesmaids' dresses.

"Look at what I picked up at the dressmaker to-day!"

She pulled all of the fabrics out of the bag and put them on top of the magazines on the table. My mother picked up a baby blue linen piece, while Treasure and Auntie "oohed" and "ahhed" over a sage-green cashmere piece. There was a garden of colors on the table and my eyes to drifted from piece to piece. I picked up one rose-colored organza piece and another white satin piece and I felt the two between my fingers, pleased with how creamy smooth the fabric felt in my hands.

"Child, this fabric is like butter! Just gorgeous," my Auntie said as she lifted a violet organza swatch to her face.

"If you talkin' butter, you'd best take this into consideration, particularly if you're planning on me being in this wedding," Treasure held a light yellow cotton piece up to her face, which contrasted beautifully against her rich cocoa skin. Just like how the yellow of a sunflower's leaves are offset by the rich darkness of the seeds. Isn't God's nature a beautiful thing?

Though everything I had seen was attractive, I hadn't found what I was looking for. I continued to search through the pile, swimming through striking flower prints, subtle plaids, and heavy taffetas until I found a bright red silk piece. *Gosh, this is my dream fabric.* I wanted my bridesmaids to be contemporary, classic, and just a little bit sexy. They were, after all, representing me!

My grandmother came over to my side of the table and took the swatch out of my hand and rubbed it between her fingers.

"That's it, baby, that is it!"

Treasure leaned over to see the fabric Grandma was holding.

"Channa, this is good. I'm gonna pick me up a F-I-N-E man at your wedding wearing this color. Lord have mercy, save me now!"

She fanned herself like she was in heat.

We all laughed and moved on to more details of the wedding. I couldn't believe how much there was to do and how much they had already done.

I looked around at three generations of women all coming together for this event—for my event—and I was truly thankful to God. We worked on different projects. I on the honeymoon, Treasure on the bridesmaids' dresses, my grandmother on the church, my mother on the flowers, and Auntie June on the cake and caterer. Yet our conversation never faltered. There were only five of us in the room, but by the noise we made calling, laughing and singing, one would have thought there were four times as many people in the house. We knew each other so well that we could talk up a storm without ever having to hear what the other person had said. I closed my eyes to sear the memory into my brain. My mother, dressed in tweed, sat to my left. Always classic, I could smell her Chanel N° 5. It transported me back to when I was a child sitting in the kitchen with her snapping peas for dinner. I saw so much of myself in her face—the strong nose, full mouth, and striking eyes. My grandmother sat to her left dressed in a crisp white blouse and black skirt, with the same nose, mouth, and eyes. To an outsider, it would have looked like one person at three different points in her life. To my right was Auntie June, who always smelled of cocoa butter and was always prompt in getting her hair dyed every six weeks to stay on top of her gray hair. She looked every bit the diva. And Treasure, dressed simply in blue to my Auntie's right, was laughing. She laughed louder than anyone I knew, and could instantly take me back to being a rebellious teenager with big earrings, bright red lipstick, and a b-a-d attitude! I opened my eyes and saw the picture clearly in my mind. I promised to always remember every part of this moment: the smells, sights, and all the songs we sang. These ladies had made my life so unique and strong.

Whatever these proud women put their minds and hearts to would end up being so much more fantastic than anything I could have imagined for myself. I reached over and grabbed my mother's hand.

She whispered, "I'm so proud of you. You're going to be a stunning bride."

We had been working for hours, debating whether the bridesmaids' dresses should be long or short when I heard my stomach growl over all the chatter.

"Who's ready for dinner?" I asked.

My mother spoke up first, "Dinner? Oh yes. Go to that place around the corner."

"What they servin' there?" Auntie June asked.

"Down-home cooking." My mother shook her head with each syllable as if she were tasting the good food as she spoke. "Ribs, potato salad, greens, fried chicken, everything."

"I'll have oxtails, yams, and some of those mustard greens if they make them up good." Treasure didn't hesitate once she heard the words "down-home cooking."

"Amen!"

Grandma raised her hand like it was Sunday and the preacher spoke nothing but the truth.

"You know people don't make good greens right no mo'. I'm going to have the fried chicken and potato salad, but you best get me extra sugah because you know how they make potato salad, they never put in enough sugah. You tell them that too. It's good, they just too light-handed with the sugah."

"Don't you have sugar here?" Treasure asked.

"No, ever since my sister came down with Sugah, I've been keeping it out of the house. No sir, I'm not trying to be like that."

Everyone nodded in agreement with Grandma not wanting diabetes.

"I will have fried chicken, kale greens, and macaroni, but only if they just made it. I don't need any greasy old macaroni when I can cook it up here in twenty minutes, and ten times better."

"OK, so Grandma, you want chicken and potato salad with extra sugar. Mama wants chicken, kale greens, and macaroni. Treasure wants some oxtails, yams, and mustard greens. Auntie June, what do you want?"

In unison, my mother, grandmother and Treasure said, "Baby back ribs with extra sauce, biscuits with honey!"

They all fell over into laughter, followed by my Auntie June.

"Chile, you know I like my baby back ribs, why you even have to ask?"

"OK, OK, I got it," I laughed. "I'll be back in a few minutes."

I went back down the hallway to grab my purse and sweater repeating the order in my head. *Kale greens, mustard greens, potato salad extra sugar, macaroni no grease, fried chicken, oxtails, yams, ba-beeee back ribs, biscuits and honey. Kale greens, mustard greens, potato salad extra sugar, macaroni no grease, fried chicken, oxtails, yams, babeeee back ribs, biscuits and honey.* We were fixin' to have a feast!

I opened the door, ready to get us some grub when I was greeted with a lonely, crisp white envelope on the stony gravel outside. *Huh? What's this?* I stepped out and looked up and down the street for anyone who may have left it, but no one was on the sidewalks or driving off in a delivery truck. The envelope had Andre's business logo as the return address. I snatched it up playfully, thinking he must have been playing one of his little teasing games. He often left little notes in my coat pockets or under my pillow, detailing what sexual position he wanted to try out later in the evening or what romantic getaway he had planned for us that weekend. I thought of the lazy time we spent laying out on the fine sand beaches of the Hamptons, with nothing for miles but the two of us, a blanket, and a bottle of champagne. The bright blue of the ocean filled my eyes as the excitement of being with Andre filled my heart. I stepped back inside and shut the door with my foot as I opened the note, anxious to read what plans he had in store for me.

Only, the note wasn't a cryptic invitation hinting at a New England bed and breakfast. Nor did it detail some new position too raunchy to make it into the Kama Sutra. The note wasn't even from Andre, but it did have his name.

"Andre and I are having a baby. You can get married but I will always be with you both until the end of time. Please call me with any questions at 555-3435."

I shook my head and closed my eyes. *Ahhhh.* I couldn't have read that right. I couldn't have read what I thought it just said. I slowly opened my eyes again, hoping, praying to find something different, but I didn't. *Andre and I are having a baby.* My heart sank deeply into my lungs for a moment. I lost my breath before going completely numb. *My Andre? Not my Andre.* I didn't know what or how to feel, but I knew exactly how to act. *Please call me with any questions.*

I was like a zombie as I wandered over to the phone that sat on an end table next to the doorway. *I will always be with you both until the end of time.* It was written as simply as a letter from the cable company. No emotion, no explanation, nothing that belied the end of everything I thought was true. Just a couple lines of text ending my life. The letter wasn't even signed, yet someone was implying that she was having a baby with my man and that she would be in our lives forever. *And you can't tell me your name? Uh-uh. Call me with any questions. Oh, I got questions. And she better have some answers.*

I already had the phone number memorized as I dialed it into the phone, looking around to see if anyone was nearby. A woman answered.

I half-whispered into the phone so no one in the house could hear me. I heard nothing more than the loud but distant laughter in the dining room.

"Hello...did someone leave a letter on my mother's front step in Brooklyn?"

"Yes. That was from me. My name is Erica."

She sounded classy, but she had to be crazy leaving me a note like that at my mother's house where I was planning my wedding.

"You're Channa, right?"

"Yes I am, and how do you know that?"

My heart was racing as I awaited her response. I could feel my pulse in my eyes. I was having trouble seeing. Everything was hazy around me, except for her words, which were painfully crisp and clear. I shook my head and tried to clear my eyes, but nothing worked. It was like my mind was shutting down.

"Would you hold on a second?" I asked.

"Of course," she said confidently.

I put my head between my legs and took a few deep breaths. I prayed no one would hear me in the hallway and come to find me curled into a ball, deaf and nearly blind with panic. I tried to slow down my breathing and waited a few seconds for my pulse to slow enough so I could see again. After what seemed like eternity, I returned to the phone.

"I'm back," I said calmly. "Continue."

"I-I work with Andre and...well, I do more than just work with him. We've been dating, and...I think I should just tell you up front that I'm White. Andre told me that's what he prefers."

"Oh, that's what he prefers? Prefers? That's what he prefers?! Look, I don't know who you are or what you want, but don't disrespect me by leaving notes in front of my mother's house. Anyone could have found it! Are you crazy?"

"I understand why you might be upset." *Ya think?* "But I didn't mean any disrespect." *Ain't that some mess right there?* "I just wanted to get in touch with you." *Honey, you don't want no touch from me right now, believe that!*

"I don't live here. Why would you think you could get in touch with me here?"

There was a heavy sigh on the other end of the phone.

"Helllooooo!!! I asked you a question. Don't get quiet now. You were bold enough to leave a note on my mother's doorstep, I'm sure you're bold enough to talk. Do you hear me?" The shock was beginning to wear off. I was pissed.

"I knew you were there because I saw your car," Erica said hesitantly.

I was frantic, my voice somewhere between a whisper and a scream. "Saw my car? How do you know my car? Are you stalking me? What the hell is wrong with you?!"

"No, no, no. It's nothing like that. I work with Andre. I've seen you dropping him off before. That's how I know your car. I live down the street and I was shocked the first time I noticed you leaving your mother's house, but that's how I knew where you were. I had my sister to leave the note on the doorstep. I didn't mean to scare you."

She was unbelievably calm, telling me that she didn't want me to be scared."Scared?! I'm not scared. I just want to know what the hell is going on, so you'd better start talking. Fast!"

With that, her voice started to shake and I could tell that she was intimidated by my reaction, but what did she expect?

"Umm, well…it's like this: Andre is only marrying you because it fits in with what his family desires and expects. He knows they would never be pleased with the baby or me, but he has promised to never leave us. I know this may be a bit much for you to swallow right now, and I don't mean to upset you…"

"Well it's too fucking late for that! What did you think you were going to do, make me happy? Was I supposed to just open my arms and say 'welcome to the family'? Do you think I would sit down with you and my date book and work out a reasonable Andre-sharing schedule?"

"I understand why you are mad at me, but once you think about it, you'll see that it's only fair that I tell you. I've known about you, and now you know about me. I'm just keeping it real."

Shhplinnngg! With that I slammed the phone down, disconnecting the call. Did she actually just say she was *keeping it real*? I didn't know if she was mocking me by talking "Black" or if she really spoke that way. I ran back to the dining room, sobbing and waving the note around. I couldn't hide what was going on.

The fussing and laughter stopped flat as everyone's face registered shock from seeing my transformation. I'd just left with a smile on my face, and now I could barely catch my breath between deep, painful sobs. My mother's hands went over her heart as if the sight of me stopped it from beating.

My grandmother rushed to my side. "What's wrong, Channa?"

"I found this outside."

I held up Erica's note as I fell into the closest chair.

My mother quickly grabbed the note and read it.

"Channa, please! This is a bunch of bull. Andre loves you

and those women on his job probably see that and are jealous of you. You'll see when he gets here and we straighten this Jezebel out."

My mother had seen the business logo, read the heartless line, and concluded that someone Andre worked with was spitting lies trying to break us up. I wished it were that simple.

"No, Mama, I just spoke to her. I called the number and... Ahhhhhh, I can't believe this is happening!"

The words could barely fall from my quivering lips. My body was on fire with bottomless emotions of rage, sorrow, and hurt all at once. I was no longer numb and insensitive to the situation.

"As a matter of fact, Treasure, hand me that phone next to you on the bookcase. I'm not waiting until he gets his ass over here later."

Treasure passed the phone over to me and I punched each number key forcefully with my middle finger like each key was one of Andre's eyes. When he answered, I didn't give anything away. "Hey baby. It's me."

"Hey, how're you ladies doing over there? Are you getting everything ready for the wedding?"

Andre was cheerful and unassuming.

"Oh, a few unexpected things have come up, but we're figuring out how to deal with them right now."

"I know you'll do it perfectly. You always do. I'm just going to finish up here so I can leave work behind and get back to you."

"Leave *work* behind? Funny. I just got a letter from a lady who says she works with you."

You could hear a pin drop in my mama's dining room as my relatives stood around waiting to hear Andre, as if I had him on a speakerphone.

"Really? I don't know who that could be, baby."

I dropped my calm tone and went straight to sistah-with-an-attitude.

"Hmmm. *Baby*. Don't baby me! It's the White woman who says that she is carrying your baby! Does it ring a bell, now?"

There was dead air on the other end as Andre tried to ignore my question.

My words flew out of my mouth like darts. "Hello? Andre? Cat's got your tongue? Why are you so quiet? Or are you trying to figure out which White woman you've knocked up and who got in contact with me? Are there really that many? I didn't think you had it in you, but I guess I'm wrong."

"Channa, I don't know who you're talking about. I love you and I'll be over around six to pick you up. I want to see this letter. I don't know who would do something like this. I really have no idea what you're talking about. I don't know what's going on."

Andre was stern; he didn't sound if he was lying or covering up anything.

"OK," I replied slyly. "I'll see you later then."

I hung up and turned to face my family's perplexed faces. They didn't know what to make of the letter any more than I did—everyone except for my mother. She blindly defended her future son-in-law.

"See? What did he say? This woman is crazy, I'm telling you, she doesn't want to see you two happy. That's all. She's a liar and a damn fool thinking you'll fall for that."

My mother's eyes were pleading with me. She loved Andre, and already considered him her son. She must have, she was fighting so hard for him.

"Yes, Ma. He said he'll look at the letter when he gets here tonight. But he doesn't know what it's all about."

I tapped my fingers on the dining room table. *Tap- tap-tap*. I had to be sure. I needed to know my next move.

"I'm telling you, Channa, your mom's probably right. This is all some prank. Andre will take care of it when he gets here."

My cousin Treasure had joined my mother in Andre's dream team defense.

"I don't know...I just don't know."

I loved Andre with all that I had, and wanted to spend the rest of my life with him. The way Erica's letter was able to get to me was unnerving. If anything, she was able to cause doubt, and I was going to get to the bottom of this situation myself. If this woman was crazy and making things up, then I needed to find out before I ended or committed my life to Andre. The next number I called was Erica's.

"Hello?"

It was her. I'll never forget a voice.

"Erica, this is Channa. Look, I've had some time to think about what you said, and you're right. It's only fair that I know about you. Now I need to make things fair for everyone involved. Do you think you can help me?"

I barely finished my sentence before Erica replied, "Why yes."

I may have been Black and she White, but there are some things that are simply universal to the female way of thinking. She must have sensed what I was planning and was eager to assist.

"Good. I need you to come by my mother's. How long would it take you to get here?"

"I can be there in ten minutes."

"Good, but I don't need you to be here until 5:40 this afternoon. Please make sure you are on time, and I mean not even one minute late. I want to talk to you woman to woman, and I want Andre to be here as well. Is that OK with you?"

"That's fine. I'm tired of playing games with Andre, and this needs to come out. I'll be there."

"Oh, don't park in front of the house," I added in.

I wanted to see Andre's face when he first saw Erica in my mother's house. I thought his expression would tell me the truth, even if his mouth was speaking lies. If he saw Erica's car out front he'd have too much time to prepare excuses.

"What did she say?" Auntie June wanted to know what was going on as I put down the phone.

"She lives down the street. She'll be here twenty minutes before Andre gets here.

"Down the street?!" My mother was shocked. "Where? How long has she been living this close?"

"I don't know, Ma, but we'll find out soon enough."

No one cared about the food I'd forgotten to get. I walked out to the living room and sat down on the couch, staring into space. Next, Grandma walked in and sat down on my right, taking my hand. I put my head on her shoulder and started to cry.

"Channa, you got to be strong. The devil is giving you a test, and you need to be ready for the fight."

"I'm not going to fight, Grandma. If Andre was with that woman, she can have him."

My mother was standing over me, but I hadn't noticed through my tears. She sat down on the other side of me and patted my leg.

"Channa? Andre loves you. He would never do anything to hurt you. You know that, don't you? And even if he made a mistake..."

"Made a mistake?"

I sat up and looked at her. She couldn't possibly think I could forgive something like this.

"What, do you think he could have tripped and fallen on top of her and got her pregnant on his way back up?"

"Channa, I know you're upset, but you don't need to talk to me like that."

My mother looked hurt and worried, and I don't think it was just because of what I had said. These accusations were threatening her happiness as well.

"I'm sorry, Ma. I just don't know what to think right now."

Treasure and Auntie June were sitting together on the love seat looking just as worried as the rest of us. We all sat in silence waiting for our questions to be answered. My mind ran rampant, wondering when Andre could have been cheating.

Was it the nights he said he was working late? Could it have been when he said he was playing ball with his boys? And where? At the office? In our bed?

My stomach turned with the thought of Andre's dark head between lily white thighs. Meanwhile, I'd been living a lie.

My thoughts also went to hope. *What if this woman is lying? Why would somebody just up and lie about something like that? Is she just some office temp who wants him and thinks this will get me out of the way? Or has she just lost her damn mind? If I find out she's lying, she's gonna have all five of us giving her the beat-down!*

I wanted Andre to look at her and say, "Who are you?" I wanted Andre to come in, look at her and say, "That's the girl I caught stealing office supplies. I had her fired, and she's trying to get back at me." I imagined him pulling me off of her mangled body and whispering in my ear, "She ain't worth it, baby, you know you're the only one for me."

But I would only sink back into the pain. I imagined having to call my bridesmaids and tell them that there is no wedding and having to call the priest to cancel. There would be no wedding! There'd be no wedding. I imagined us all going back into the dining room with all of the work we'd accomplished and splitting up again to cancel everything. I imagined having to go back to my lonely bed, my lonely tub, my lonely kitchen counter—all of the many places that reminded me of him. The places I'd made love to Andre would stand like roadside markers of remote historical locations. *This is the rug where Channa and Andre made love after deciding they'd get married.* I would need a tour guide for my broken heart.

The doorbell rang promptly at 5:40. I answered, and there she stood, every bit of a size four with her short, straight auburn locks and hazel eyes. I looked at Erica and felt a stabbing pain in my stomach as I viewed her protruding, rotund belly. She was carrying my man's baby in that massive ball sticking out from under her jacket. I wanted to rip her face open with my long manicured nails, but at the same time, I didn't want to cause injury to an innocent baby. So far, Erica did not appear to be lying about anything. Before I could invite her inside, my mother ran behind me yelling obscenities at the top of her lungs.

"How dare you come to MY house talking all this mess to MY daughter about MY future son-in-law? Are you out your mind?"

She continued carrying on like a madwoman until Treasure came and calmly escorted her into the living room.

Erica looked shocked to see my mother go off on her like that. She probably didn't think anyone would be there except for me, and then later, Andre. Well, I already knew she wasn't that bright.

"I apologize for my mother, Erica, but I'm sure you can understand where she's coming from. Please, come in."

I stepped aside. She walked in cautiously. She was probably watching out for another shrieking Black woman in a dark corner.

"I'm really sorry it had to come to this. I...I just wanted you to know what kind of man you are marrying."

I could feel my eyes burning with tears. I tried holding them back, yet my voice and face remained like stone. I kept ownership of my public emotion. They weren't going to see me sweat.

"Well, I'm sure that wasn't your only intention, but I still appreciate you exposing the truth, if it is the truth."

I closed the door and then led her to the living room where everyone else sat waiting for Erica to explain herself. My mother was looking at her so hard that I thought she was going to burn a hole in her stomach. The rest of my family seemed to be confused as to whom to look at—Erica, my mother, or me. No one spoke for what felt like forever until my mother yelled at Erica again.

"You home wrecker, how dare you come into my house like that! Who do you think you are?"

Erica started to move as if to leave, but I stood up and she sat back down.

"Listen, we're never going to be friends, but I respect you for trying to do the honorable thing. Please stay so I can hear what happened and make the right decision about Andre. You owe that to me."

Erica didn't say anything. She sat back down with her eyes on the floor. I then turned to my mother. "Mama, I really needed to hear Erica so that I know exactly what to say to Andre."

My mother started to protest, but my grandmother intervened and said, "Let the child, hear what she needs to hear."

There was no way my mother would argue with my grandmother, so she stayed silent and Erica began.

"I know you all must think I'm a horrible person, but I never meant for any of this to happen." She seemed ashamed as she continued speaking, "Andre and I met at work three years ago. We started talking one day, and he innocently asked me out to lunch. It didn't start out as anything romantic, but that changed as we began having dinner together. Eventually, we stopped getting separate rooms when we went away on business trips. There was no sense in lying to ourselves; we both quickly realized we wanted more from each other."

"This tramp is full of it! Listen to her, talking as if Andre loves her. He doesn't love you. He loves Channa. They're getting married! Do you hear me?"

My mother jumped up out of her chair and lunged toward Erica.

"Ma! Please. I need to hear what she has to say."

I pleaded with my mother to remain silent while Erica told her story. My mother folded her arms in a huff and plopped back into the sofa. I turned back to Erica, who was still staring at her feet.

"Please, Erica. Finish it. ."

"Well, he told me how he did care for you, but he also loved me, and if this was a perfect world, his family would accept me. When I told him I was pregnant, he told me he would never leave you. I didn't plan this, but there was no way I wasn't going to keep my child, so I figured it was only right to let you know just what you were getting into. Andre said he was going to take care of me and the baby."

Just as she finished, the ancient grandfather clock sitting in the hallway sounded loudly as it struck six o'clock. *Ding, ding, ding…*

"Why the hell are you living in the community? Did you move here to watch Channa and Andre?"

My mother could no longer contain her heated outbursts. Erica looked down at her shoes. Everyone else in the room, including myself, felt sorry for the girl. As she was talking, I noticed how young she was. She couldn't have been more than 24, and her pregnant belly seemed to overwhelm her slight frame. The sound of the doorbell echoed throughout the house when Andre rang, not knowing what awaited him on the other side of the door.

Auntie June got the door and flung it wide open to reveal Erica with her swollen tummy, standing next to me. Andre stopped short, not fully entering the house. His face said it all, and if it didn't, his words did. He started a vicious verbal assault on Erica.

"Why are you here? Why are you trying to destroy my relationship? Get out of this house. Get out of here. Now!"

Andre had a look in his eyes I'd never seen before and I was frightened for Erica. But the facts were there. He knew exactly what they both had done.

"Andre," I intervened, "Don't come in here acting a fool. We have a lot to talk about."

"No, she has to go. Now! Now!"

He pointed to Erica, never taking his fuming gaze off of her.

"No, she's staying right here because you need to explain to me why you think it's OK to have your White girl on the side while you show off your trophy Black girl to your family.""This woman is crazy. Channa, listen to me. We can work this out. She's out of the picture - she's out of her mind!"

Out of the picture? I had still hoped he'd convince me that Erica had lied. I hoped that nothing that came from her mouth was the truth. But now, *she's out of the picture?* It was true. He had slept with her, it was his baby, and my world was crashing around me at the speed of light. I felt dizzy from taking too much in at once. "She's out of the picture, Andre?"

Andre's face turned blood red. He was busted. He confirmed the unforgivable.

Erica began to cry, "Andre, you said you'd never leave me, you promised."

She always knew about me and didn't care. She just wanted Andre, even if she had to share him.

"Shut up! Why the fuck are you here?!" Andre yelled at Erica again.

"Yeah, get out!"

My mother was backing him up.

"No, I said she wasn't going anywhere. Andre's going to tell me what he was doing with this White girl and then they can both get out!"

My grandma, aunt, and cousin sat around stunned as they watched the fiasco in my mother's home unfold."Channa, you've gotta hear me, she's over. Her and I are over. Trust me. Please. I-I was out of my mind. I lost it. I fucked up. I fucked up. Channa, don't turn your head, please, trust me."

Andre was taking deep breaths as he spoke. Tears were falling down his face.

"I don't even know if that's my baby. I'm sure I wasn't the only one she was sleeping with. We can work this out.

Channa, let's just go somewhere and talk. Me and you, just me and you, come on. Please."

"No. Andre, it's over. I don't want to hear anymore. I don't care if it isn't your baby. You made your bed with that woman, now you're going to lay in it! Here's your ring. I can't trust you."

I slid the canary diamond ring that once symbolized my future off of my finger and back into the hand of the man whom I once believed in wholly.

"And if you knew she was sleeping with other men, why would you tap her nasty ass? You could've brought some shit home to me! The wedding is off, Andre." I pointed to Erica. "Take your baby's momma—or whatever she is—and get out! Get out, just get out!"

Andre whirled around to Erica, seizing her by both arms, and shaking her brutally. "You see what you did? You see what you did? I don't ever wanna see your stupid ass again!"

He threw Erica to the floor like she was a rag doll and headed for the door.

"Andre! Andre!"

Erica limped on the floor and called out behind him.

"You said you wouldn't leave me. You said you loved me! Andre! Andre!"

Andre never looked back and stormed out, slamming the door loud enough to make us all jump.

The women ran to Erica's side, but I remained standing, watching the door as if I could see him leaving through it. After witnessing Andre's act of cheating, and then tossing his pregnant lover around like a bag of garbage, I realized that I could let him go. The liar, the cheater, the abuser. Yet Erica and her child would be connected to him for life. I went to her side and held her hand as we both cried for the man who didn't deserve either me or Erica.

Chapter 20

After I walked Erica, who was still crying, to the door. I heard myself tell her, "Just take care of that baby. The baby is all that matters." It was mechanical, I know. But I just had the wind knocked out of me, and I wasn't even the one thrown to the floor.

"Oh my God. I-I can't believe he would do that to me," Erica finally was able to say. "But I guess I deserved it. I knew about you and I didn't care. I just wanted Andre. You didn't have to stand up for me like you did. And your family didn't have to help me up. You all had every reason to kick me while I was down and you didn't. You're all such good people, and knowing that makes all of this hurt even more."

"I gotta be honest Erica, I don't know what's driving me right now. I know I'm hurt and angry, but no man is ever supposed to put his hands on you like that."

I couldn't even look at her. My eyes were fixed on some odd spot just over her shoulder. God must have been moving my lips. All I wanted to do was to curl up into a little ball and cry.

"I'm sorry, Channa. I am. I really am. Please tell your mother that I'm sorry."

She walked out the door with her head down, her shoulders shuddering. I bet she cried all the way home. As soon as Erica left my mother's house, we went to work dismantling the wedding plans. Despite the shock of comforting my ex-fiancé's pregnant lover, we all knew that the sooner we took care of the situation, the better. My relatives immediately jumped into separate tasks to help me with the pain.

I staggered into the dining room where I heard the rustling. My mother was gathering up all of the flowers and shoving them into old grocery bags. The tears had soaked her beautiful cheekbones, and it made my heart break for her. As she shoved stalks and stems into the bags, she muttered to herself, "no-good hussy. That no-good hussy."

Auntie June shoved fabric swatches back into the bags Treasure brought. She was silent but obviously distraught. When she got to the red silk piece we all loved, she squeezed it in her hands until it disappeared inside her clenched fists. She shook her head like she was trying to wake herself up from a bad dream. *Wake me up too, Auntie. If only this could be a dream.*

Treasure picked up the box of the colorful frostings and cake samples. She gave me a sad look and shrugged. She sulked out of the room and we heard the garbage disposal turn on.

Grandma stacked one magazine on top of the other until she had a tall mass in the center of the table. I knew she couldn't lift them all, and I went over to help her. I reached for the bottom of the stack and she put her hands over mine. The top quarter of the magazines fell and our eyes met. From there, it was a blur. I began to cry hysterically as I ripped the covers off the fallen magazines. Grandma didn't say a word; she took the next magazine and began to rip it apart too. Through my tears and glossy shreds of magazine paper, I saw that my mother joined in, and then Auntie June. I heard my mother's sobs as I caught a breath from my own. By the time Treasure came back, my mother's dining room was a mess.

When I returned to my home, I continued the cleansing process. I removed all pictures and memorabilia from their spaces and threw each and every letter, picture, clothing item, and gift that reminded me of Andre into the fireplace. I curled up in a blanket, watching my future burn up in smoke. By the time the fire went out, there was nothing left of him, and very little left of me.

I sulked for a few weeks before going to Jamaica where the tropical drinks, sandy beaches, and laid-back island lifestyle started to bring me out of my funk. I wore nothing but a bikini and sarong; ate nothing but fresh fruit and fish; did nothing but relax, read, and toil over the nagging question of what went wrong. *Why would Andre do such a thing? Did he really prefer White girls and used me as some cover-up to make his family happy? Had he loved me at all?* I thought it was possible that he did love me, but was just a cheater. The way he threw Erica around after I told him it was over seemed to defend that. I didn't think he'd put his hands on a pregnant woman that he loved just because his parents preferred me to her. No, I believed Andre loved me, but he lost me. I thought about calling him and asking why he cheated, but I couldn't trust him anymore. I don't think he even knew the meaning of the word "trust."

The day I flew home from my island vacation, my friend Max invited me to a password party whose host was an eccentric movie director and a friend of a friend. If you knew the secret word, or were fashionably dressed and dropped the right names, you were in the party.

"Channa, it's Max," she said warmly. "I know you probably aren't over your break-up yet, but you've had enough time to think about him while soaking up the rays on the beach. Now you need to party! Go get your hair done, and meet me there."

Max was right. I had wasted enough time worrying about Andre. I wrote down the address and made a hair appointment where I'd get my hair dyed to match my perfect tan. *Let's find out if blondes really do have more fun.*

As planned, I met Max at the party. The password was

the host's favorite movie, *The Godfather.* It was at a dimly lit loft, yet I was still able to see all eyes on me as I strolled in, tossing my new golden tresses courtesy of my stylist, Ms. Clare. I flaunted my sun-kissed glow from the Jamaican vacation. My white short suit was the perfect complement to my tan and new hair color.

Max rushed over smiling, and gave me a big hug, "Lady, Jamaica has been good to you. I'm so happy to see you smiling again."

It was true. I had my signature smile back in place and hadn't realized it. She knew I was tired of speaking about Andre. This party was just what I needed to get my back my life and to change my vibe.

"I'm soooo glad you showed up. Some old-ass man is sweatin' me, and he's got the dragon. The breath is killin' me!"

We laughed as she pointed him out.

"No he didn't come out the house with some Hammer pants on!"

"Yes he did. And *he can't touch this!*"

Max did a half turn like she was on the runway.

"Uh-uh!" I laughed. "Max, you're crazy!"

We took a position near the director's gigantic poster of Al Pacino. It was time to see and be seen.

After a half hour of turning down drinks and dances, I was approached by this F-I-N-E, cocoa-chocolate man.

"Do you want to dance?" he asked me in a deep Brooklyn-soaked accent.

I loved it! This man was so fine, looking every bit the cover of *GQ Magazine.* And he was looking at me as if no one else were in the room. But, I had to play it cool and not let him know what kind of an effect he was having on me.

"And you are?" I asked with a slight smirk, tilting my head enough to let my hair fall over my shoulder.

"Kevin," he said with a smile that revealed his straight and perfect white teeth as he extended his hand. "Kevin Dean Walker."

His smile did it. The flirt inside me could no longer be repressed.

"Well, Kevin Dean Walker, I am Channa Renée Jones," I purred like a pussycat and offered my manicured hand.

Never dropping his gaze from my eyes, he took my hand in his and raised it to his plush lips, gently kissing it.

"Shall we?" he asked.

His eyes widened for a split second as he raised his perfect eyebrows, showing his confidence in my answer.

We hit the floor, commanding everyone's attention, dancing in sync as though we'd been partnered for years. And just like that, my faith in men was restored.

We've been dancing ever since. Kevin's world collided with mine just when I needed a new love, and he filled the job superbly. Years later, after Dr. Patel's debacle left me paralyzed, and some of the people in my life just left me, Kevin stayed and reminded me that I was a WOMAN throughout my recovery. I learned that no matter what drama faced my life, Mr. Walker would not leave. He wasn't always perfect, but he was always there, which was enough for me.

Chapter 19

It is 2004, and my gaze is fixed on the flashing lights and mountains of brick and mortar. I can feel myself fall into the mountain, rough to my touch, but stable beneath me. My feet are grounded, but my eyes see the sky. My ears are keenly aware of the harmonious integration of the symphony down below. Coughing, laughing, moaning, honking, bumping, cursing, kissing, crashing, yelling, whispering. I can smell wet pavement and sweat, and sweet, and anger, and passion.

Though I am oblivious to the specific sights, smells, and sounds, I am focused on everything as a unit. The windows to my soul put up their seductively long shutters. I soar into a world of hustle and bustle beneath me as my mind races with what I see and what I want to feel. Chocolate-colored uniforms distribute highly anticipated, self-ordered pleasures. The hurried and aggressive click clacking of the Prada pumps that command the pavement merge with my own heartbeat. Pedestrians roar colorful epithets at vehicular weapons that do not respect a citizen's right to walk. The city is entrancing.

So is he.

I smell his animal getting closer. He comes up behind me and I say to myself, *not this time*, but even as I think it, I know I want him as much as he wants me. My breath catches in my chest as I feel his body press slightly against mine. I can feel everything, every inch of him though he only is skimming my body.

A hand reaches around me and pulls my stomach in close to him. I throw my head back over his shoulder, my long brown hair cascading over both of our bodies as if we were one. He twists my nipple gently. Both nipples stiffen at the slightness of his touch. "Don't stop," is what I want without thought. My body ignores my mind's pleas and leans deeper into him. His fiery palm is instantly felt. The nape of my neck is ignited with flames as he runs his lips along my skin.

It is that time of the month, so I unlock my comely, sensual lips to object, but seemingly before I speak, a massive and powerful hand tenderly strokes them. With his touch, he persuades my tongue to remain silent. He wants me, and what he wants, he takes.

Like a knight, he undrapes himself and kneels before Queen Channa. My baby pink summer skirt rises like I'm Marilyn Monroe standing over a manhole. I want this man, whole. My thong is pushed aside. It's discarded like yesterday's paper. My moans fade in and out between moans of ecstasy. He knows how to make me do the things I would be ashamed to do with another man. He knows how to make me want to do them.

I am abruptly swept off my feet. Strong muscular arms stretch my desire-filled body across the seemingly pure plains of the Italian imported sofa. It is deep, thick, soft, and pure white. I feel like we're on a cloud, and he knows the route to take me to heaven. I move my hands along the expensive fabric. I am only aware of the couch and my man.

He snatches my skirt from my body as if it were a rag. His hardness brushes inside of my leg. His arms extend higher, whisking my sleeveless Donna Karan away. I am suddenly reminded of my Aunt Flo's monthly visit.

"No," I say in a gasp, "we'll make a mess."

He gets up, moving with the confidence and agility of a jungle feline. My eyes follow every leg muscle movement.

He makes his way to the bathroom adjacent to his office, taking his time getting back to his waiting victim. His dick sways from side to side leaving me captured in its trance.

"Use this."

He hands me a Knicks player's towel. I grab the towel. Its unique orange and blue hues disappear beneath me. He places his body back between my legs and spreads them. I still hesitate. I am afraid the monthly proof of my womanhood will leave a stain no cleaning crew will be able to get out. Yet part of me wants there to be a mark of my presence, of this moment when we are one body, sweat and sex. Channa was here.

My pussy senses my hesitation, and becomes tense. He senses my tenseness.

"Stop fighting me. Open your pussy for me, Channa Reneé Jones."

He is well aware that the sound of my whole name coming from the depths of the baritone he possesses made me crazy for him. He takes his index finger and traces a familiar trail that starts at my belly button. His finger slides down, slowly, bringing me to heightened desire. I want him to touch me, touch it, touch me there. Finally, the soft tip of his finger hits my clit and all hesitation goes away. His finger goes down further and twirls itself around my tampon string, he pulls it out and we both know exactly what we want to go in. Staring only at my fleshy flower of open blooms, he drops his last hindrance into his wastepaper basket. He licks his lips.

"Mmm, you are so nasty. You know it's yours. Fuck me, baby."

His head readily descends. His face fades. I am met with the full view of his high-priced, skilled barber craftsmanship. The swirl of waves on his head hypnotizes me as I wash my hands through them. His hardness pressed solidly against my inner thigh and swelled hitting my rum drop causing my body to twitch. I-95 was twelve inches of pure addiction. I called it I-95 because it's a big highway everyone knows takes you north to south. I move into a realm of bliss and rapture, letting him take me wherever he wants to go along his route.

He grunts as he hungrily strokes his manhood in and out of my starved body, which heeds his body for every demand. He slides his cocoa-chocolate fingers between my lips. I suck at them as if they were I-95, but not quite. He likes it rough, and I clamp my teeth down around his long thick fingers.

"Tsk! Ahh."

For him it is a pleasurable pain.

He grabs my ass with renewed vigor. I grab his ass and force his love rod to penetrate deeper. He's locked in my pleasure, squeezing me tightly, breathing heavily, grinning slyly, grinding deep within my insides, causing them to dance with delight. I am flipped over with familiar strength and ease. A red light is a foreign concept to I-95. I am face down on the couch as he enters me swiftly without missing a stroke. My body presses into the couch farther and I am lost in him. I tremble as I fall into the pure, plush white material beneath me. Colorful juices flow from my honey hive. He is right behind me the whole time.

"Ooh, Channa. Ooh, Channa."

My ears are met with immense gratification as he speaks tenderly. His hands explore the contours of my shape. He is gentle with me, but I want him rough.

"Deeper! Go faster. Faster! Harder!"

He complies.

My mind is adrift again, this time to unwanted territory. While feeding my starving hunger for lust, I am interrupted with my hastily discarded thoughts of Carl. My man. Earlier uncertainty and guilt are washed away. Carl is no match for Kevin's bloodthirsty infatuation. Will Carl be able to tell? Will he know my walls have been stretched far beyond the widths of its natural memory? Can his animal pick up the scent that another left behind? Can Carl look into my eyes and see the relief from long awaited satisfaction? Will my body show the signs that I was with another man? I've been with Carl for some time now and I know he loves me with all his heart. He is so kind, so sweet, and so pure. Carl is a great guy, and his faithfulness is a quality that is desired by so many. I am lucky to have Carl. But having and wanting are two separate things. I try to fight it, but I keep seeing Carl smiling at me as if being with me is his sole key to happiness. I can almost hear him telling me how much he missed me after I'd taken a trip, and it feels like he was lost without me. If Carl knew Kevin only needed to say my name and I'd melt into a ball of clay, ready to be molded into his sexual whims, Carl would be devastated. I don't want to see the light stolen from his eyes. I don't want to hear the heartbreak in his voice. I don't want to feel for Carl at all while I am with Kevin. I try to turn my mind off and let my body move on autopilot through nature's course.

I don't care. I do not care! Care! I only want to feel Kevin. I want him now, yesterday, and forever. I am amazed at the primal, unthinking level of our love. It is difficult not to allow my body to want him without getting my mind in the way. It is both erotic and familiar.

His thrusts get faster. I feel him throb and pulsate and I know it's time. Kevin pulls out of me and pulls my head back by my hair. His juices spew forth from his love fountain down the side of my cheek. He falls to his knees and I turn to see his face. Kevin leans in as if to kiss me only to lick the creamy crimson from my face. I stretch my tongue to taste what spilled nearest my lips and the saltiness reminds me of the treasures of the earth. His tongue meets mine, and he feeds me from his mouth. Hungry, I take it all, sucking the sticky residue from the pink, moist spoon. I press my hands to his shoulders, ready to shift my weight to bring him to the floor, but he grabs my wrists and stops me cold.

"Hold on. Let me get up so you can clean yourself off."

Kevin stands up and takes the towel off of the sofa and wipes his face with it before handing it back to me. He goes back to his desk and reaches into his brown Louis Vuitton briefcase searching for his palm pilot. Once he finds it, he speaks.

"Do you need me to call you a car?"

"Can I use the bathroom to wash up?" I say softly, dabbing my face with the towel.

"Sure. But make it quick. I'm meeting Tyshawn for drinks to discuss some business. We need to go over this contract again and talk about this commercial we're doing for the team. It's going to be great, and I can't wait until the deal with the sponsor is completed."

"I'll be out of your hair in a minute so you can run off to your important little meeting. And, no, I don't need a cab. I can take myself home"

My skirt is on the floor next to the sofa. I pick it up and stand to put it on.

"C'mon. It's not like that. C'mere."

I walk over to his desk, adjusting my skirt. He pulls me down to his lap.

"I can't help that I have a meeting. There's nothing I can do. I can make it up to you later. There's a new premiere next Friday I thought we could swing by. We'll have the whole evening to ourselves."

"And what about the next morning?"

"Oh, I'm sorry baby." Kevin smiled sheepishly. "I have to get up early for another meeting. You know how important it is that I'm prepared."

He pats me on my rear end. His dark set brown eyes gaze into mine in wait of my response.

"Of course I do."

It wasn't that long ago when I was wheeling and dealing in the corporate world.

"So, do we have a date?"

His lips touch me tenderly on my face, his kiss releasing the tension of my cheek.

"Come on, we'll have fun. You like fun, right, Channa Renée Jones?"

He knows I can't resist when he is like that.

"Call me Thursday."

I slam the door shut with a thunderous BANG! I storm down the hallway, furious with myself that I had again let Kevin in. I wanted to hate him, to push him out of my life and hook up with someone so much better that I would never look back.

I can't believe this shit. All he does is fuck and leave. He never spends the night at my house and I'm not allowed to spend the night at his. Even now, I was being quickly moved from his office. Damn! Is there any place where "we" can stay together after our intense lovemaking? I've also never known a scout to take such a personal interest in a player's career once they've been recruited. He's not meeting Tyshawn. Humph, more like he's meeting Tashia.

But, as always, my anger subsides the moment I leave his building, turning into restless anticipation for Friday when we will again have mind-blowing sex. I'll pretend to be mad when he came to pick me up. He will sweet talk me over lobster and fine wine and take me to a movie without ever taking his eyes or hands off me. We will end up leaving the movie early to have one another as many times as we can before dawn. The same thing has happened a thousand times before, and I know it will inevitably happen again, but I can't stop myself. He is my lover. My to-die-for-dick, and the man for whom I lose all good sense. I need his passion and his drama like I need air. I want him to be my husband, but for the moment, if it was all I can have, I am fine with having Kevin as my ten-year date.

Chapter 18

Kevin Dean Walker was a dream maker in every aspect of his life. Personally, he came from a troubled, yet privileged, background. Jamaican born and English reared by a two-parent household, Kevin was the perfect son who lived up to his parents' every expectation. His father was a cheater who gave Kevin two half-siblings during his parents' marriage and expected Kevin to be as flourishing with the women as he was. His mother was an extremely understanding woman who loved Kevin so much that she dismissed all pain in knowing her husband was a cheater. She wanted Kevin to be successful academically and professionally. On all accounts, Kevin made it; he was center stage and star of the family. He slept with more women than his father could have ever dreamt of, without ever being involved in any baby mama drama. He graduated with honors from the prestigious NYU Law School. He later went on to a high profile, high-salary job.

Professionally, he turned impoverished youth basketball players into wealthy adult basketball stars working for the New York Knicks in a job for which many would have given their first born child. He was Head of Operations of New Talent and attacked his job with fervor. Unlike many scouts who sat in the stands watching the game silently and left without saying a word to the young players, Kevin would hang around after the Rutgers games late into the wee hours of the night, getting a feel for the street kids. He trash talked with them, drank with them, partied with them, flirted with women with them, and most of all, played with them. At 6-foot-6 inches, Kevin took his A-game to test playground legends and future NBA superstars by getting down and dirty with them. For every bounce of the orange ball, for every piece of pitch-black gravel embedded under his skin, for every drop of salty sweat that burned his eyes, and for every blood-red cut received during one of his all-out games, the players respected him even more. There was no one in the NBA who could fulfill the dreams of not only the men with the talent of bouncing a ball, but also the men who wanted to have power—the kind of power he possessed and could help others possess as well.

Kevin didn't just use his keen eye for detail for his career. He put the same dream-making focus and dedication into his social life as well. He took his dates to the classiest restaurants and to only the most exclusive nightclubs. He was as agile on the dance floor as he was on the basketball courts, keeping up with all the latest dance crazes, and commanding all the attention through the flashing lights. That was just about all a woman needed in a man with hands as big as his.

Mmm. Just look at him walk into the room. Soft hair, sharp suit, expensive watch, and confidence for miles, I could see every woman's head turn in his direction. His dark eyes, so dark they were almost black, would make short contact with everyone. His full and perfectly squared lips showcased his pearly white teeth in a flirty grin as he scanned the room for the woman he wanted. I could almost hear them wonder, *Ooh! Who's he with?* Then his eyes would sparkle as they met mine, his mouth opening into an even bigger smile. *That's right, ladies, he's with me.* Kevin Dean Walker was my dream maker. *He-ayyyhe was all mine!*

From the moment I met Kevin, I knew I couldn't just let him go. I didn't know much about him, but there was something in his eyes or his smile, or maybe even in the way he walked, that told me that he was going to be more than a fling—this handsome man was going to become a regular part of my life. I was more than happy to have him.

For our first date after our chance meeting at the password party, Kevin took me to a hot new club in the city downtown. I wanted to make sure this fine chocolate specimen of a man would want me as much as I wanted him, so I made sure to dress to my finest qualities, which meant something short, red and T-I-G-H-T! I showered, curled my long, light brown locks, and carefully applied make-up to accentuate my eyes and full lips. I dabbed perfume in all the important places and put on my new Gucci dress and matching Gucci heels. I took one look in the mirror and knew that there was no way any man, including Kevin Dean Walker, could resist me.

Kevin picked me up at my home in a jet-black Range Rover, and we made our way through the city in style. We pulled up right in front of the club and walked past everyone in line, going straight to the bouncer at the door. Kevin flashed his smile, shook the bouncer's hand, gave his name, and we walked right in. *Now that's V.I.P. treatment.*

The club was crowded and dark, with the only light coming from a small silver bulbs that hung from the ceiling. All eyes were on us as we made our way out to the center of the dance floor, though I was only focused on Kevin. Facing him, I grabbed the back of his legs and dipped so he could get a view of my round, plump breasts. I wanted him to picture his manhood being thrust between them with just enough sweat on them to move his dick in and out with ease. I turned around, and started to grind my round booty in his groin. Now he had a full view of how wonderful his oversized manly hands would look gripping my tiny, feminine waist while he took me from behind. He vibrated, sending a shock to my rum drop. Knowing I was the source causing the shock, I kept winding my hips as I arched my back to push my ample cleavage out further. It was a profile that would drive any man watching to the brink of madness. I was putting on a show for my *new man.* Our whirlwind courtship had just begun. I wanted to give him something to think about when he got home.

He vibrated again, but this time it was his cell. It was cute at first, but it did not take long to annoy the hell out of me. As we got deeper into the relationship, the cell phone would become a constant source of tension. He never picked it up, or checked to see who was calling while in front of me, and after a year of asking him why, I never mentioned it again. Even on later dates, we would go back to his place or he would come to mine, but Kevin never answered his phone, not once. Kevin's intention may have been to make me feel more important than the callers, but to me it felt like he was hiding something, or someone. That cell phone would sit in a drawer or remain in one of his pockets while we made love. I would hear it vibrate a short distance from where we were, but as long as I knew Kevin was mine when I was with him, I learned not to care.

One morning, after a particularly exhausting night with Kevin, a piercing ring snapped me out of my much-deserved rest. Groggy, I lifted my head off my pillow. The clock on my nightstand read 7:39 a.m. The ringing wasn't coming from there. I rolled over, reaching for Kevin, but of course, he was gone. I slid out of bed and wrapped myself in my old pink bathrobe and went searching for the unfamiliar sound. The shrill ringing continued, and I followed it to my bathroom. Kevin's phone was sitting on the vanity. He must have left it by mistake. I was the bird dashing to catch the unattainable worm. I thought to myself, *no wonder I didn't know the ring, he never takes it off vibrate.* The phone rang one more time before abruptly going quiet.

I looked at the phone and debated what to do with it. Hmmh. I knew he needed his phone, but he should have already reacehd the stadium, by now. I opened the phone to see if he had any of his personal numbers stored. And when I came to the screen, I read the ICON: 1 missed call from R.W.

R.W.? At 7:39 a.m.?

Curiosity had overtaken me, and I decided to listen to the message to see just who this R.W. could be. I pushed the button and waited anxiously. A woman's voice came through.

"Baby, this is Roshanda. Are you up? This is your wake up call."

Baby, this is Roshanda? Her voice instantly set my flesh afire. I was livid. My jaw dropped in painful amazement at this hoochie who was comfortable enough with Kevin to call him at 7:39 a.m.

"You wanted me to call you, sweetie, and get you up," the message continued, "Baby? Are you up?"

I had to put the phone down before I heard anything else. I mumbled obscenities beneath my breath.

"Soft-talking bitch callin' MY man."

Dammit, I don't think so. Who the hell is this lady who obviously feels too close and too comfortable with MY Kev? Mr. Walker has been seeing me for the past seven years. I dated him freely and openly. I risked the comfort and security of *my own* committed relationships with another man. Kevin was the man with whom I shared my heart with while dating others. The man that I hung around with, in hopes that he would one day turn to me with brown eyes full of sincerity, lifting me in his strapping arms while making this heartfelt declaration, "I want only you, Channa Renée Jones!"

Ms. Wake-Up Call could throw a wrench into all that.

My fingers red from fury, I picked up the phone and deleted the message. But that wasn't enough. S*he could always call back.* So I pushed the button to return her call.

The ring was too long, but she answered.

"Hello."

"He...He-llo." My voice cracked, throat full of saliva and vinegar from anticipating the confrontation. "You just called for Kev."

I could end her, and I knew it. The silence was thick and I leaned back on the counter and pulled my robe tighter with my free hand.

Finally, she replied, "I'm Kevin's woman. Who are you?"

Her words were fully enunciated and each syllable correctly accented and pronounced. She reminded me of Erica. I knew I had to be a lady, so I replied calmly and coolly.

"Well, *I'm* Kevin's woman, and have been for seven years. So, you couldn't possibly be *his woman.* He doesn't have a committed relationship with any woman. He has a woman in New York, Atlanta, L.A., and I'm the woman in New Jersey."

The heat felt good as it left my body. My voice was strong, dominant. I was not the one to be messed with.

"So, you see, you couldn't possibly be his woman, lady, or whatever it is you claim to be."

She fell silent again. I knew I hit her hard with my words. I waited for her to say something else. I was ready for her. I had to make sure she never talked to Kevin again. *Shit! She's going to tell Kevin. Damn, I hope this chick doesn't have caller I.D.*

"I see that you're on Kevin's phone." *Shit!* "Did you have sex with him?"

The way she said it just sounded so clinical, impersonal. I had to let her know that it was no visit to the dentist. A sly grin crept across my face as I relished in giving her every minute detail, blow by glorious blow, of the wild night spent with Kev.

"Oh, of course!" I sang. "And the dick was good, as always."

There was a deafening hush as her end went cold. I could hear her hurt and confusion in the silence and I knew I messed up. I had taken my anger out on her and she wasn't ready for it.

"I thought I was in a committed relationship," she answered weakly, sobbing.

I imagined brokenhearted tears streaming down the

cheeks of the faceless voice. I could picture her sitting alone in her apartment, dressed in sweats with her hair piled up on top of her head, looking a hot mess. I'd been there too.

"How could you do this?" she whispered into the phone.

I didn't know if she was angry that I was sleeping with Kevin, or angry that I told her.

"Do what? Tell you the truth? You should be thanking me."

Yeah, I went there. I didn't want to hurt her, just make her understand. I was just like Erica, keepin' it real.

"It's best you know that you aren't in a committed relationship. It's only fair. I can tell you things about Kevin Dean Walker that would really leave you speechless on the other end."

I felt bad, but she hung up before I had a chance to save my butt. Now it was just a matter of time before I had to explain myself to Kevin.

I put Kevin's phone on the nightstand, making sure to put it on silent so that I wouldn't get any more calls from women dreaming they were Kevin's one-and-only. If anybody was ever going to fill that position, it was going to be me.

As I lay back down alone in my bed, an intense wave of regret and anger swept over me. R.W. Roshanda. I was mad at myself for losing control with a woman that didn't matter—for turning my passion for Kevin into something petty. I wanted to hurt her because her very existence hurt me. I thought Kevin had other women, but KNOWING it was different. Actually speaking to one of them made his womanizing so much more real. I started to imagine them alone in her home in Los Angeles or New York or Atlanta, going out to places Kevin and I would go, laughing the way Kevin and I laughed, making love the way Kevin and I made love. I could hear her voice, so classy and clear, saying, "I love you, Kevin."

I felt my stomach lurch and bile rose up my throat. I had ruined it with Kevin. I knew it. Once Roshanda told him what I'd done, he wouldn't ever trust me again for giving up his secret to her.

Then I started to get a little angry. Why should I be worried about what he would think of me? He was the liar and the cheat. He was the man that only entered his women's initials in the phone just in case anybody saw. I wondered whom he would have told me R.W. was if I had just seen the name and not heard the voice. Robert Williams? Richard Walters? I knew whatever name he gave me wouldn't have been a Rosanna or a Rhoda or a Rita. He was the one who was trying to hide his true self, while I was completely out there for all to see.

I ran my hand over the spot where Kevin had been just hours ago, and smelled the pillow that still contained traces of his cologne. If I shut my eyes hard enough, it was like he was still there with me. I still wanted him to be there with me, even though I was angry with both of us. I hated him and loved him, and at 7:45 a.m. with Roshanda's voice still ringing in my ears, it was too much to take.

In a fury, I took the pillowcase off his pillow and threw it to the floor, but the bed still smelled like him. I ripped the comforter and blankets from their neat tucks around the corner of my bed and threw everything into the center, panting from my fury as I went. I pulled everything from around my bed that smelled like him and threw it in the mix, including my old robe. Naked, I scooped it all up and ran down to the laundry room to ram it all in into the washing machine. I had to get rid of him from my mind by getting rid of him from my bed. I dumped twice as much detergent in the machine as normal and put it on a double wash, heavy soil. I needed as much help as I could get to wash Kevin Dean Walker out of my life.

Exhausted, I fell to my knees and started to cry. I could wash the sheets as much as I wanted, but it wasn't going to help me get rid of him one bit. Despite all the women, and there were tons of women he was lying to, I still desired him like a fool. It wasn't because of the things "on paper." At the core of me, I didn't care that he was Head of Operations with the world-famous New York Knicks, Juris Doctor from NYU, wealthy, single, and with a big, juicy dick. I wanted him because when I was with him, he made me feel like I had it all. My mind, body, and soul craved him.

My love for him was something of a rare oddity, allowing him to be in my life without pushing him into commitment. In all other areas of my life, I was a pusher—I pushed myself through college to graduate and became the top of my class. I pushed myself through graduate school to get an MBA. I pushed my way past racial and gender discrimination to get an executive position at a multinational corporation. I pushed myself through the mental and physical anguish of being paralyzed to come out on top once again. With Kevin, though, there was no pushing. Instead, I used the tender patience of my love, sweetness, sexiness, understanding, and of course, my GOOD P-U-S-S-Y to guide him into commitment. I wasn't on my time frame with Kevin. I was on his, and it was finally starting to get old.

I went back to my naked bed and laid in the center. I opened my arms and legs out to take up the whole space. I tried to fall back asleep, but my mind just kept going back to Kevin and what I needed to do to turn things around—if things could still be turned around. I wanted him to be sleepless without me, when he couldn't spoon me and feel me safely nestled into the contours of his body. I wanted him to hate every morning when he couldn't wake up and say, "Good morning, Channa baby." I wanted him to not be able to eat or think or function without me by his side. Most of all, I wanted him to desire me, need me, love only me.

I wondered if Roshanda was calling Kevin's work or home at that moment, to tell him everything I had told her. Even if she kept quiet, I knew I didn't know for sure that he was loyal to me. Heck, we were both seeing other people.

I closed my eyes and fell into a dark sleep, resting for the drama that I knew would unfold that day. My dreams and nightmares would have to wait until I woke up.

Chapter 17

I pulled into my cobblestone driveway. I was pleased as I took in the landscapers' skilled maintenance of the neighborhood's foliage. Hedges were perfectly trimmed with not one branch or leaf left astray. Gardens were grown from seeds that were deliberately planted so that when they sprouted, beautiful arrays of nature's hues would decorate freshly manicured lawns. I tapped the button right above the windshield on the driver's side to open my garage door. Yeah, moving to Montclair, New Jersey was definitely a good decision.

I entered my garage and parked the car. After pushing the button two more times, the door closed behind me. I unlocked the door leading to my kitchen and walked over to my main hallway where I had a Bible laying on a long marble table. It was opened to the Book of Job, which tells the story of a man who lost his family, money, and for a time, his will to go on. He never lost faith, though, and because of this, God replenished Job's losses ten times. I have been Job. I'd lost my job, my home, my friends, and even my will to live, but like Job, I put my faith in the Lord and was blessed tenfold. I kissed my hand then placed it on the Bible, thanking Him for all that surrounded me. Not just for the gorgeous home, but for my family and friends who stuck by my side when I too had lost everything. I repeated this ritual every time I walked in and out of my home. This is how I never forgot that God was with me always.

Feeling a little hungry, I went into the kitchen to find

a snack suitable for my craving. I placed my purse on the round glass kitchen table and caught a familiar glimpse of my cell phone's flashing light. I had missed a call. *Funny, I didn't hear the phone.* I flipped it open with my thumb and dialed "star" plus "one" and "talk", and waited for the message.

"Hi, Channa. Are we still going to eat after work? I know, I said I would be at your house before sixish, but I'm stuck at the firm."

It was Carl.

"I need to tie up some loose ends, OK? I'll grab something at Whole Foods down over on Bloomfield. I'll get your favorites—vegetarian chili, garlic bean dip, and those blue chips that you love. Channa baby, I'm sorry. You know I'm just trying to make a living, that's all. You know your poor paralegal boyfriend is trying to have millions just like you."

Millions. I thought back to a time when a can of beans and one measly frank had to be stretched among three people for three days. It's amazing how things change. I also remembered a time when I wouldn't have given a struggling paralegal the time of day, but I've changed. It used to be that if Channa Renée Jones did not spot Pradas on his feet, and Gucci on his back…NEXT. Now, I'm dating a common, nine to five, working man who'd never be able to afford the high- priced restaurants and tiny blue boxes from Tiffany's to which I was accustomed. No, he was perfectly content with the mediocre health food menu and a night of cuddling on the couch.

While some things had changed, Kevin Dean Walker had remained a constant. I've always had more than one suitor, one always being Kevin. He is the same man I've been secretly allowing to drain the sweet nectar of my honey hive for the past ten years. I was always ignoring my commitment to other men without any thought of how "my boyfriend" felt or how he would react if he found out about Kevin. I refused to allow my love life to remain in the confusing mess it's been during the Walker dynasty. Kevin was either going to have to shit or get off the pot. Either way, there were big sweeping changes that needed to be made in my life. I just didn't know where to start. That was where having true girlfriends, without jealously and pettiness came in handy. Only another woman would be able to connect with me and truly understand what I was going through. I hadn't spoken to Arnelle or Deja in weeks and needed to catch up. Forgetting about my hunger, I decided to go upstairs and call my girls.

My feet followed the trail of steps leading to the second level of my home. I placed my hand on the wooden railing of the staircase and trotted up the first ten steps. Counting steps was a method I used when I had to learn how to walk all over again. At first it was a bargaining chip, "if I can make ten steps, I'll take a break." Then, I counted to measure my success: *one, two, three*...was so much better than no steps at all. The fourth step was an achievement over the third, and so on. After the tenth step, I turned to my right. The rest of the carpeted staircase opened up wide to greet me as I ascended to my bedroom to place my cell phone on its charger on my dresser. I plugged it in and placed it down on the dresser's lacquered finish. I went over to the nightstand near my custom-made, massive cherry wood bed with smooth delicate carvings on the posts and picked up my cordless phone.

I dialed Arnelle's home number. Arnelle was a woman who worked with me at Morgan Pharmaceuticals when the company was trying to railroad me. She appeared to be a typical, All-American, White woman who was climbing the corporate ladder at a steady, persistent pace. Yet her looks were deceiving. After knowing her, that saying had a whole new meaning. Breaking through the glass ceiling was not a difficult task for a Black woman if the executives believe you are White. No one would have ever guessed her dirty little secret. Whites spoke freely around her, and she was privileged to conversations that would never have taken place if they had known who she truly was.

She was a good friend. When Richard Greene, my bigoted boss, tried to sabotage a very important presentation I was scheduled to give before the head honchos in Puerto Rico, she was right there to save my butt. Somehow, Richard had corrupted my files on my laptop, just hours before I was due to speak to a large group of men who held my professional future in their hands. I had spent days compiling my data, making my speech perfect, and putting together a killer Power Point presentation. Suddenly, everything was gone. Arnelle was the only person who offered me a heads up to a potential problem.

She overheard office rumors of Mr. Greene having it in for me. He was plotting something major to embarrass me in front of my colleagues. When I realized my presentation was gone, Arnelle came to my hotel room and turned my panic into relief. More computer savvy than I was, she recovered every bit of information I needed to wow the top-level execs. We watched Richard turn red with hatred as I delivered the presentation of my career.

But knocking them dead in Puerto Rico wasn't enough to keep my job after I'd had a series of accidents, one of which paralyzed me. Richard Greene managed to spin some tale and got me fired while I was helpless in a hospital bed. Arnelle was the one who broke the news that she was offered my job, but I didn't blame her. She stayed around when my other so-called friends left. When my malpractice suit went to court, I saw her in the audience. Had it not been for family and friends like Arnelle, I would not have made it out of those darker periods.

Arnelle answered in her classic, White-collar voice after the third ring, "Hello."

"Hi there," I chimed.

She immediately recognized my cheerful voice. "Channa? Channa, is that you?"

"Of course it's me. How are you?"

"This is great. I was thinking about you a few days ago. I didn't know if you still needed time to get everything together after the trial. I know it can take months, sometimes years, to get your life back on track. I wanted to give you enough space before I checked in on you. I'm so glad I didn't have to wait long. How have you been?"

"Ahh, you know. I can't complain. Well, I could, but what's the point? I know I've seen worse days. Remember Puerto Rico?"

"I hate to see people use their position and power to keep others from progressing, and that is exactly what Mr. Greene was trying to do. He was going to have you fired, not because your work was unacceptable, but for his own personal reasons. And he was going to use sabotage of all methods? Wiping out your presentation wasn't right. Wrong is wrong, and I couldn't watch it happen."

"You were really there when I needed you to be."

"Those were some crazy times. You probably don't want to see the inside of another courtroom any time soon, but you should sue."

"I am. I filed an E.E.O.C. and Division of Human Resources Complaint before the malpractice trial even started. My lawyers said I probably wouldn't have to go to court because my case was so strong. They'll settle in mediation."

"Good, Channa. I'm glad it's all over."

"I agree. I also wanted to thank you for the flowers. When times get rough, you really find out who your friends are."

I heard my wise grandmother's words come from my lips so naturally. I was listening when she spoke, and I know now more than ever how right she was.

"Channa, it was nothing. I just believe in doing what's right."

She was never one to arrogantly take credit for performing a life saving deed. She always showed up just in time and ready for action. She was in my life for a reason.

"Well, you have to let me treat you to dinner," I insisted.

"Oh no, Channa. You don't owe me anything," Arnelle resisted.

"I know I don't, but I am not taking no for an answer. So

how is Wednesday night?"

"OK, OK. I am dying to see you and catch you up on the latest gossip at Morgan."

"Sounds like a plan then. Let's say I call you Tuesday evening to confirm."

"I am looking forward to hearing from you, Channa. Oh, I can't wait to see you."

I could tell by her voice that she really missed me, and that she really cared.

Making dinner plans reminded me I was hungry, so I went back downstairs to the kitchen. I went to the cupboard to grab a bag of barbecue potato chips and sat down at the kitchen table to call Deja. I needed to sit down. Otherwise, I'd be falling on the floor in laughter while I was talking to her. Deja was always so animated that it made for a lively exchange. There was never a boring moment with that girl. Finding true friends was not easy, and I needed to reach out to the few I had left. I dialed her cell phone and she answered in her sweet southern drawl after the first ring.

"And where the hell have you been?"

"In my skin…Hello to you too."

I laughed at Deja's tough guy act. I knew she was happy to hear from me. She was one of my oldest and dearest friends. We met while attending Columbia University in pursuit of our MBAs. She was from Georgia, and sweet as a peach. She could be a little hard to swallow at times, but her intentions were always sincere, and her advice always on point as if she were in my head and knew just what I needed to be told.

"You ain't funny, gurl! I am not laughing…OK, yes I am."

We cracked up at her inability to maintain the hard-hitting persona.

"Gurl, it's good to hear from you."

"Whatever. So fill me in."

As always, we jumped right to the point.

"Well, you know I'm planning this wedding and I'm losing my mind, Channa! Arrangements, settings, appointments with caterers and other people who want my damn money... I didn't know it would be this much work."

Deja was about to take the plunge.

"Well, if you need any help, you know I'm here for you. Just name the time and place."

"Oh, I will. You won't get outta helping me. You know I'm gonna work that ass overtime, so get ready. How are you feeling these days, gurl?"

"Don't worry; I'm ready for anything you throw at me. Everything is finally looking up over here."

"I'm glad for you. I'm glad that whole damn trial is over and you got what you deserved. Ten million dollars, that new beautiful home, but best of all, you are literally on your feet! That damn doctor. I knew he was a fraud. Poking needles in somebody's back and he don't know what the hell he's doin'. Gurl, you shoulda sued the shit outta his ass, just like you did. He wasn't even licensed to perform those treatments to your spine."

"Yeah, he's out of business. So what else is going on?"

I sat and listened as I tried to discreetly feast on the bag of chips. *Crunch, crunch, crunch.*

"Well, that crazy cousin of mine, Jason, is doing all right. He was able to keep his manager's position, but you know he had to drop out of school to work full time."

"Well, that's good, isn't it? I mean, he had to become responsible one day."

"Hell no, it's not good. *One day,* was sure as hell not *today*. Those babies were born two days apart. He just tossed his future away with not just one, but two kids at the same damn time? He's only twenty! What kinda shit is that? At least the two babies' mothers are getting along, finally. They bring the kids by so that they can play together and grow up as a family."

"Finally? What was going on?"

"Gurl, they were in his mama's house fightin'. You know

it was building up, and one day it exploded. They were bringing the babies to be watched by their grandmother, and they got there at the same damn time. Well, once they got to the door, one of the girls got an attitude because the other girl rang the doorbell before she did. What kind of young-ass shit is that?"

"So they were fighting on the porch over who rang the bell first? They are very young."

"Gurl, my auntie got to the porch and they were throwin' down! I mean, on the ground rolling around like two mad lions. My auntie snatched both their asses up and asked what the hell was wrong with them."

"Deja, stop. Get out of here, Jason's mother?"

"Yeah gurl, they left the babies by the door and coulda straight rolled on them while they were acting like fools and done some real damage. She took them both inside and told them they had to cut out the foolishness and start acting like women who had children now. Auntie told them silly girls to put their children first. She said she wasn't gonna have her grandbabies rollin' around fightin' in her house, and their mamas wasn't gon' be doin' it neither."

"Really?"

Jason obviously had a problem and needed to be blamed more than anybody. Any man who thinks it's OK to be unmarried and populate the earth with his seed through the wombs of many different women is crazy. And he was only twenty, so his days of baby making were far from over. This was only the beginning, and if they didn't get the boy some professional help, he'd only get worse. Deja's rehashing of events that could not be changed was starting to make me sick, and I didn't want to hear anymore of it.

"I just don't understand those girls. They are both stupid if you ask me. They are both still in love with him, and he's still sleeping with both of them. They've worked out some ridiculous schedule to split up Jason's time between them, and talking about what is best for the kids. They took my

Auntie's advice and interpreted it in their own sick way. Auntie said whatever keeps the peace. Isn't that outrageous?"

"Yeah, it is."

I remembered making a snide remark about sharing Andre with Erica the day she made her presence known. I was about to mention it to Deja again, but I knew neither one of us wanted to talk about Andre anymore. Deja would sit and listen to me talk about him when I first met him years ago, but she had threatened to glue my lips together with her weave adhesive if I didn't stop talking about him. So I knew I had talked too much about him in the past and also in the present. Enough had been said on the subject of Andre.

"So, enough about me. How is that man of yours, Carl?"

"Carl is fine."

"Carl is fine."

She poked fun, mimicking me to a tee.

"Fine? That's all you have to say? Well, I guess I didn't ask the right question. Let's try this one on for size...how is Kevin?"

Deja knew every detail of the fiasco I had been going on with Kevin. Her nonjudgmental advice always made me comfortable enough to discuss specifics that I would never reveal to another living soul.

"Kevin is still Kevin."

"Just as I figured. What has that man done now?"

"He kicked me out of his office right after he finished screwing me on my period."

"What? Why? Why?! Wait, you had sex on your period? Eww, you nasty heifer."

"Leave me alone, yes on my period. I'm not the only woman who gets it on when she's got her menstrual. I'm not the first and I won't be the last."

"And neither, will I, hahaha. I know how it is; I was just messing with you. Shoo, I know how my men like it. Anytime, anywhere, and they don't let a red light stop them. Besides, there are other holes if you know what I mean."

"Ah-ha-ha! You are something else, Deja. But yeah, he rushed me out saying he had to go meet one of the players for drinks."

"Isn't that something? Another player? Gurl, he was probably going to meet one of his other women for drinks. What does he think you are, a booty call?"

"No, he thinks he's just *dating* me. I know, I'm starting to feel like a booty call. But you know how it is with me and Kevin. I love him. I'm just at my wit's end. I want him to be all mine. Do you know it's been ten years? I want a commitment."

"If you wanted him to commit, you should've left him eight years ago and made him chase your ass. Men like it when they have to chase you. You always make yourself available to him."

Like I said, Deja's always on point.

"Now, let's get back to this period thing, don't you make a mess doing that?"

"No, not if you lay a towel down."

"Oh, I see, and what about him? Doesn't he get bloody?"

"Why are you acting like you don't know about having sex on your period?"

"Channa, I just really want to know if you used a condom with him. Please don't tell me you're still not using protection."

"Deja, it's been ten years and..."

"Uh-uh, don't even finish. You know you can't come up with an excuse to tell me I'm wrong. Damn, that man has got you sprung. You doin' all types of craziness."

"He's good I've never felt anything like it. Besides, I'm sure he doesn't have anything. I'd notice something after all this time. Kevin is in the best shape of his life...oooh, you should see his chest. It's chiseled like a Zulu Warrior...and he has a spear to match."

"Damn. There you go, off into la-la land. Please let me find a man that makes me want to give him some while

I'm bleeding just because his body looks damn good. That's what I need. I need a well endowed bodybuilder that makes me lose all good sense."

We cackled like two hens.

"But seriously, child, you are going to have to change the way you deal with Kevin. There's nuttin' you can do to make another person change, Channa. If you want them to change the way they treat you, then you have to reject the treatment you've been receiving so far. You can't let things continue the way they are because they will never change."

My phone clicked and I told Deja I'd call her back. Whew, saved by another call. I knew everything Deja was saying was right, but that's not what I wanted to hear. I picked up the other line. My mother's number was on the caller ID.

"Hey, Ma," I answered enthusiastically.

"Hey, Sunshine. How are you feeling?"

"I'm feeling well. What about you? Is everything OK?"

"Everything's fine. Don't worry about me. I wanted to know if you were going to your physical therapy on Wednesday. You know it's important to keep strength in those muscles."

Uggh! The last thing I wanted to think about was my disability. I was trying to spend my time focusing on the positive.

"Yes, Ma, I know."

Tango began barking loudly.

"Ma, I have to let Tango out before he has a conniption."

"OK, baby. I just wanted to check on you."

"All right, Ma. Thanks. I love you."

I hung up and opened the door to my backyard. Yeah, I now had a big, beautiful backyard. No more walking the streets with a Pooper Scooper. Now Tango could just go out in the yard and do his business. Life was even better for the dog.

I sat on the wooden park bench I had in the yard that was lined with Jersey's finest cherry trees. The flowerbed was blooming beautifully. I wondered if life could always be this good as I contemplated the previous years' heartache. Seeing Tango run through the yard with such speed and agility made me wish for past times when I was able to move with the same vigor.

I got up from the bench and grabbed Tango's ball sitting beside a tree. A few cherries had fallen with the rain from a few days ago and left red dye spots all over the ball. I tossed it to the other side of the yard and yelled for Tango to fetch it. He darted in the ball's direction and skipped back to me with the retrieval. We played for a few minutes then I decided to go back inside to wait for Carl to arrive with dinner. *Oh yeah, and I said I'd call Deja back.*

I headed to the kitchen and picked up the phone and hit the redial button.

"Hey gurl, I just finished walking Tango."

I could hear feet shuffling and people talking in the background.

"What's all that noise behind you?"

"Gurl, I was on my way out the house when you called me the first time. I gotta get my hair braided. I'm trying to save some money and cut back on the perms."

"Oh, I hear you."

I heard it, but I couldn't picture it. At the first sight of any new growth, Deja was at the salon and telling the hairdresser to put in a really super strength touch up. She had to maintain her impeccable appearance.

"Yeah, you know I had to stop going to the Dominicans. They used to be reasonable and I didn't care if they couldn't speak English, as long as they knew how to lay these naps down. But now they've gotten hip. Nah, they ain't charging thirty-five bucks for a no-lye anymore, they want to charge what the black folks are charging these days."

"No, get out of here. How much is that?"

"Forty to fifty bucks for a no-lye. Can you believe that?"

"Well, you know, Deja, I am letting my perm grow out. Yeah, child."

"Channa, now what the hell you doin' that for? You know you have hair covering every section and crevice of that head, and your head is the size of a beach ball. How you gonna let all that grow out when you know good and damn well that once the heat and humidity hit it, you'll be looking like Buckwheat's grandmother gone wild?"

I laughed uproariously as I envisioned an old Aunt Jemima with her hair sticking out wildly in a hundred different directions from beneath her scarf.

"Aw, why you gotta go there? It's not that bad. That stuff on your head is a whole lot worse than mine, and you know it."

"I'm just sayin' you're my gurl, and I'm only looking out for your best interest. You can't walk around looking like you just took your finger out of a light socket."

"Whatever. So, what are you getting done?"

"Something I won't have to tend to for months. You know, they tiny micro-braids."

"Oh, OK, Bo Derek."

"Uh, not quite honey. Bo had cornrows in that movie with the little man, what was the name? Ten? Anyway, micro-braids don't lie down flat. They hang free, almost like your own hair. You know, like Brandy when she was on Moesha."

"Damn, that's a million and one braid. Deja, how long does that take?"

"Gurl, I don't know and I don't care. I'm not spending a penny for the next few months on this head. I still can't believe those Dominicans went up on the price. They can *beso me culo*. That's right. They can *kiss my ass!*"

"So, where are you getting it done?"

"I'm headed to the building now. This girl that lives in the projects is gonna do it for me. She's only charging me fifty bucks for all that work. I just had to buy the hair. She's good though. She did a coworker's hair, and it came out really good. It lasted for at least three months. And, Channa, this damn girl, the braider, is only fourteen!"

"Well, she's already an entrepreneur."

"Yeah, there are a lot of entrepreneurs living in the projects of Southwest DC. I'm sure some will come and ask me if I'd like to sample their crack rock...*first hit's free*."

Although the statement was probably true, I doubled over clutching my stomach at Deja's hilarity.

Catching my breath, I said, "But this is one businesswoman who's on the path to making make an honest living."

"I know, which is why I'm going to pay her $100. I want her to keep doing hair and see that money can really be made in it if her work is of good quality. We have to encourage our youth to follow a legitimate path, and sometimes showing them that good money can be made if they do right. This will help motivate them to make money legally."

"Listen to you. I guess the MBA that you got in finance taught you the value of a dollar."

"Gurl, I know the value of a penny! Yeah, and I have to pass that knowledge on."

"You're right, but since when are you a social worker?"

"Channa, Deja has always loved the kids."

"You are so silly, and I'm shocked at you, Miss Black Chanel. You are lowering your standards and stepping one of those four hundred dollar shoes inside the PJ's?"

"Gurl, I'm slumming it, but I'm not stupid. You think I'm gonna come in here dressed in my regular clothes? Oh, HELL to the NO. They ain't robbing me and throwing my body in a dumpster out back. Not to-day."

"Stop it Deja. You're killing me."

Tears were forming in the corners of my eyes from holding back the laughs.

"I just hope they don't kill me. Damn, look at this place. You know the rats are runnin' things. I think I see a trap bitten in half."

"What?"

"I just found the damn building the girl lives in. They all look the same, and not all of them have letters on them. I have to take the elevator up to the ninth floor."

"You'd better make sure it works. Or you'll be taking the stairs."

"Oh, it works. If it didn't, Deja would be takin' her ass back Northeast. I'll be damned if I'm takin' the pissy-ass stairs all the way to the ninth floor. Uh-uh, she'd have to bring a chair down and do my hair outside."

"Now you know that not all projects have staircases that smell like piss, you just happen to be in a bad one."

"Yeah, you're right. Oh, here's the elevator."

I heard the elevator door open and imagined it was one of the old fashioned models as the sound of the gate sliding back came through the phone's receiver.

"Oh, uh-uh. This is nasty."

"What's wrong?"

"This elevator is all wrong. It smells to high hell and heaven in here. What the hell is wrong with people? They don't believe in pissing in toilets? Since when is the elevator the place to relieve bodily functions?"

"Deja, it can't be that bad."

"Oh yes it can. My nostrils are gonna be stinging for days with the smell of human and rat piss. I can't believe people are this damn nasty in this day and age. They got working toilets in their apartments. That's just nasty."

"I told you. You're just in a bad PJ. Not all of them look like that."

"What? I didn't catch that."

"I said you knew you're in a bad PJ. Not all of them look like that one."

"Hello?"

Deja must have been losing the connection in the elevator.

"Hello? Deja? Can you hear me?"

"Damn, my phone is going in and out, Channa, and I'm almost at the floor so I'll give you a call later."

"OK, and be safe."

"Don't worry, I said I wasn't stupid. You know I got a knife on me. Bye-Bye."

Oh, that Deja is a trip. Sweet as a peach, just don't cross her, she'll cut ya. I laughed some more and rubbed my cheeks, which hurt from smiling nonstop.

Chapter 16

Carl showed up not too long after I finished speaking to Deja. The doorbell chimed to the melody, *Hallelujah*! I hurried to the door and there he stood, all five feet and eleven inches of him. Not the height I'm used to seeing, but he was charming, kind, and gentle which made up for his lack of height.

Carl was raised in a single parent home in Houston, Texas. He paid his way through Texas A&M by working two jobs. Now, he attended classes at New York Law School three nights a week. He worked hard all day and loved to unwind in my arms. I greeted him with a kiss on each cheek like a Hollywood diva.

"*Muah, muah*. Hi baby, how was your day?"

Damn, I sound like June Cleaver.

"I really want to thank you for bringing the food, but you do know I would've cooked."

I took the bags from him and placed them on the kitchen counter, smiling to myself that we were eating supermarket takeout. I knew it was hard for Carl, with his tightly gripped budget and practical approach to life. My Carl who didn't even see the point of getting a double mocha grande from Starbucks. That was actually how I met him. He was ordering a plain cup of decaf, two sugars, and skim milk down at the Starbucks at Whole Foods.

Sheesh! I thought as I fumbled through my purse with my head down trying to locate my wallet when I heard the ridiculous order being placed. I had to get a view of the perpetrator of such a horrendous crime. What kind of person would come to STARBUCKS and pay two dollars for a cup of coffee? He had to be very cheap, but wanted to fit in with the crowd, so he paid two dollars for a Starbucks cup filled with decaf coffee, no less. I found the entire exchange senseless. I looked him over and attempted to make sense of the situation.

I got to the counter as I was scouting for my wallet in this mess of a purse that I had once called orderly.

"Please, a double shot mocha cappuccino, extra sweet. Thanks."

It rang up to $3.59. I pulled out a five-dollar bill and paid the cashier. After collecting my change, I went down to the end of the counter to make my mocha pick-up, and there was Mr. Cheap Decaf. He smiled at me. *Here we go*, I thought. *Well at least he has all his teeth, and they are straight and white.* I smiled back, noticing he was a very nice-looking man. I wondered if I would ever be able to date such a regular guy. After all, I was used to the Mr. Kevin Dean Walkers of the world. The rich, high-powered executives who would never be caught dead ordering decaf from Starbucks. I was still pondering what life would be like with Mr. Cheap Decaf when he interrupted my thoughts with his voice.

"Hi, I'm Carl. Do you come here often?"

Oh, no he didn't just use the oldest line in the book. Who does he think I am, that I'm going to fall for this one? Do I come here often? Ahhhh. What a cornball.

"Hi, I'm Channa. And no, I'm not a caffeine-o-holic."

That much was true. I treated myself from time to time, but I didn't need Starbucks like some people I knew.

"Well, that's too bad. I was hoping you'd say yes and we could meet one day for a cup."

Is he kidding? He can't even buy himself a real cup of coffee, and now Mr. Cheap Decaf wants to treat me? I didn't want him to go into cardiac arrest upon seeing that my coffee cost more than two of his.

"Well, maybe some other time."

I turned my attention to the goings-on behind the counter to find out what was taking so long with my order. I usually didn't mind waiting, but I really wanted to go before he started another conversation. Darn it. Too late.

"Well, how often *do* you stop by? I'll tell you what, how about I just give you my number, and the next time you're in the area, you can give me a call? We can share some stories over a nice hot cup of Joe."

Cup of Joe? Who is he? Humphrey Bogart asking Lauren Bacall down to the café for a cup of coffee? I'd only heard that phrase in old movies. *This guy is a walking book of clichés.* But what the hell? I hadn't been out in a while. What did I have to lose by taking the number? He was cute, and maybe I'd be able to get past the overuse of corny-ass comments.

"That sounds good. Do you have a card?"

I hoped he was at least an entrepreneur with his own business that he'd invested his money in. That could explain the cheap decaf.

"Uh, no, but they've got pen and paper behind the counter."

He smiled at me again, and it made me laugh. There was something about his smile I liked. He asked one of the workers behind the glass counter for a pen and piece of paper.

Another worker placed my coffee on the counter in front of me and I thanked him. I grabbed it, and the piece of paper with the phone number from Carl's hand. I told him that it was nice to meet him. As I left, I had a second thought about calling him. He wasn't really my type, but maybe that's just what I needed—a change of pace.

It was almost three weeks later when I had a hankering for Starbucks. I figured, *why not?* and went into my bedroom to find the paper on which Carl had written his number. It was in the top drawer of my jewelry box with the bracelets. He just wasn't important enough to put into my cell phone. Then, looking at the paper, I wondered, "What if he doesn't remember me? It was three weeks ago." I started to throw the number away, thinking that he probably applied his "Do you come here often?" line on dozens of women daily. Then I thought of his smile. It was bright, and seemed to light his face with an entrancing glow. *And hey now, wait a minute. I'm Channa Renée Jones! I make a hell of a first impression.* I cast aside my doubts and picked up the phone by my bed.

"Hello?" The voice was jovial.

"Hello, may I speak with Carl?" I asked confidently.

"This is he. Who's calling?"

He was curious, but pleasant. That was a good sign that he didn't have a bunch of bill collectors calling him day and night.

"This is Channa, we—"

"Oh, the woman from Starbucks! I'm surprised you called."

"Well, I've been really busy and just got a free moment."

You always have to make them think you're busy, even if you're not.

"I wanted to know if the offer for coffee still stood."

"Of course it does. I have a pretty full schedule myself, so if you'd like to set a date and time, just let me know and I can tell you if I'm free."

"OK, well, I'm looking at my calendar, and I'm free Tuesday."

"Ooh, Tuesday's no good. I have class. What about Wednesday afternoon?"

This was not as easy as I thought it would be. I just knew for sure that whatever I suggested would be taken.

"OK, then Wednesday it is."

The rest is history. After going on a few dates and spending time really getting to know Carl, I found him to be not only good-looking, but also an intellectual. I knew that was a hard combination to find. I enjoyed the time we spent getting better acquainted, and I knew that he savored every minute. He was a protector who would keep me safe in his love. He learned of my shortcomings, and didn't run to the mountains screaming for mercy. He was a good fit for me, well, at the time.

Now there we were, about to spend a quiet evening in the safe confines of my home. He opened the bags and began to remove the white food containers. I headed to the refrigerator.

"Carl, what do you want to drink?"

"What do you have?"

He was now sitting at the table opening containers, trying to figure out what was in each.

"Uh, let's see."

I skimmed the shelves and noticed that it was time for food shopping.

"Hmm. Carrot juice or wine?"

"Carrot juice sounds good to me. What's up, doc?"

He cracked himself up. He was still corny, but I loved him. I was glad the open refrigerator door blocked his view of me rolling my eyes and shaking my head in awe as I wondered where he came up with this stuff. We sat at the round table across from each other, preparing to indulge in our meals.

"That's your favorite veggie dish, right? There was a new girl taking orders today, and she downright confused me. I know what I usually get, but I wasn't sure for you this time."

It wasn't that the vegetarian chili was my favorite. It just was the least greasy food item to eat. I had to watch my shape even if no one else was.

"No, this is it. Thank you, baby."

I dug into my chili with a hearty appetite. Carl got himself a grilled chicken sandwich and tossed side salad with no dressing.

"Good, I just wanted to make sure. So what did you do today?"

"Nothing really, just spoke to Arnelle. We're meeting for dinner later this week. Deja is still crazy, and my mother called to check on me. What about you?"

"Well, I'm researching some cases for one of the lawyers. He's got a client who is suing her former employer for racial and gender discrimination. This can be a landmark case for the firm if it's won. I want to do an impressive job with gathering all the research they need. I just don't want it to interfere with my studying for school. I guess I can do both."

"You've got a lot on your plate, but remember you're the same man who worked two jobs while taking a full course load every semester in college. And doesn't New York Law school has an excellent law library? You can use it after class instead of going to the office. The old dusty books at the firm are not as updated with new case law. Just use the school's library."

"That's why I love you. You know just what to say to keep me focused. I'm going to do that."

He smiled at me as if to say, "You are something else, Channa."

"I don't offer my candid advice to loved ones frequently, so you'd better follow it."

We finished our dinner chat and moved into the den, my special room, located in the far left corner of the house. See, there just seemed to be something out there in the world, something out of my control that wanted to cause me harm. I just felt it in my bones. Before I moved into the house, I had the den painted all black. I read in one of those home-remodeling magazines that some believe black to be the color of protection. The color "black" would repel against the world's unseen evil forces. I felt particularly safe when huddled in there, like the wickedness was left at the doorway, because the outside forces that tried to destroy me could not penetrate the blackness. I couldn't tell anyone the real reason the room was black. They'd think I lost my mind. I'll never change it, though. It keeps me sane.

We cuddled up on the couch in the center of the room while we watched our favorite prime-time programming.

We had the same taste in television programs. We never had horrible remote control fights like most couples. He liked all of the *Law and Order* shows, as well as *CSI.* We were kept in suspense as we watched the scripted drama unfold as each crime was solved. After the last show went off at eleven, Carl gave me *the look.*

I gave him credit. He held out until bedtime, but now it was time for him to collect his prize. I looked up at him grinning slyly, and I knew what was on his mind. It had been on my mind too, but now it was time to act. He'd been banished for the past week by my evil Aunt Flo, my period. I ran my hand over the bulge in his pants and headed upstairs to the bedroom. Heeding the signal, he was on my heels all the way.

Once we reached our destination, he laid me on the bed and climbed on top of me.

"Channa, you don't know how badly I wanted you all week."

He said the same thing every month. I obliged.

"I wanted you too, baby."

I knew I was lying, but I did it so well, even I started to believe myself after a while.

"Oh, Channa."

He said my name, and the first thing that popped into my head was how Kevin said my name. I pushed the thought out of my head and went back to concentrating on loving the man I was with. Carl continued kissing my neck feverishly, as if he couldn't wait to push himself deep inside the moisture puddle being created between my legs. His kisses were quick and forceful as his lips pressed hungrily against my flesh. It was effective, but it wasn't Kevin. No matter how hard I tried to get that man out of my head, I couldn't. Not even when my Carl was trying to make love to me.

I decided to stop fighting it and just go with the flow. I closed my eyes and just pretended Carl was Kevin. As soon as I did, my little moisture puddle turned into the Grand Rapids. I reached up and held Carl close to me as I grinded my pussy against the bulge that had grown considerably since I first touched it downstairs. He was ready and so was I. He unbuttoned my shirt and buried his head between my breasts as he pecked at their softness. I ran my hands over his back and up under his shirt. Then I stripped it off of him.

I imagined his chest was Kevin's as he pressed his body firmly against mine. It was warm, but not as muscular. I just had to contiune fantasizing. Carl stood up to remove the rest of his clothing, and then he slowly took off my remaining garments. He was naked, and his dick stood at attention, saluting me before entering. Once Carl penetrated me, I waited to see if his reaction was any different from other times. I was riddled with guilt and expected him to immediately jump up and insist on knowing whose big dick had been inside his pussy. But he didn't. He just moaned in relief.

"Finally. I couldn't wait for this, Channa."

"Neither could I K..., just don't stop."

I almost slipped up. Thank goodness their names both start with the same sound. I pulled it off because Carl became very excited. I felt him swell even harder inside me. His strokes were rapid and hard. I slowed the sway of my hips to get him to calm down. He was a starved wolf. I wanted more time to take in the moment, to pretend Kevin was making love to me.

Needless to say, at the rate Carl was going, he finished a bit more swiftly than usual. It was normal right after my period went away. He was backed up, and at the first feel of relief, he was sure to explode. His strokes became more hurried, and he ignored my hips' suggestion to slow down as he continued to quicken his thrusts.

"Oh, Channa."

His head flew back, his back arched, and he quickly collapsed as he laid on top of me in a sweaty lump. As Carl remained motionless, I wondered why I couldn't get Kevin to stay the night and curl up with me the same way Carl always wanted to. I stroked Carl's back, feeling guilty for conjuring up thoughts of Kevin to put me in the mood. I just couldn't help myself. I didn't choose the times Kevin invaded my thoughts without my permission.

Carl's warm breath tickled at my neck. "Whew, that felt so good, baby."

"Mmm-hmm! It was all I could think about all week."

Lying again. I had already been with Kevin earlier in the week, and could only think about getting back to him.

"I know you wanna lay on me all night, but I have to use the bathroom."

"Oh, I'm sorry. You're just so soft, Channa. I love the way you feel next to me."

Carl rolled off to the side, but one of his hands lingered on my thigh.

"I'm only going to be gone for a little while. Then I'll be right back to let you appreciate all this softness."

I withdrew to the bathroom to wash up before bed. Carl was in a resting position on the bed, ready to drift into his never-never land. I got under the blanket and turned my back to him for a comfortable night of spooning. My booty was comfortably and safely snuggled into his crotch with his arm draped around my waist. After a few minutes, I heard Carl begin to snore quietly. He didn't have a loud foghorn snore. Carl was a snorer, but it was a cute little snort that could barely be heard.

I took in the room's silence as it took my thoughts back to Kevin. I had a perfectly good man snuggled next to me, but that wasn't good enough. I was pining for a man who didn't snuggle with me, who never stayed the night, and who was probably out doing who knows what at that very moment. At least I knew where Carl was during the day, and I knew where he wanted to be at night. I had just what I wanted, but it was coming from the wrong man. I went to sleep thinking about Kevin so much, I kind of got my wish. I did have sex with Kevin that night, even if it was only in my dreams.

Carl bounced out of bed wide-eyed early the next morning, waking me up. Carl was extremely handsome with his little sexy body and pleasing personality. His fair golden complexion seemed to glow on most days, and although he was not as tall as I was accustomed to, he had a very manly stature. I mean, at five foot eleven and almost two hundred pounds, there were plenty of women who would want such a delicious catch. He had just been to the barber the day before, so his Caesar was freshly cut, making him look like a new man. He snatched the towel from his waist and began drying himself off. He walked back into the bedroom with the towel draped over the top of his head, the excess material hiding his face. With his face covered, I pretended I had Kevin in my bedroom after a night of smoldering hot sex. *Good morning, Sexy.*

Once Carl finished dressing, he found me sitting on the radiator across from the bed.

"Channa, why are you sitting over there?"

"It's cold, and I'm parking my booty right here until the heat comes up."

"Well, you wanted to keep the old boiler system. Why not get central heating?"

"Why? When the old boiler tank works just fine."

"Yeah, it works so fine you're cold and sitting on a cold radiator. How long does it take for this whole house to get warm?"

Carl smiled. He was teasing me.

"That doesn't matter. I am not paying to have central heat routed all through here and turn my life upside down with contractors and more bills. No way. The old tank in the basement works just fine."

I said all of this with my arms wrapped around me, rubbing my shoulders with the palms of my hands.

I watched him tie his shoes and make his way over to me.

He stroked my hair and looked at me lovingly for a moment.

"I'm happy you're in my life. Really. I just want you to know that."

"Of course you are, Carl. Who else do you know with such an effective heating system?"

We laughed at my little joke.

"Seriously, there's nothing more I want to do at the end of my stress-filled days than to get back to you. You're a breath of fresh air. My sunshine. My girl, my girl..."

I became bashful as he broke into song, serenading me as I sat with my derriere on the radiator.

"Stop it. You're going to be late."

"That's OK, as long as I'm not late getting back to you, everyone else can wait."

"Well, you'd better get moving. Don't keep them waiting too long. They may not want you when you get there."

"Oh, they'll want me. Give me a kiss."

I obliged, looking up to greet his beautiful, full lips with my own lips. Mah, mah, mah.

"I'll call you later to find out if you want me to bring dinner before I come over."

"Good. I don't think I'll feel like cooking tonight."

"All right then, baby, I'm Audi 5000!"

Geez, who still says that? Carl was on his way to face the world, and I was left to wonder "why." Why couldn't I just get Kevin out of my mind? Why couldn't Kevin act this way toward me? Why couldn't he act like he didn't want to leave my side? Why was Kevin always in a rush to end our passionate moment of love making? It was time to make some changes both with the way I acted, and how Kevin treated me. He was going to have to commit to me, or someone would have to have me committed to the crazy house.

Chapter 15

Uggh! The sharp ringing of the phone jolted me from a peaceful night's rest. I looked over at the digital alarm clock that my mother encouraged me to purchase. The numbers were large, and that's just what I needed when the sleep was still in my eyes. My eyesight had gotten weaker over the years. My family and friends tried to convince me to get LASIK eye surgery. But, I was just fine with being called "four-eyes," or popping in my Acuvue contacts. As I always said, it wasn't cool to have to tap around with a cane *and* a blind person's walking stick just to get through he world. No way, it wasn't for me. I wasn't going to go blind because another Dr. Patel decided to try his unskilled hands on my precious eyeballs. My value for the sense of sight ran deeper than the Nile.

Rrrriiiinnnnngggggg!!!

It was 10:33 a.m. *Who is calling me so damn early?* Anyone who knew me was well aware of the fact that I slept late since I never got a full night's rest. *If it is a telemarketer, he is going to get ripped a new asshole.* My mother kept at me to call Verizon and get "call intercept" to stop rude ass pushy sales people from getting through and waking me in the middle of my rest. I needed to stop being cheap and just pay the extra eight dollars for peace of mind.

"Hello."

"Channa, just wanted to chit-chat while I'm getting m hair done."

"Deja??? You're still at that child's house? It's 10:30 a.m.!

Please don't tell me—"

"Nah, gurl," Deja interrupted. "I left and came back. Tied a scarf around this nest and went home. You know how I like to get an early start."

"Damn! What kind of hairstyle are you gettin'?"

"You know, the thousand braid style. I told her to braid them thin as a single thread. You know, I need to hot curl and style my hair however I want. I don't care if it's in braids."

"OK, but was I the person on your 'to call' list? You know I sleep late. Shit, Deja, you outta everybody knows that I have to pee every four hours and I don't sleep the whole night."

"*Tch*! Channa, don't give me the act. I know that Carl spent the night and you were doing your thang. You old nasty-ass heifer. You had sex with Kev when you were on da rag and a couple days later, you hittin' it with Carl. Nah, I don't feel bad 'bout wakin' yo ass up. Get-up, nasty ho."

"I should hang up…"

"Oh, hell no, you shouldn't. You gonna sit right there while I sit right here and talk to my ass while this girl braids my hair."

"So how much more hair does she have to braid? Are you at least *half*way done?"

"Channa, I don't know, and I don't give a damn. If it takes three days to finish, then that's how long it takes. I'm not giving those Dominicans a dime, and the Blacks can forget about it. I don't know when they thought it was cool to start charging these Beverly Hills salon prices."

I accepted the fact that I wasn't going to get my sleep and sat up in the bed. *Damn, this girl can talk.* I settled into the conversation.

"I know what you mean. I'm still not sure what I'm going to do with my hair yet, but I know I'm letting that perm grow out."

"Well you need to do it under a wig. Don't think you got that good stuff that'll just lay down when it's natural. If it was, you wouldn't need a perm."

"Deja, I got this. I know what I'm working with here."

"I hope so. You just as confused 'bout your hair as you are 'bout your men."

"I'm not confused about my men. I know who I want, I just don't know how to make him want and feel the same thing."

"Well, you better make up your mind before Carl finds out."

"He won't find out."

"Why won't he? You think you can keep this up? And for how long before Carl gets hip to da game?"

"I don't think about it. I always meet Kev in the city. There's no way Carl would ever catch us. I mean, he's too busy between work and school."

"Stranger shit has happened." *I know that's right. Like gettin' a note on your mama's doorstep.* "You think you got drama? The gurl that's doin' my hair. Wait. Wait a minute, hold on a sec."

There was a muffled sound from her placing her hand over the receiver.

"OK, Channa, I'm back. Just wanted to make sure it was cool with my new hairstylist if I told my best friend, who will not repeat a word to anyone, what happened last night."

"What the hell is going on over there?"

"Well, my hairdresser's older sister is a nasty heifer like you, only she can be because she's young. Nobody cares about a young, nasty heifer. They expect it. But an old, nasty heifer like yourself? Uh-uh. Anyway, she's eighteen and been seein' this one guy since high school, but he got locked up for about a year for hustling. She was supposed to be faithful and all that stuff, but then she met this other guy who had a bigger dick and was sprung."

"Deja! How do you know all of this?"

"Her sister told me."

"I thought you said she was fourteen."

"She is fourteen, but she's grown as hell."

I heard both of them laughing.

"Anyway, gurl, so the first boyfriend got out of jail last week, but he already heard 'bout his girl's messin' with this other guy. Other girls got big mouths and were tellin' their boyfriends who were tellin' their brothers who are locked up and you know everybody's locked up together around here."

"Did you even take a breath just now?"

"Shut-up and listen so you can learn something! So, he got out and went to his old girlfriend's house and told my hairdresser's sister he was done with her 'cause she was embarrassing him in the streets. She thought everything was cool, but then last night, he got drunk. And, *guuurrrrlllll!* He came bangin' on the door like he's the po-lice. No one was saying anything and he was yellin'. I was in the kitchen, and my hairdresser's sister was in the back with her new man. Well, the new man got bold and went to the door. He opened it, and told the other guy to leave, but the old boyfriend refused to go and said he wanted to talk to his girl. The new boyfriend got mad, and they started fightin' right there in the hallway. Couldn't nobody break them up. They were like mad dogs."

"Damn, that's the PJ's for you. Y'all lucky nobody got shot. Seriously."

"Yeah, well, that's gonna be Carl and Kev if you keep it up. Fighting over your pussy 'cause you confused 'bout who to give it to. All this damn fighting goin' on, my cousin Jason's babies' mamas, these two guys, yup, you next, Channa. You know things happen in threes."

"I'm not confused."

"Then what are you gonna do?"

"I don't know."

I was sitting upright in my bed with my back against my headboard, wondering what I'd plan on doing.

"Only confused people say, 'I don't know.' Let's try to narrow it down. Who's nicer?"

"Come on, you know Carl is a sweetheart, and Kevin is sweet to my body."

I closed my eyes and sighed, thinking how lucky I was to have such great guys in my life.

"Yeah, especially when he's kicking you out right after you fucked."

"Deja! Who are you telling my business around?"

I could almost see that fourteen-year-old girl with Deja's nest of hair in her hands, and her mouth open after hearing all of that.

"Oh, calm down. Don't nobody here know you. OK, let's see…who's the better lover? Never mind. You don't have to answer. We see who you let screw you when you're bleeding."

"Damn, Deja."

She wouldn't let up.

"But yeah, I'm starting to get sick of this."

"You *just* startin'? Gurl, I was sick around year five. Anyway, you need to get sick enough to throw up or something. You gonna have to make a choice sooner or later."

Deja was always right.

"I know, Deja, and I will. I just want Kevin to know for sure. I hooked him. I just don't know how to reel him in."

"Hmm...let's see...give me a little time and I'll think about it and get back to you."

"OK, Deja. You know, I'm kinda glad you woke me up."

I stretched like a cat, thrusting my fist up to the ceiling and let out a loud yawn in her ear.

"Ugh, you hussy. Why you yawn in my ear like that? I know that's my cue."

"Oh please. You're a much bigger hussy than me. Just think about what we talked about and I'll call you later."

"I will, Channa. Lata."

I sat on the bed for a few minutes absorbing everything Deja just said. That girl knows she can talk. I got out of bed and headed to the bathroom. *Might as well start my day since Deja had to wake me up.*

After showering, I was in my walk-in closet with a towel wrapped around myself, still dripping wet. I knew I wanted to be comfortable, so I settled on a sienna-brown fleece jogging suit Deja gave me for Christmas last year. She knew how tired I was of physical therapy and said, "If the exercise doesn't make you feel good, at least you'll look good." I did. I worked the hell out of that suit. It hugged my frame, showing off just enough to tease the onlooker. I brushed my sleek, chocolate brown hair into a ponytail. I noticed my roots were growing out. *Shoot, Deja doesn't know what she's talking about, I don't need the super relaxer she's always demanding. That girl's crazy.*

I threw on my brand new running shoes, and headed off to volunteer at the hospital to hold newborns left behind after birth. They didn't deserve to be abandoned by the rest of society just because their mother's didn't want them. With all the blessings I'd been given by God, it was a great way to give back.

I pulled my white Mercedes-Benz S Class into the hospital parking lot and closed the roof on my convertible. The car was a present to myself after winning my lawsuit against Dr. Patel. He put me in a wheelchair, but these were MY wheels. I put myself on these. I chose the hard top convertible because the idea of having cloth over my head as I sped down the turnpike or over the George Washington Bridge did not sit well with me. And I was privileged to park in the handicapped space that was, thankfully, so much closer to the facility. But I still hated seeing the logo on the disabled parking placard I had to hang in my windshield. It reminded me of difficult times.

With the memories, I also thought of my victories, and was overcome with the need to recite the Lord's Prayer. *Our Father, who art in Heaven, hallowed be Thy name...Yes Lord, deliver us from evil...Dear God, thank you for all your help and for saving me. Thank you for listening to me. I know I am a sinner, Lord. I know I haven't been all that you've wished for, but I am trying. Lord, please don't frown on me.*

I crossed myself, stepped out of the car, and walked in to the doors of Newark Medical. I headed up the escalator to the second landing and walked over to the large, circular desk that sat in the middle of the floor. I leaned over the counter and batted my eyes at Mr. Packer who was sitting in his chair reading the sports page. Tyshawn Morris was on the cover.

Mr. Packer was an older, fifty-something gentleman, but you know what they say. Black don't crack, and I wasn't able to pinpoint his exact age. If I were into older men, I would definitely give Mr. Packer something to pack.

"Good morning, Mr. Packer."

I put on my best schoolgirl voice and reached into my purse for my volunteer ID.

"I am here again today."

"Hi, Ms. Channa, no need to pull out your ID. I know who *you* are."

He got up and stood close to the counter and let his eyes roam all over my body like a dirty gym teacher.

"Mmmhmm, I know exactly who you are. You look real nice in your jogging suit. Brown suits you just fine. Mmmhmm, yes indeed."

Like I didn't know that? Your eyes aren't failing, Mr. Packer.

I enjoyed putting a smile on a man's face, and loved the deep soothing hums that came from the depths of his belly. His voice was raspy and older than his age, but still sweet enough to coax a cat down from a tree.

I headed down the hallway and looked at the people walking past me. I really hated Newark Medical. Homeless men who had nowhere else to go used real and fake illnesses to get sent to the hospital. This seemed to be their action every time the weather cooled off. There weren't enough rooms or gurneys, so they sat in the hallways with their busted feet in the middle of the floor. The only reason I dealt with stepping over all those people was my never-ending love for the babies.

I got to another set of elevators and entered as soon as the doors opened. The elevator carried me to the fifth floor, where Nurse Comfort was there to welcome me. Yeah, there was actually a registered nurse named Comfort. Comfort was a Nigerian woman who was the head RN in the nursery. She was down to earth, and well, her name said it all. Nurse Comfort took me over to the rocking chair in the maternity ward where we waited for one of the other RN's to bring a baby over. The other nurse came and nestled a tiny little boy in my waiting arms. Then she went over to tend to other babies. Nurse Comfort and I looked down at the little tyke and his eyes were wide as he cooed at me. I smiled and lightly tickled his belly with my forefinger.

"Channa, I bet you want one just like this one here, one day?"

Nurse Comfort smiled. Her teeth looked like pearls in contrast to her dark skin.

"Yeah. He's definitely a cutie. I'd love to have my own one day."

I turned back to the baby. "But I'll take you for now, little guy."

The thought crossed my mind to actually take him as I stared into his innocent eyes. I wanted to rescue him from the hospital and give him a fair start in life.

"You'd be a great mommy. I see it all in you."

"Thanks, Comfort. I sure hope so."

And with that, I started to hear the faint ticking of the biological clock everybody talks about.

"I see how you hold the babies. You love them. You have a lot of love in you that will make you a good mother."

"You are really sweet, Comfort. I know I'm going to spoil my kids silly."

Comfort and I giggled at my statement.

"I bet you will. Well, let me leave you two and get back to my duties. I'll see you before you leave."

"OK."

She turned and took one last look at me, holding the baby, and then left the room. I held that beautiful little boy in my arms and gave him a bottle. After burping him, I rocked him and sang a lullaby.

Hush little baby, don't say a word.

Mama's gonna buy you a mockin'bird.

An hour passed before I rang to tell Comfort that "Baby 08504" was asleep. The nameless babies left behind by mothers too young, too high, or just too selfish to want their own flesh and blood were simply given numbers for identification. The number was representative of the month, day and year of the child's birth. Baby 08504 was born August 5, 2004. This abandoned baby remained nameless until either the mother felt some shame and came back to claim him, or when social services came to enter the baby into the system. My heart broke every time I thought of the fate that awaited this baby and many other babies like him.

I had been thinking about a life with Kevin so much lately that it carried over into my volunteer work as well. I looked down at Baby 08504 and thought about what would happen if I brought him home.

"Kevin!"

I fantasized coming in my front door with the baby carrier in my hands.

"Kevin, I have a surprise for you!"

Kevin would walk out of the kitchen, still sharply dressed in an Armani suit after a long day at work, and stop dead in his tracks when he saqw the surprise I had for him.

"Who do we have here?"

He'd laugh, changing that gorgeous, seductive smile into a dopey, playful grin meant for cooing at babies.

"Honey, this is Kevin Jr. He's our son."

I'd smile like I just hit the lottery.

I imagined Kevin being happy about the baby. He would feel that his life was complete. *The perfect job, the perfect home, the perfect son, and of course, me. Ahhh.*

Nurse Comfort tapped me on my shoulder and interrupted my daydream. She placed the baby back in his crib.

"You know, DYFS is coming to get him next week."

Comfort looked into my eyes, seriously. She wanted to shake me out of my daydream world, so I would understand the reality. Social Services was taking "Baby 08504".

The image of Kevin bouncing "Kevin Jr." was in the air faded in my mind.

"Yeah, I know."

Back in my car, I made my way toward the New Jersey Turnpike on my way to New York. I was going to lend my assistance to the Gay Men's Health Clinic. My thoughts rested on the men I was going into the city to see. These men kept me grounded. There they were, living with HIV and AIDS, and they still managed to maintain high spirits. When I was working for Morgan Pharmaceuticals, I marketed drugs for people living with these diseases, but I never really had the individuals in mind. I only thought about my salary and all the money I made for the company. Now the money and politics involved were not corrupting my motivation. I was working first hand, one on one, with people who were HIV-positive. All that mattered that I made a difference. Now, I was able to give them more than any drug ever marketed for this group.

I volunteered at GMHC by talking to the men, encouraging them to keep going, and by showing them love. Society had turned its back on them. Strength was gained not just from some drug, but also from others who refused to give up on them. I knew the industry could be impersonal, and sometimes unforthcoming when it came to complete effectiveness of some drugs. I wanted to speak to these people as an ex-professional from the industry and give them the inside information they needed. I didn't tell them anything that was untrue about Morgan's HIV meds. I just wanted them to have realistic expectations so they knew exactly what medication would actually help lower their viral load and which ones would ease their pain.

I was merging onto the turnpike from the exit lane when my phone rang. I pressed the dashboard button to answer on the speakerphone mode.

"Hello, Arnelle."

"How do you know it's me? I called your car, right?"

"Yes. Obviously, you don't know how advanced the Mercedes is."

We both laughed aloud.

"Are we still on for dinner this Wednesday?"

"Oh yeah! I was supposed to call you, right? I'm sorry, I forgot."

"It's OK. No need to explain. But we're still on?" she asked.

"Of course."

"Good. I'm going to Louisiana next month and I wanted to see you before I left."

"Really? I've been meaning to get down there," I said.

Of all the wonderful places I'd been privileged to visit, I'd missed out on Louisiana.

"I never have the time these days to take a trip."

"Well, you should make the time to go. Channa, you shouldn't stay holed up in that house. There's always a party going on down there. You'll have a ball when you do find the time."

"Yeah, I guess I'll have to see about moving some things around in the coming months."

"Channa," Arnelle was suddenly excited, "you know what? Why the wait? I'm only taking my kids with me, and it would be great to have you along for the trip."

"Oh, I don't know Arnelle..."

"Nonsense. I won't have you say no."

"OK, let me think about it and we can talk about it more

over dinner."

"Sounds good."

I imagined her giving a thumbs-up to the phone.

I was at the tollbooth and paid to go through the tunnel. Some maniac in a blue Ford stationwagon almost took my front end off as I started back into traffic. I slammed on my breaks to let him go.

"Arnelle, I have to go. Some idiot almost hit me, and I'm about to go in a tunnel."

"OK, Channa, be careful and I'll see you Wednesday."

We hung up and I made my way to the crowded city. I parked in a lot down the street from the center and walked in the glass door embossed with the center's logo.

"Hi Channa, Miss Thang. How you doooinn'? Lookin' kinda gloom and doom wearing all that brown. Honey child, you look like a stick of shit. You know we don't like things that look sad or shitty. Sch, Ho-neee!"

I looked to see which of my admirers was paying me such a compliment. It was Tyrone. Tyrone had one of Deja's super strength relaxers in his shoulder length hair, which he dramatically flung across his back whenever he spoke. He was wearing what he thought was a fierce silver sequin tank top with pink sweat pants that resembled my brown ones. He had on a matching pair of pink and silver Pumas.

"You know, if I didn't like you, Tyrone, I wouldn't let you say the things you say to me. I almost got into a car wreck on my way to GMHC, so you should be nice to me."

"Huh, you should've been nice to yourself this morning when you got dressed, honey child."

"Uh-uh. If I didn't know better, I'd say you were jealous you don't look as good in sweats as I do."

Tyrone threw a hand to his chest feigning shock.

"Oh, don't lie to yourself, girlfriend. This diva looks fab-u-lous!"

Tyrone used his other hand to give a snap on each over-emphasized syllable of the word "fabulous." He sashayed to the center of the room and back as if the floor tiles were a runway. Everyone in the room cracked up. He placed his hand in front of his face and snapped his fingers again.

"Oh please, Tyrone. I didn't wear this for you. There isn't anything in this jogging suit you want."

"Well, you right about that."

Tyrone looked me up and down like he was sizing me up for a catfight. Then quickly changed and smiled.

"Huh, you know I love you, Miss Chaaaa-nnaaa!"

He hugged me and I squeezed back, letting him know he was loved too.

We went to a room where a few of the other men were waiting to hear me speak about the importance of practicing safe sex, the different HIV drugs available, and the power of prayer. We had a brief question-and-answer session, and I was done. Before I left, I spoke to Tyrone privately to make sure he was taking his meds regularly. I loved Tyrone's spirit. I hated to see him weak and lying in a hospital bed with a hospice nurse saying, "The only thing we can we can do for him at this point is to make him comfortable." I'd seen it happen with other patients who didn't believe the medicine would be of any real help since it wasn't an actual cure.

"Yes, Miss Chaaaa-nnnaaa! I'm takin' my meds. Now take your ass to the mall and get something with a little more sass before coming back up in here."

Tyrone flicked his overturned hands in a shooing motion.

I laughed and left. But I couldn't stress enough to Tyrone and the others the importance of staying alive long enough to see a cure. Taking their meds on a consistent basis was one way to ensure that.

On my way out, I grabbed a quick bite to eat from the hotdog man whose cart was on the sidewalk outside of the center. Then I called Arnelle to change the date for dinner to Thursday. I needed more time to think about this trip. She agreed, and we decided to meet at Houston's on Central Park South and 27th Street.

Chapter 14

I arrived at Houston's five minutes late and caught Arnelle's attention when I entered.

"Hey girl, over here," she said, waving and smiling like an anxious child.

I walked over to the bar and greeted her with a hug.

"I just got here a few minutes ago. I ordered a gin and tonic with a twist of lime."

Hmph, a gin and tonic is such an ordinary drink for such an extraorindary lady. I looked at her as she continued to ramble on about the ride over and parking. She was dressed in a blue business suit with her dyed brown hair pulled into a tight, English schoolteacher's bun. Her ruby red fingernails were tapping nervously on the bar as she spoke. She didn't look like any of the other white females around. Her lips were a bit fuller and her nose was just a tad flatter.

"I'll have a bottle of mineral water for now, thank you," I said as the bartender approached me.

He handed me my green bottle and Arnelle and I went over to the hostess's station to give our names for a table. Arnelle beat me to the punch.

"Arnelle Taysha Arroyo," she said before turning her attention back to me.

I stumbled backward in shock. *I never knew she was Latina. Her last name is Arroyo? Since when? Oh, we need to sit down so she can give me the inside scoop.*

The hostess escorted us a minute later to a booth on the left side of the restaurant.

"Your waiter will be with you shortly. Enjoy your meal ladies."

A sexy young man with a Sean Connery, "Double-0-Seven" thing going on, came to the table.

"Good evening, ladies. My name is John and I'll be your waiter for the evening."

Dag. He even sounds like Double-0-Seven. John handed us our menus and listed the specials for the night. We gave our orders and he walked off.

"So let me tell you about what's been going on at Morgan." Arnelle patted the table like she couldn't contain juicy gossip any longer.

"Yes, do tell. How is my old boss?"

"Fired!"

Arnelle's face lit up like a Christmas tree. Her hands stopped tapping—she was relieved to get it out.

But I picked up where she left off. I slammed my hand on the table. "What?"

"Yeah girl, he got caught with his pee-pee in the cookie jar. He was dating another manager and using company money to pay for dinner and hotels. That man didn't even have the decency to pay for his own affair."

Arnelle resumed her laid-back calm.

I sat back in my chair, stunned.

"Get out of here, Arnelle. Who?"

"Becca Winston."

"Uh-uh! That tight ass?"

"Yup! And when her husband got wind that something was going on too—"

"Husband?!?! Oh, uh-uh!"

"When he suspected, he pressured Becca to admit to it when she came in late one night. She broke down crying and told her husband everything."

"Damn."

"Then her husband called Human Resources about the possible misuse of Morgan's expense fund. You know Morgan was obligated to investigate that kind of claim after the call, and they uncovered the whole thing. They got rid of Richard Greene AND Becca Winston."

"Ohhhhhh, this is such music to my ears. I can't believe it. This is fantastic. Oh, I'm sorry, heh, heh, I know I'm wrong, but I'm so excited to hear this."

I leaned forward, laughing with Arnelle as we tried not to take pleasure in another's misfortune, but hey, he made his bed and now he was lying in it.

Arnelle pulled herself together first.

"So, Channa, what have you been up to? The last time I saw you was over a year ago, and you were in a wheelchair. Now you're getting along without it just fine."

"Yeah, you know, that was a difficult period for me. I was so against that contraption at first because I didn't want to appear helpless. But once I finally realized it was just a tool to help me get by until I regained my strength, everything became easy."

"Wow, that sounds like a tough transition."

Her eyes ached for all I'd gone through.

"Oh, it was. I was in the hospital when I got the letter of termination from Morgan."

"I'm so sorry about that. Really, Channa."

Arnelle played with her silverware, diverting her eyes from mine. She had been the one to send me that letter, which also informed me that she had been given my position.

I reached over and put my hand on top of hers.

"I was never mad at you, Arnelle. There's no need to apologize. It was Morgan who deserted me, not you. I know you had nothing to do with what happened. Richard Greene had been after me for months."

Arnelle sighed and looked at me again. I saw that her eyes were glassy with tears that never left her lower lids. I must have told her what she needed to hear.

"I'm glad to hear that. I worried so much that you thought I was out to get your job. But it wasn't like that. I always had the utmost respect for you and looked up to you. When

I found out what Richard was doing, I just wanted to stop him but, I didn't know how."

"Of course, Arnelle, I know you only tried to help me. But losing my job was a humbling experience. I had no idea where my money would be coming in from. Suddenly, I had hospital bills to worry about, as well as credit card bills. I had used my plastic cards like it was a "Food Stamp" a.k.a EBT card. I needed to stay afloat while I was out of work. I had to live. You can't imagine the sight at the welfare office when I applied for assistance to pay basic living expenses."

"I had no idea you had to go through all of that, Channa."

"I'm telling you, it was something else. I never knew how many places were not handicap accessible. The welfare office didn't have a ramp, and the side door was locked, so no one could enter through it. That was a federal violation. I had to depend on complete strangers who were standing in front of the welfare building to lift my wheelchair up three steps to get inside the office. By then, I didn't have the power and energy to fight the injustice. I just wanted money to pay my bills."

"You should have contacted me and let me know you needed money. I would have helped you in any way I could."

Her expression seemed caught between horror and outrage.

"Thank you," I said, smiling to reassure her, "but my family was there. I was fortunate enough to be able to stay with my mother and grandmother, and they took excellent care of me. If I didn't have them, I would've ended up forgotten in some nursing home or shelter."

"Did you go through some type of rehab program to be able to get rid of the wheelchair?"

"Yes, I was at Relsnek."

"Oh, I've heard of that place. It's supposed to be a superior rehabilitation clinic, one of the best in the country."

I assumed Arnelle kept up with the trade through medical magazines and journals.

"Relsek is the best. But that didn't mean my stay was pleasant. You know Christopher Reeves went though Relsnek too? Still, even with Relsnek's knowledge, I still had to place all of my faith in God. I didn't have control of my bowels, and had to have them cleaned daily by a nurse. The snap of latex gloves brings back memories of those days every time. Most of the nurses were very thoughtful and tried to make the process as painless as possible, but there was one nurse who was rough and insensitive."

I shook my head.

"I was there for 120 days, and I counted."

"You really pulled through, and didn't let it keep you down. I really have a whole new respect for you. It's terrific to see you didn't pick up a despondent view on life."

"I couldn't with all of the support I had around me."

I knew if I kept talking about those days, I'd cry from recalling all of the pain, disappointments, and outpouring of love.

"That's enough about me."

I leaned forward and looked at Arnelle seriously.

"Arnelle, can I ask you something?"

"Sure, go ahead."

Arnelle took a sip of her drink.

"What's the deal with your last name? Arroyo? And your middle name, Taysha? I didn't know who you were when you were talking to the hostess."

"Oh, that? Well, my husband was Puerto Rican. You know how it is in the corporate world, and especially at Morgan. Everything's in a name. If they see Arnelle Arroyo on the application, they won't even call me to clean the carpets. Even those jobs went to white contractors. So, I just use my maiden name, Johnson, at work."

I sat there looking at her speak, and thought how the woman with two faces never ceases to amaze me. This woman had more shit with her than an asshole itself. Arnelle was a trip. *Who knows what world she's going to spin my mind into next?*

The young Sean Connery came back with our drinks. Before I could take a sip, Arnelle said, "Oh wait. Let's toast, Channa."

We raised our glasses and she continued, "To a better life, good friendship, and love. Yes, true love."

"Yes, it is true love."

I repeated her words, my mind wandering to Kevin for a second.

"You know, I've been dating this guy for ten years. We go out all the time and have the best sex I've ever had with any man. He is so passionate and strong. I just love being with him."

Arnelle raised her perfectly shaped eyebrows. "Sounds good so far."

"Yeah, but we've been seeing each other for years and he won't commit. I don't know what to do to make him see the light. You know?"

I frowned a little and took another sip of my drink.

"Oh, that's an age-old dilemma," Arnelle sighed.

"I know. And my poor boyfriend..."

"Boyfriend? Ooh, Channa, you're bad."

We laughed.

"I know, I know. I love Carl, but he's just so, so...safe. He's predictable and stable. I want to settle down in the dream life with a husband, children running around in the backyard. I want my nuclear family. I feel those motherly instincts starting to kick me, hard. And I know I can get all of that with Carl. But, he's just not Kevin."

"Girl, trust me, kids are nice, but they aren't everything. Who needs to be safe? You should always be happy first. Safe is boring, and it still doesn't guarantee you'll be together in the end. You'll have your kids and no man and wishing you had that best sex guy in your life again. Forget about Carl."

I was taken aback by Arnelle's honesty. I would have thought for sure that this married woman with three children would understand my need to develop a real home life. *There's so much more to this chick than meets the eye.*

"Well, I guess you would know better than me, but I think I'm ready for it. I always go to the hospital and hold the babies who've been abandoned by their mothers. There's this one baby boy who I've become a little attached to. He's being picked up by social services next week, but something in me wants to take him home."

"Then why don't you? Adoption isn't a bad idea. You'd take motherhood on your own terms."

"I don't know, Arnelle. I mean, I've been tossing the idea around, but I don't know if it's really for me. I know I want a baby, but then again, I also know I don't want to take on that responsibility by myself. And what if I get rejected by the agency? I don't know if I'm ready to handle that. I don't know what it requires to adopt. I don't know what type of people they're looking for. Being told, 'No, you can't have that baby', by some pencil pusher who only knows me on paper is not something I'm ready for."

"Well, at least you are mature enough right now to know you aren't ready. Children are work and there are plenty of women out there who do not believe it until they have one. By then, it's too late. You can't take the baby back. I'm sure many of the girls who abandon their baby at the hospital fall into that category."

Arnelle perked up again, saying, "So, when do you think you'll be ready?"

"Maybe once I'm married. Then I can try it the old fashioned way and have one of my own."

"Unh, marriage isn't all it's cracked up to be either. That's why mine is over."

I flashed back to Arnelle saying, "My husband *was* Puerto Rican," but the realization didn't minimize my shock.

"Since when?" I said.

It's one thing after another with this chick. What's next? She's a CIA spy, a femme fatale and she's here to assassinate me? Everyone at work believed Arnelle was a white woman, married to a white man. All of that was being revealed to me as untrue.

"I've been divorced for a while."

Arnelle's face was blank. She could have been recounting a story she read in a magazine, but I felt it was a true story and one very difficult to tell.

"He took me through hell with his beatings, night after night. I was bloody and tired of being sore all the time. I had to get out of there before he got to my kids."

Beatings? I was floored and couldn't believe my ears.

"My kids stay with my mother, only she doesn't live in West Virginia like I've told people. She's in New York. Brooklyn as a matter of fact. They're over in Red Hook."

My mouth was already open before I spoke. "Red Hook Projects?"

"Yes. I'm looking to buy a house soon and get them out of there. I've been saving like crazy. My ex really messed up my credit."

I was speechless. A frog had crawled into my throat and decided to take a squat. I had to take a sip of wine and tried to eat a shrimp. Just then, my phone rang. I reached into my purse to pull it out and saw Kevin's number on the display. I couldn't have been happier. I didn't have a clue of what to say or ask Arnelle.

"Excuse me. I have to take this."

I stood up and headed for the ladies' room where I could sit on one of the couches in the powder room. *Talk about saved by the bell.*

I let the phone ring as I walked through the restaurant, not just to give the other diners respect, but to give Kevin the idea I wasn't jumping to take his call. Although inside… *hop, hop, hop.*

I answered the phone just outside of the ladies' room door.

"Hello?"

"Channa Renée Jones. How are you?"

His voice was like velvet and made me melt like a silly schoolgirl.

"Hey, handsome," I said.

I'd made it into the powder room and plopped down on the couch as planned.

"I'm fine. What are you up to?"

"Just wanted to know if you were free to go to the movies to see *Ladder 49.* It's premiering this Friday."

"And you just have to see the crowd's reaction."

"You know me. I always like to go on opening night. So, it's a date?"

Hmm, listen to him, just assuming I'm available.

"I don't know, Kev, I have to check my schedule."

I faked a little strain in my voice like he had me at a bad time.

"Oh, come on. Channa, you know you have time for me. And if you don't, you'd better make some."

"Hold on Kev."

I paused like I was rummaging through papers as I rumpled a piece of paper towel I ripped from the dispenser on the wall.

"Umm, let's see, when did you say it was again?"

"Fri-day. Come on, Channa, are you free?"

Kevin started to sound impatient. *A-ha, join the club.*

"Well, I can move a few things around. Wait, no, I have to keep that appointment, so I may not be able to."

"Channa. Are you serious?"

Kevin sounded like I was one of his star players who missed a lay-up.

I knew I was beginning to become annoying. But, I had to keep up my act. I let out a long, breathy sigh as if he'd worn me down.

"OK, Mr. Walker, I'll break the appointment just for you. But this movie better be damn good."

Kevin laughed, "Good. We can eat at Ruby Foo's over on Broadway and walk down to the theater afterward. There's nothing better than some delicious Asian delicacies and walking through the brisk, New York air."

Yeah, for you, I thought. He always did what he wanted to do without giving a second thought to what anyone else may have wanted to do. Ruby Foo's was out of my way, and sometimes the walking could really take a toll on me. I was about to suggest a change of venue for dinner, maybe somewhere in Bloomfield, when I quickly bit my tongue. I didn't want to take the chance of bumping into Carl. I just had to be careful and I already knew that Kev wanted to control the date, as usual.

"OK, Kev, now let me get back to dinner."

"Dinner? Who are you eating with?"

"Hmph, wouldn't you like to know?" I snickered. "Smooches."

I blew three kisses into the receiver before disconnecting. I looked at myself in the mirror to be sure everything was in place, and went back to see what bone Arnelle was going to let fall out of her closet next.

As I approached the table, I could see Arnelle was almost finished with her meal. I sat and took a serious gulp of water.

"I think I'm just going to wrap my food up and take it home. I'm not feeling so well."

"Channa, what's wrong?"

I could see Arnelle was disappointed that I was leaving so early. But honestly, I needed to take a breather. She had hit me with a lot, and I still didn't know what to say about the domestic violence situation. I could tell she thought that my leaving had something to do with her, so I attempted to find out more on the Louisiana trip.

"Well, you're still coming to New Orleans, right? There's a Creole Heritage Conference at Tulane on the 12th and 14th of November. It's good to get out and meet other people of mixed races and different heritages. These experiences will be great for my kids and to see other light skinned black people like themselves."

What in the hell is she talking about? I couldn't utter a word as she went on about this Creole Conference. *Is she serious? Did this actually exist? A conference set up for Creoles? Should I go? Should I keep this woman in my life?*

"Channa, I appreciate what you've shared with me today, and I want to be able to be honest and share my true self with you, as my friend. I hope I haven't said anything wrong today, and I hope you still come to Louisiana with me. It'll be so much fun. Since you love to eat, I know you will love this food. These shrimp you are eating here taste like rubber tires, but in New Orleans, they are cooked with extra virgin olive oil, sweetest white wine, and just enough spice. The experience will last forever. You'll be spoiled rotten and won't want to come back to New York. Also, the clothes. Boutiques have the greatest finds. You have to see Baton Rouge too. The countryside is beautiful, especially during sunrise."

"I don't know, Arnelle."

A trip like that was something you took with people you'd known forever. Every time Arnelle spoke, it seemed like a new person was coming out.

"Your kids don't need some stranger tagging along."

"They'll love you. You're not a stranger. You're my friend. And, you don't have to hang with us the entire time. Enjoy the sights, or just relax."

"Well, I haven't done too much traveling. And, I have a lot of bills. I don't know if I should take on something so big."

"Channa, you travel back and forth to the city all the time. With this, there are security checkpoints and what not, but other than that, it's no big deal. And I'll hook you up with my travel agent so you can get the conference rate. We get a great deal on rooms. We should, there are a lot of Creoles coming."

"But I'm not Creole."

I really felt on the spot. How could I let Arnelle down gently?

"Nobody has to know that you're not Creole. You don't

have to go to the conference or anything. I'm just getting you a better deal so the trip will be affordable. It's only a weekend."

Arnelle looked worried. I was afraid she would take my reluctance personally.

"I just thought you could use the vacation and try something new."

"You got me. New food, new places, and faces. I'm going, Arnelle."

"Excellent."

Arnelle looked so relieved. She waved the waiter over to the table.

"Excuse me, can we please have a doggie bag for my friend's food?"

It was October 1, 2004, the premiere date for *Ladder 49*. I was standing in front of Ruby Foo's on the cool, breezy autumn night. I thought it would be a lot cooler, but it was unseasonably warm for October. I had a light jacket on over my outfit. I couldn't wait for Kevin to arrive because it had been a while since I'd seen him, and I could taste my favorite dish, Chilean Sea Bass with horseradish sauce, on the tip of my tongue. I looked at my watch, a gift from Carl, then down at my heels. I thought that I should have worn my flat red and black shoes and not these heeled black boots. *Damn, my feet are going to be killing me in an hour.* I wanted Kevin to hurry up so that we could have a seat.

I passed the time thinking about the end of the night and I just needed to get off my feet for a few hours. I would be laid on my back…then flipped over…and oh. I was getting hot just thinking about it. I hoped that we'd at least be at my place and not his office or condo when the night was over. That way, I wouldn't have to gather my stuff and be hurried out like he just found out I had the plague. I was not giving him another opportunity to kick me out after he'd had his way with me. I refused to put myself in that position again. *From now on, if we don't go to my place, we just don't have sex.* It was time I put my foot down. *Oh, who am I kidding? That man can have it wherever he wants, all he has to do is ask. I just can't keep feeling as ashamed and whorish as I did that day I was on my period.* Deja was right. I needed to change my approach with Kevin.

I stood in front of Ruby Foo's trying to figure out why Kevin didn't want to commit, but could take me to dinner and premieres. Then it dawned on me; I should just ask him. That's it. I'd just say, "Hey, why aren't we moving this relationship to the next level?"

His black Range Rover with tinted windows pulled up in front of the restaurant and honked the horn. The window rolled down and there was Mr. Kevin Dean Walker in his entire glorious splendor in the driver's seat.

"Hey, baby," he said, capturing the tone I thought heaven would sound like.

Damn. He's fine.

"Hey, Mr. Walker."

I gave him a wink and my signature smile.

"I'll be right in. I just have to find somewhere to park."

I stepped closer to the curb.

"I had to park over in a lot on 73rd. It was $25 an hour, but it is New York."

The sound of heaven went away as Kevin shouted obscenities as he hit the steering wheel several times.

"I hate paying for this shit with my money."

Uh, this shit? You're on a date with me.

"The Knicks should be picking this up, as much as I do for them."

Why should the Knicks pay? This ain't no business dinner. Do I look like I'm ready to go one on one with Shaquille O'Neal in these boots?

"Damn. Its $25 an hour?"

He pulled off in the direction of the costly lot.

I went inside of Ruby Foo's and requested a cozy table for

two. Kevin came in shortly after and put his smile back on when he saw me.

"You're looking good, Channa Renée Jones."

Oh shit, if he keeps saying my name, I'll take him right here in the restaurant.

"And I like you in those boots." Kevin leaned in and whispered in my ear, "You'll keep them on for me later, right baby?"

Daaaaaaammmmmnn!

We were seated a few minutes later and Kevin ordered shrimp, dim sum with plum sauce, miso-glazed black cod, and I got my sea bass. He drank green tea as I sipped a glass of sweet plum wine. Kevin started talking about the star player he recruited, Tyshawn Morris.

"So Ty's career is really starting to take off. This new commercial we're doing is really going to put him out there as the lead player. The owner is excited about the whole thing. He's calling me constantly to make sure I have everything I need to keep Ty happy."

I loved to hear him talk about his success. Tyshawn Morris was all over the sports news, so Kevin had to be reaping the rewards. There was even a photo of them on Kevin's desk.

"Well, that's great, Kev. So, when can I meet the world-renowned Mr. Tyshawn Morris?"

Kevin sat back in his chair, picking his napkin up out of his lap and wiped his mouth. He viewed me through squinted eyes and asked, "Why?"

"Why? Why not? You keep telling me how great he is and how big he'll be. And I've seen him in the sports clips, with his cornrows and licking his lips. What? Are you jealous I'll leave you for him?"

"No, just curious as to why you want to meet Ty."

Kevin moved the food left on his plate around with his chopsticks. He seemed suddenly withdrawn.

"Again, Kev, why not? You spend a lot of time with him.

He's like your best friend these days. And he is a starting player. So why wouldn't I want to meet Ty?"

"We'll see, Channa."

Kevin leaned forward and finished the rest of his meal in silence.

By the time the check came to the table, he'd perked up again.

"As much as I'd like to get you home and make dessert out of you, I think we should take in that movie."

Kevin stood after paying for our meal, and helped me out of my chair.

"Yes, let's go see the movie. The night is young."

We made our way to the door where Kevin wrapped my jacket over my shoulders.

We walked holding hands. My mind started drifting as I thought about our relationship. December would make it ten years of chasing our tails and running in this so-called relationship circle. No progress was being made. We still did the movies and occasional dinners. Let's not forget the trips every now and then, or should I have said 'brief out-of-town excursions?' I would meet Kevin in the town he was conducting business in and wait in his hotel room for his workday to finish. *What the hell is this shit?* My face must've said it all when I looked over at him, because he just looked at me with an expression that said, "What?"

"Kevin, why haven't we been in a relationship?"

I let the words fall out of my mouth as casually as if I was breathing.

Kevin didn't slow his pace or flinch, he kept his cool and answered the loaded question. "Channa, we are in a relationship."

He swirled his thumb over the top of my hand and gave it an extra squeeze.

"You know what I mean, Kev. Why haven't you committed yourself to me while we've been dating all this time?"

"Channa, I don't want to talk about this again. Sheesh! Whenever December rolls around, you go off and throw a tantrum."

Kevin shook his head like he was mentally whipping himself for a huge mistake.

"What? Either you shit, or get off the pot."

There, I'd said it, and it cracked him up.

"Channa," he said laughing loudly as he stopped us from walking any farther. "Channa, I like your GP. So why would I need to buy the cow when I get all the milk for free?"

He kissed me on my forehead and kept laughing.

"Hmph, keep messin' around, Kevin, and you're gonna need Ladder 49 to come rescue your ass."

I rolled my eyes at Kevin to let him know I was still mad at him for his cow comment. He thought I was funny though, and chuckled, shaking his head. Then he pulled me in tightly and kissed me slowly and passionately. My knees became weak after feeling his hot tongue seducing mine. As usual, he used his power over me. But as I stood there in his arms, my mind glanced back over the past ten years. I asked myself, *If my GP is the only thing that's kept him around, it's about to change. He's not going to keep milking this cow for free.* I was determined to make him buy the whole damn farm, and I was willing to do anything to make him do it.

Chapter 13

"Channa, Channa, Channa!"

Arnelle was yelling my name, searching through the airport.

"I'm over here."

I was chatting with the skycap when Arnelle's three children came up and hugged me one by one. I didn't know what to think. These kids had never seen me a day in their lives and were hugging me as if I was their favorite aunt. Arnelle greeted me with a hug as well.

"I'm so happy you agreed to come, and relieved you are taking a break."

She was out of breath from lugging luggage and children through the airport.

"You work so much and you don't have to. This is going to mean more for you than for the children and me. You're gonna have a good time. Just relax and I'll show you around 'The Big Easy.'"

Arnelle was dressed in neat khaki pants and a white blouse. Her matching khaki jacket was draped through the strap of her carry-on. She was ready for the trip, and her face showed that she was eager to go. So were her children, who were each beautiful and seemed to mirror her in some way.

I tipped the skycap and watched as he handled my hot pink DVF Newport canvas luggage. I used to think it was important for everyone to know that I spent money and only bought the best. If I didn't own a matching set of LV luggage, I didn't own any luggage. Now, my priorities were a bit different. It was more important to be able to recognize my bags quickly once they came out of baggage claims. No one could mistake my bright pink luggage for their own.

Flight 1036 arrived at 9:53 a.m. sharp. Arnelle and her kids took their seats in the coach section, but I couldn't travel in those cramped seats. I would practically be sitting in the lap of the person next to me in that area. I took my seat in first class and noticed Arnelle and her children were seated in the first row behind my section. She was trying to get them to settle down before take-off. Arnelle was a tolerant mother; she wanted to make sure her children had all that they needed before take-off.

"Rick, sit down. I said sit. You can have the window seat on the flight back."

Boy, she has it hard, I thought as I slipped into my spacious seat. The pilot made his announcement. His voice was smooth and sexy, just how I liked it. Then the flight attendants did their thing, and we took off.

Oddly, this flight reminded me of the business trip that Arnelle I went on while I was at Morgan Pharmaceuticals. It was a flight to Puerto Rico. That was when we first bonded. She had come up to my seat, whispering and scoping the aisles with wide eyes to warn me of my boss's plot to sabotage my presentation. At the time, I didn't understand why Arnelle risked telling me about it, but now I figured she must have felt the need to look out for me since *she* knew we were the only two Black women working in Morgan's executive level positions. She saved my behind in Puerto Rico. Now, we were on a plane once again headed somewhere hot and beautiful. Would Arnelle have to save me from something again? *Who the hell knows.*

The bell dinged and I was able to lean my chair back again. *Ah, relief.* I could hear Arnelle's children asking for soda, juice, chips, and anything else they could think of. I contemplated if and when I would be ready to start a family.

I didn't want to raise children alone. I just wanted Kevin to commit so that we could share the experience together.

Once in New Orleans, we hit the French Quarter. The streets were alive as if it was Fat Tuesday in February, but it wasn't. The city was shining as lighters sparked to allow nicotine addicts to inhale the city's charm. Glass bottles gleamed under the sky's natural light. Store displays glimmered with beads, and neon signs winked to invite patrons to enjoy all of an establishment's offerings. Mischievous laughter filled the ears of passersby. The space around us was filled with electricity that caused skin-rippling goose bumps.

"I wanna go in there!"

Arnelle's daughter jumped up and down, pointing at a store across the street from the hotel. We went inside and Arnelle started spoiling the children with Mardi Gras beads.

We looked through the selection of multi colored beads, figuring out what each color represented, when a woman came up to me and handed me a card. She was a short woman, wore all white, and resembled a creepy ghost-like figure. I was a bit fearful. Usually white was angelic to me, but this woman was no cherub. There was something spiritual about her, though. I looked down at the card that read, "Marie Laveau's Granddaughter is here for your service. Call 504-457...for your reading and help with all matters. Marie Laveau will help you get money, love, work and all that you need. Guaranteed. Call Today." I flipped the card over to a colored picture of Marie Laveau's tomb. I was dumbfounded.

"Why did you give this to me?" I asked her. "You came in off the street and walked past dozens of other people to get to the store, then bypassed everyone to come to me? Why me? Why not the lady next to me?"

There was a short black woman with dreadlocks standing next to me, and when she heard what I said, she dropped her beads and walked out of the store.

The woman in white cocked her tiny head to the left and stared into my soul. I looked at her and saw that she wore a seven-knotted handkerchief around her skinny neck. *Oh boy!* I had heard stories about a voodoo high priestess whose ghost was always recognized by the knotted handkerchief she wore. She was very trusted by her followers and extremely feared by her enemies. Apparently, this voodoo queen was very effective in her practices in the realm beyond flesh. I felt I was in direct contact with one of her followers. *Or is it her ghost?! Now I've done it! I should have just taken the card and said, thanks. No. I had to open my big mouth.*

The woman opened her mouth to speak and I felt a chill go through the room.

"Chile, ya neet hep."

Her accent was thick, deep, and country.

"Ya luv lif' it not wut it s'posed t' be. You gotta cuss on ya'. You haf bin to mini tials an' tibulations 'n it ain't ova yit. Call 'er, she kin hep."

Then she marched out of the shop without giving a card to anyone else.

Arnelle and I stood there looking at the card and then at each other. We were speechless. I wanted her to explain what had happened to me since she was familiar with New Orleans and the colorful people that lived there. My eyes must have asked her, "why?" And, still stunned, she shrugged an "I don't know."

"Stop! I'm not a girl!"

Bobby, the youngest, squealed and broke through his mother's shock. His older brother and sister were dangling pink beads in his face.

"You act like a girl," Ricky, the oldest, said.

The only daughter, Arlene, joined in, saying, "Yeah, crying all the time like a baby."

The kids didn't notice the scary woman in white, and they didn't pick up on how much she was able to freak us out.

Bobby stormed off to the other side of the store and ran his hands through the tangled beads lying in an old wooden box. His siblings stayed where they were, giggling and picking through the beads that hung from the wall.

I was still shaken by my experience but able to speak.

“Arnelle, what the hell was that? What do you think?”

Arnelle moved her attention between her smallest son and to me, saying, “I think you need to take heed and go visit Marie Laveau’s granddaughter.”

“But Arnelle, I’ve never really been into that black magic crap. I mean, who has time for all of that mumbo jumbo?”

Arnelle’s eyes darted to me.

“Mumbo jumbo? It’s not mumbo jumbo, Channa. I’ve gotten readings before, and they were always right. How do you think I knew about Richard Greene’s scheming and plotting?”

My bottom jaw could have hit the floor.

“A psychic told me there was a snake on the job who was mad at the world because he’s short.”

With that, I burst out laughing. Richard Greene was a short man who seemed to overcompensate by making everybody miserable. I had pegged him with having “Short Man Syndrome” myself.

“You’d better stop laughing, Channa. I’ve seen some pretty real things happen with this *mumbo jumbo* as you call it.”

I stifled my laughter. “I’m sorry, but come on, someone told you that?”

“Yes, you’d be surprised what a true clairvoyant may tell you about yourself.”

She looked over toward Bobby again. He held up a handful of beads and she smiled approval.

“I don’t think so, Arnelle. I mean, it was pretty weird, but…”

Arnelle’s attention was back on me.

“No, there’s no but. It was weird, and you can’t deny that you were singled out. With all the madness that’s going on in your love life, she had to sense it. I’m telling you, they take their *mumbo jumbo* seriously down here and don't just play games with people like that. Think about it. Why you, Channa?"

Arnelle got me thinking.

"OK, why not? I'll call her if it'll please you."

"Yes, it would."

Arnelle reassured me with a smile like the one she'd given to Bobby when he'd come up to us with the beads he selected.

We finally got to the hotel and checked into our separate rooms. The smooth-skinned, dark chocolate bellboy picked up my bags. He was a strapping young man, standing at 6'4" and supporting about 230 pounds of solid country muscle. *Mm-mmm. Welcome to New Orleans to me. I know his mama fed him well.* The bellboy's pecs showed through his thin, white shirt and open vest. I imagined that he developed those arms from tossing bales of hay and unloading grain from the back of a pick-up truck. On the elevator, I stood behind him to watch his cute little round booty in his black uniform pants. I saw that it hugged him just enough around the hips. *Red beans and rice didn't miss him.* He couldn't have been more than 18, but he had the body of a grown-ass man.

"How old are you, if you don't mind me asking?"

"Oh, nah, ma'am," he said as he looked down at his shoes shyly. "I jus turnt eighteen."

"I knew it. That's what I guessed, and why are you ma'aming me? Do I look like a ma'am?"

He raised his eyes slowly from his shoes and up my body and down again.

"Nooo ma'am...I mean miss."

I declare, I imagined myself as a southern belle, *I'd swear you were blushing.* I laughed as the elevator stopped and opened on my floor. He walked me to my room and placed the bags down by the dresser. I had a modest, but spacious one-bedroom suite. Just for being extra sexy, I tipped him a twenty.

"Now, don't you spend that all on candy."

"Nah, Miss, ah won't."

His eyes lit up at the sight of the crisp bill as he left.

*Mmm! If I was about 15 years younger...*But who was I kidding? I wasn't getting any younger and the young boys would soon look at me like I was an old lady. Besides, I needed to get my wrecked love life in order. *Kevin, Kevin, Kevin. Why won't you commit?* I unpacked my bags, while deep in thought. *Maybe the lady on the card could really help me. Nothing else seems to work. I'm not getting any younger and neither is Kevin. Doesn't he want a family? A wife? Kids? Doesn't he want to come home to me?*

I thought about Marie Laveau's granddaughter and sat on the bed near the nightstand with the phone on it. I reached to place a call but hesitated. *I'm a Christian, should I be doing this?* I was always taught that these types of things were wrong, but why? Weren't soothsayers and clairvoyants used in the Bible to reveal truths to men at times? And if it really were wrong, wouldn't I be forgiven for it? I sat there for at least five minutes debating. I finally dialed the granddaughter of this deceased woman who possessed powers beyond my realm. She was the only way I would ever know if Mr. Kevin Walker would commit.

Even the phone's ringing sounded eerie.

"'Lo?" said a raspy voice.

"Uh..."

I was stuck, what was I supposed to say?

"Speak chile', ain' got al'day. D'ya wan a readin'?"

"Y-yes."

"Come by 'morra at tin. Twen-fi' dollas it cos'."

Her accent was thick and hard to understand, but after a few minutes, I was able to get her address and directions. When I hung up, I was fretful. I dialed Arnelle's room.

"Arnelle?"

I wasn't even sure if I dialed the right number.

"Channa? What's going on?"

"I called her."

"Who? Marie Laveau?"

"Yeah." I was out of breath and I'd been sitting the whole time.

"Well, what did she say?"

She was excited. It made me feel a little better with her being thrilled by it all.

"She told me I can come in tomorrow morning."

"So, what time are we going?"

"Ten."

I was starting to catch Arnelle's excitement.

"Well, gimme a second. I think I remember reading something about an on-site childcare facility here at the Hilton. Let me find out and call you right back."

"OK."

I fell back onto the bed and stared at the ceiling for eternity. Or, it felt that way.

Two minutes later, the phone rang.

"Channa?"

"Yeah?"

"OK, I'm going to leave the kids with the child care service in the morning and then we can go."

"Good, I'll see you in the morning then."

I felt a wave of relief that I wouldn't have to go this thing alone.

With all the worrying I was doing, I was surprised to get such a peaceful rest. I awoke the next morning to the bright Louisiana sun and was ready to hear what the voodoo priestess had to say. I called Arnelle's room at about 8:30 a.m.

"Are you up?" I asked her, knowing good and well that if she wasn't up before I called, she was now.

"Yeah girl, these kids had me up at seven, but the childcare center serves breakfast at 7:30 so I took them down there already. I was just about to call you to see if you wanted to meet early enough to get some breakfast."

"Oh, you know I'm ready for some French Quarter food. I'll see you in the lobby at nine."

"OK, see ya then."

I needed to shower and get dressed. *Hmm, what does one wear to meet with a voodoo queen?* I settled on my purple blouse and black slacks and made it to the lobby by nine. Then we headed toward Chartres Street, window-shopping and people watching as we made our way.

We came near a Café Au Lait and were seduced by the aroma of freshly brewed coffee and sweet cinnamon bread. I pictured the glazed sweet cream from a warm doughnut running down my fingers as I sipped a hot cup of Joe. I giggled to myself as I thought of my corny Carl and pulled Arnelle to the café. A waiter dressed in a white button-down shirt, black pants, and a red apron tied around his waist came to the small steel table we chose. We ordered *beignets* and two cups of French vanilla coffee.

"Mmm. Did I die? These *beignets* taste like heaven," I gushed, licking the powdered sugar from my fingers.

"Mmm-hmmm."

Arnelle moaned with damn-near orgasmic pleasure. Just then she looked at her watch and her eyes could have popped out of her head.

"Look at the time."

It was almost ten. We'd been enjoying the beignets so much, we lost track of time. We gulped down our coffee and stuffed what was left of the treats in our mouths and darted out.

"Wait, I didn't leave a tip," I said and dashed back to place $4 on the table.

Fortunetellers lined Chartres Street, giving readings to tourists. Extra tall seven-day candles burned calmly next to cards spread with faces like no deck I'd ever seen. I spotted Marie Laveau's shop and stumbled over the doorstep, looking for the doorbell button. I rang the bell and waited for a minute. No answer, so I rang it again. *I made an appointment and psyched myself into keeping it. I'm not turning back now. C'mon, lady.*

A voice rang out from above, "Who dat be callin' on Marie t'day?"

Arnelle walked out to the sidewalk and looked up at the woman leaning over her balcony, yelling, "We have an appointment."

I heard a loud buzz, and opened the squeaky wood and glass paned door to a dark stairwell. We made our way to the top and Marie was standing there, waiting. The woman was dressed in all white, like the lady with the cards, and her complexion was very fair. She led us into an apartment that was filled with the pungent odor of unwashed geriatrics who probably should have developed lung cancer years ago from their pack-a-day habit. The once-white curtains were a dingy yellow from cigarette smoke. Old Asian rugs littered the floor with ragged ends from years of foot traffic. Five chandeliers hung overhead, and there was salt on chair's seat cushion.

Marie only looked at me.

"You be comin' for da readin'. Chile, you is de one who needs mah hep. Yes, chile, 'tis you. Come now in de utter room, I will do it there."

Arnelle tugged at the back of my shirt when Marie turned for me to follow her. I looked back at her, and she cut her eyes up at the chandeliers as if to say, "Who decorated?" I understood, and snickered a little as I turned to follow Marie.

Marie took the head seat at the rectangular dinner table in what would be the dining area. I walked through the colorful beaded partition separating the dining and living areas.

Marie peeked back to Arnelle who was a few steps behind me, and said, "You stay. Ah need ta know who energy am readin'."

Arnelle understood, and plopped down in an old recliner

next to a window with a view of the sorcerers below.

I sat in the chair to the right of Marie and nervously rubbed my hands over my thighs. *Here we go.* I worried about what Marie had to say, but knew I needed to get it over with. There was a deck of playing cards sitting on the table in front of me.

I was instructed to pick the cards up and shuffle them while concentrating on my question. It wasn't a regular deck of fifty-two cards with kings, queens, jacks and tens that fell together easily when you pretended you were a casino dealer. The cards were larger, and worn down. The edges were soft and frayed. The ink had faded or rubbed off. I could tell that the cards had been in use for quite some time, but they might have belonged to the original Marie Laveau.

Will Kevin commit to me? Will Kevin commit to me? Concentrating on my question was the easy part. It seemed like a broken record that played in my head day and night.

"Chile, de cards don' lie."

Marie turned over each card slowly, nodding occasionally as if the cards spoke to her.

"Yessah, you haf bin afflicted by anuda woman who don' like you t'much. She dark 'n' tall. Her jealousy was t'much and she wan' you t' suffa. She wen t' a lady who worked nasty roots on ya. Yessah, she took ya to de graveyard and buried ya. Mmm, hmmm, buried ina small coffin, small 'n black wit small nails. She buried ya' picha wit some 'erbs 'n put ya ina fresh grave."

I was floored. But how could I know she was telling me the truth? Everything was so general. She could have said it to anyone. I was still skeptical.

"Chile, ya' had tree life changin' accidents. Dis happin' cuz you wuz in de graveyard. Da dead wuz tryin' to come for ya' but God said, 'NO!'"

Marie slammed her hand on the table and startled me.

"Ya hear me, chile? Why ya' look like ya' seen a ghost? Don' worry, I kin hep. I kin send it back. Trust Marie, chile."

I tried to get up from the table. I paid Marie, and she

gave me a list of things to come back with the next day so she could rid me of my demons. She said she was going to give me a spiritual cleaning with a special bath. I looked at the list as I walked in to meet Arnelle. Marie needed a dozen eggs, twelve lemons, nine small white stick candles, and beer. At the end of the note, she wrote, "Wear all white cept your unda-wear. Don wear unda-wear at all."

Arnelle and I made our way down the dark and narrow staircase and waded through the crowds on Chartres Street to get back to our hotel.

"I am not ready to go pick up the kids," she sighed.

"You can hang in my room for awhile."

"Anywhere as long as no kids are screaming and you're telling me what happened in there."

Arnelle raised an eyebrow. She was fishing for information.

"Well," I started, "She said I got roots put on me by some tall black woman."

"Really?"

"Yeah, that's what Marie said right before she said she could help me."

"How?"

"It might be some type of spiritual cleansing. She gave me this crazy list and told me to come back tomorrow in all white and no panties."

I handed the list to Arnelle and she glanced over it and handed it back.

"Channa, I've heard about these cleansings. They really work if someone has put roots on you. But she had to tell you something more. You were too skeptical going in."

"No, that wasn't all she said."

"Then what? What did it?"

"She said that I had three life altering accidents. How could she have known that?"

"See, look at that! I told you, you never know what's going to be said. The real ones always come out of left field with something you didn't expect them to know."

"I guess, Arnelle. This is weird. I never believed in this stuff, and now here I am ready to go back to this old lady's apartment with no panties on. What am I getting into?"

"Don't get worked up, Channa. I told you it's a way of life down here. There's nothing weird about it."

"I hear what you're saying, but I'm not used to this."

"Look, you're making a big deal out of it, and that's why you're worried. Once you realize it's perfectly normal and nobody down here is judging you, you'll be fine."

I hope so, I thought. I was going to head back to Marie Laveau's tomorrow, and I was going to do everything she told me to. How did a simple twenty-minute reading turn into a two-day event? Marie Laveau's granddaughter was going to help me get what was due to me. *I hope this works.*

Chapter 12

I awoke the next morning with an even stronger resolve to make Kevin commit. I'd barely slept a wink trying to figure out how Marie knew about my accidents. I popped out of bed, eager to get over to Marie's so she could wash away the curse that stood between Kevin and me. But first, I needed to rinse off the funkiness from the day before, so I walked over to the bathroom and began running the water for a morning soak.

I stepped out of my skimpy nightgown and eased into the tub, turning off the faucet on my descent. I needed to contemplate what the day had in store for me. *Would this thing with Marie Laveau really work? Was Marie telling me the truth or was she just trying to make a buck?* We hadn't discussed a price for anything. I became afraid that she'd charge me some outrageous amount, and if I refused she would put a spell on me so bad the other one would look like a walk in the park. *How much does a spiritual cleansing cost?* I wondered if I could research it on the Internet at some website like spookyrituals.com or schoolafool.edu. *Maybe I could call around the neighborhood and do some comparative shopping? Maybe someone would advertise, "We honor other priestess' coupons."* I just couldn't believe I'd gotten myself into some creepy mumbo jumbo stuff. But I wanted Kevin, and there was no amount of money too much, or voodoo too crazy.

I got out of the tub and wrapped the fluffy towel around my body. I checked the mirror to make sure my hair didn't get wet, as my mind traveled beyond the earthly realm. *OK, let's do this.* I finished drying off and applied enough lotion to rid myself of any ash. If I had to walk back to Marie's place with that dress on, the least I could do was to make sure I wasn't ashy when that old lady did whatever she had to. I turned on the television, and saw that it was going to be a hot one. It was already eighty degrees outside.

I slipped into the pure, lily-white dress with an empire waistline and wide shoulder straps I had bought the day before. It flared slightly at the bottom and came to my ankles. The dress wasn't really my style, but I needed something white and didn't have time to go on a major shopping expedition for something I probably wasn't going to wear again anyway. I bought some gaudy white platform sandals with an open toe at the same store I found the dress. *These things are ugh-ly. Like UGH, these shoes are ugly.* I strapped them up and looked in the full-length mirror. I looked like I was headed to some coronation to become Kevin's queen. I grabbed the small white purse I had bought too, 'cuz you know girlfriend has to match. Then I headed out to the elevators.

"'Excuse me, ma'am."

The elevator doors opened and revealed the young football player bellboy.

"Now, what did I tell you about calling me ma'am?" I replied jokingly.

"I apologize, miss. Are ya havin' a nice stay?"

He wasn't as quick with his eyes this time, as he gave my body a scan.

"Why, yes I am. Thank you, young man," I cooed. "You are such a gentleman." I said it in such a singsong flirty voice that I surprised myself. I still had it

"Well, have yaself a good day, miss...and, by da way, I like yur dress."

Stepping into the elevator, I turned to look into the long mirror and realized why he was looking at me. He had stared at my breast, then my crotch. *Ahhh. Dammit. My nipples.* My nipples must have caught a breeze because they were about to pop through the cotton dress. Looking down, I saw that I could see right through the bottom half of the dress in that light. *I should have put on a slip.* I gave myself a mental beat down. But it was too late; the elevator doors were about to open to the lobby. *Aw hell, this is New Orleans. The French Quarter's 9th Ward. I'm sure they've seen worse in these parts with all the Girls Gone Wild videos.*

The elevator doors opened, and I saw Arnelle standing outside biting the nail on her forefinger, looking back every time she heard the hotel doors swing open. She appeared to be much more uneasy than myself. I was the one who was getting the "spiritual bath."

"Are you OK, Arnelle?"

I put my hand on her shoulder and some of her tension subsided with my touch.

"Yeah, I'm just a little worried for you. I mean, are you sure you want to do this? I know how unsure you were before."

We began to trek the same path to Marie's we'd taken the previous day.

"Arnelle, I'm not going to let you freak me out at the last minute. I have to do this."

"I understand. OK, I won't say anything else about it. Good luck, I'm sure it will work out. I'm just worried about you, Channa. Anyway, the kids are going to have a ball while we're out."

Arnelle made a grand attempt to change the subject.

"Really? Why do you say that?"

"Well, I checked out the brochure in the room, and did you know that the Hilton is ranked number one when it comes to their child care center's activities for children?"

"What kind of activities do they have for the kids?"

"All types of stuff. They have arts and crafts workshops that I enrolled the kids in. They get to make as many Mardi Gras beads as they want. Maybe that will stop them from trying to steal each other's necklaces."

"I hope for your sake it does. I know it's much more peaceful for you when they're all getting along. Ooh, let's stop here."

There was a small grocery store on the way to Marie's place and I still needed to pick up the ingredients she requested.

Arnelle and I made our way through the small, tight aisles of the little country shop. I had a small basket and gathered the everyday products that Marie could use to change my life. It took no time at all and we headed to the counter to pay for the items.

"Is everything OK?" I asked Arnelle, who looked to be in another world.

"I'm fine. What about you?"

"I'm not as scared as I thought I'd be."

"Well, that's all well and good, but I'm going to be right downstairs just in case. And, if you are not down in an hour, I'm calling the cops. Got it?"

We reached Marie Laveau's, and my finger began to quiver as I went to ring the bell. Maybe I was a little more nerve racked than I thought. I took a deep breath to calm myself as I heard Marie's call out from the window above.

"Come up, chile!"

I turned to Arnelle and said, "This is it. I'll see you in about an hour."

"Yes, or I'll be back with the police."

I hugged Arnelle, and thanked her for being there for me. I opened the door to head up the elongated staircase. *One, two, three…* Counting each step, I thought about how Marie's words from the day before kept me from getting any real sleep. She actually told me that I experienced three life-altering accidents. My skepticism about clairvoyants and fortunetellers was beginning to wane. My eyesight, however, was still intact, yet I could hardly see in the darkened hallway. The only light was peering down on me from Marie's apartment where she stood atop the staircase waiting to greet me. She had on a white outfit again. The light surrounding her frame made her appear angelic.

"Come 'n, chile," she said once I reached her.

I scurried in and took a seat on the couch opposite the dining room table that was now occupied by nine small white plates arranged in a circle. Behind the plates, there were of glasses filled with water, or some type of colorless solution.

Marie walked over to where I was sitting.

"Ya brung wut I as' fo', chile?"

Without saying a word, I simply held out the bag I'd been clutching so tightly. I hadn't realized just how tightly until Marie had to tug at the bag to get it away. *OK, cool, calm, collected Channa has left the building.* I was going to hold it together and not let Marie see me sweat, but I was anxiously expecting the unexpected. Marie began searching the bag and muttering in her heavy, raspy accent

"D'candils in ah?" I wasn't sure if she was speaking to herself or to me. All I was really able to understand was when Marie looked up from the bag and said, "Good."

Marie moved toward the table, taking one candle out of the bag at a time, placing one on each plate. She reached into the pocket of her white housedress and pulled out a small jar decorated with a brightly colored flower pattern. She then squirted the contents into the air over the table. The scent pouring from the bottle was light and airy like a garden, yet I wasn't familiar with the aroma. I sat perplexed on the couch, watching her perform her ritual and wondering just how long it was going to take. But I wasn't crazy enough to interrupt her with silly questions. *I just hope Arnelle didn't jump the gun with the boys in blue.*

Once Marie was finished spewing the powerful scent from the small bottle, she turned her attention to me.

"Stand, chile."

She thrust her shoulders back like a soldier accepting orders to go into battle.

I immediately took to my feet as if part of her troop. Marie looked me over from head to toe and summoned me to the table.

"Now chile, ya' need ta light da candils, right t' lef."

I picked up a box of matches that was sitting in the center of the table. Marie stopped me right away, placing her bony wrinkled hand over mine.

"No chile. Don' mess wit da match. I git it f'ya."

Marie walked over and picked up a small white candle that sat by the matches. It wasn't one of the ones I bought. This candle had been in Marie's possession for quite some time. The wick was withered and black. Not to mention, there was barely any wax left to call it a candle. I watched as she lit it off of a seven-day candle that was burning.

"Ah alwin keeps mah flame a'burnin'."

She handed me the lit candle, saying, "Use dis, my chile. Nah light de candils."

Marie stood beside me and led my hand to the candle at the top of the circle.

"Dis way. Go t' da right slow, chile. Clockwize, frum right t' left win yah light in de circle. Undastand? Lak ya lightin' de numbas on yo' watch. Dwelve, den go to one, den two, den tree, fo', 'n s' on. Neva, neva, light candils for good anti-clockwize, only if ya doin' bad. Den it be dwelve, 'leven, tin, nine, and so. Yeah?"

I couldn't speak, and I barely understood Marie. I was still in awe that I was there, performing a voodoo ritual. I simply nodded my head, yes. Once I lit all of the candles, Marie took my hand and led me to the bathroom. *All that's left is the beer, lemons and eggs. What could we possibly do with them in the bathroom?*

I was bowled over. My Catholicism was quickly called into question. I immediately noticed the saints that hung in every corner of the room. There was no window, and all the light was coming from many lit candles that were in tall, glass jars. The floor was an old mosaic pattern of brown and white. Smack dab in the center was a claw-foot bathtub. I looked to the saints again and wondered if I was doing the right thing. There was Saint Michael, sword in hand, captured in his masculine pose standing over the devil's slain body. Michael was the saint who protected Catholics from the Devil's reign.

Then I saw a picture of Saint Anthony, the saint of lost causes. Tears began to roll down my face as I fought internally with my faith. Marie obviously believed in God and trusted in the powers of the saints. *Would she really be able to help me?* Maybe voodoo wasn't so bad after all, and God would forgive me for this indiscretion. Maybe there was nothing for which I needed to be forgiven. Maybe this was the way things were supposed to be done and I just never knew it. The tears continued to flow as my gaze focused on the figure standing next to the tub. It was the Blessed Mother Mary towering in the center of the saints occupying the walls.

Hail Mary, full of grace, the Lord is with thee...

I stood before her many times. I knew she wept for me. The emptiness I'd felt throughout my life's hardships had come back. I had been aching for Kevin in a way that had gone beyond the flesh. The Blessed Mother was there for me.

Blessed art thou among women...

The statue of Mary was so life-like that I was able to look her directly in the eye. My 5-foot-8 frame only rose two or three inches above the Virgin Mother. At her feet were flowers and lit multi-hued seven-day candles. Of course, she understood my feelings. She wasn't just among women. She was the mother of us all. Why hadn't I taken my woes to her about this? Why had it come to this? Even with Her there, my faith was on the fence.

And blessed is the fruit of your womb...

Mother Mary was holding her beloved baby Jesus in her arms and her neck was draped with wooden rosary beads. The figurine made me panic, and I began crying profusely, heaving deep breaths between soulful sobs. I knew. She had carried me too. Had She carried me there to Marie Laveaus's?

Holy Mary, Mother of God, pray for us sinners now and at the time of our death…Amen…Amen…AmenAmenAmen.

Pray for me. If I was wrong to be there, I would need it.

Marie's deep drawl interrupted my frantic thoughts.

"Chile, stop yo' cryin'! Yah haf to cleen yo'self. De evil mus' b' off ya, chile or no good iz gon' come. Take off ya' clothes! Now do it befo' ya make de speerits mad cuz you waste dey time."

She spoke so forcibly and I was so vulnerable that I damn near jumped out of that white dress. Marie had already drawn the bath for me, and now that I was expected to submerge my body in this liquid, I couldn't keep my questions to myself any longer. There was an oil-based swirl that wasn't mixing with the other substances I assumed to be water.

"Marie, what's in the water?" I asked timidly, still sniffling away.

"Chile, I tell ya cuz you not gon' do wut I do, yeah? De sea salt cleans you from all evil livin' 'round ya. Suga in it t' sweetin' yo' lif'. Yella flowas keep yah frum harm. High John de Conkawa Awl 'n root t' give ya strenf to git wutcha wan. Den las', sandalwood awl and powda to make it work lak lightnin'. Ya know, it gif it dat 'xtra pow, a lil' punch yeah? Also, rue awl and flowa t' protect ya. Now, ya undress 'n ya know wut in de wata. Are we ready, yeah?"

I nodded my head "yes" and started to make steps toward the tub.

"Whoa, chile, I don' tell ya to git in yit. Ya mus' lissen."

I stopped dead in my tracks and waited. Marie then went into the grocery bag and pulled out each lemon, one by one. She rubbed each one over my body, and then cut each in half with a very questionable kitchen knife. *Damn, Marie's packin'.* She then took out an egg and handled it delicately between each hand and rolled it over my head, eyes, face, neck, chest, breasts, arms, thighs, calves, and then my feet. After she finished rubbing my feet with the egg, she stood abruptly and threw the egg to the ground and we watched as it shattered.

Seemingly satisfied, Marie next grabbed the beer. *Are you gonna take a swig? It isn't even noon.* I heard the hiss of the compressed air finding its way out of the can's opening. *Hmph, I sure could use a drink too.* Just then, Marie began to raise the beer slowly above her head. *I know she isn't about to douse herself with beer and drop into convulsions on the floor from the power of the spirits.* But the can made way to the space above my head. *No, she isn't, No! No! No!* I had my hair pressed at the salon before taking the trip, and it was looking good. Before I could protest, Marie tipped the can and I cringed feeling the cold liquid drench my entire head. I watched in misery as the white suds from the beer formed puddles at my feet. I was furious, but I didn't say a word. *Damn, damn, DAMN!*

"Gwon now, git in de tub, chile. Git in!"

I put my right leg in and noticed the water was pleasingly warm. The oils sent me on a heavenly journey, as the saints felt more like friends, and not warnings to hightail it to the door. Marie stood over me, speaking French. I could only pick up a few words from taking the language elective at Howard. It sounded like she was repeating the 23rd Psalm. My thoughts were scattered as I wondered what would be in store for me once this was all said and done.

After the prayer, Marie told me to get out of the tub and handed me a towel to dry myself. The whole experience had me out of this world. There I was naked in this woman's house who I'd known less than 48 hours. I was sticky, I smelled like beer, and I could feel my hair frizzing up. I looked at my watch and noticed I had been in Marie's for almost an hour. *I'd better call Arnelle before she gets the po-po.*

Marie picked up the bag and I figured all that was left were the eggs. *Why ask me to buy a dozen if you only used one? You gonna make us an omelette?*

"Chile, ya cleen naw and wut ya wan ya kin haf. Da

spells gon' 'n da black coffin c'not harm ya. So, speak. Wut ya wan?"

Suddenly, it seemed silly to go through all of that just to get a man. Most women don't have to do this just to get someone to love them. But most women didn't have a chance with Kevin Dean Walker.

I was still a little embarrassed and spoke lowly, "I want my lover to commit."

"Speak up, chile. Wut?"

My voice grew stronger with resolve as I stated it again.

"I want my lover of ten years to commit."

"Ya sho?"

"Yes," I said firmly. "I've never been surer of anything in my life." I knew I wanted my lover and wasn't waiting any longer.

Marie closed her eyes and began rocking back and forth chanting something under her breath. She then opened her eyes and stared at me.

"Chile, ya sho?"

Something in her eyes begged me to say no, but I ignored it, thinking the lady would think that I would ask for something more substantial. She was persistent, however.

"Chile, my sweet chile, 'r ya sho? Dis one is no' righ fo' ya. Dere is anudda man woo loves ya dearly. He de one you shood seek. 'is love's pure 'n gentl'. I kin see deeper dan you. Ya mus be sho', chile."

"Yes."

I answered with even more authority this time. I could not understand why this woman was asking me the same questions over and over. And it sounded like she was bringing Carl into the mix. *Didn't I tell her already that all I wanted was Kevin?*

"Chile, I knew wut ya wan befo' ya tol' me. I was hopin' da saints wood change ya' min'. I worry wit dis man, ya git mo' den ya as' fo' wit 'im. Gwon, look in bag."

She sat the bag down on the floor in front of me. I opened it to glance inside but hesitated to touch anything for fear of ruining the hard work and cleansing Marie had just finished.

"Marie, can I touch these things?"

"Dey yose, chile. I tell ya wut t' do wit dem. Don' ever let any-yun see wut ya doin'. Don' tell dis man wutcha doin' t' 'im 'n don' tell dat friend of yose waitin' outside."

Marie was laying down her law and raised her voice to reinforce her rules.

"Ya hear me?"

"Yes, Marie."

She seemed very serious, and I wasn't going to lie to her. If she didn't want me to tell anyone, then no one would ever find out from me.

"'Kay. Dere is fo' candils, a red clof, incinse, and a juju bag. Don' opin de juju. Keep it on ya body win ya wit 'im 'n take off onlee win ya sleep alone. Yeah?"

"Yes."

"De instructions in de bag. I wrote 'em down fo' ya t' look at. 'n befo' I fuhgit, take a egg n' put one in each room of ya house fo' nine days. Den find a street wit fo' way stop sign n' tro' each egg down n' da centah. Y musn't fuhgit. De evil will stay in de egg 'n ya mus git it out de house afta nine days! Undastand chile?"

"Yes."

Marie placed her hand on her hip and than cocked her head to the side.

"Chile, is all ya know how t' say is, yes?"

"Yes."

She shook her head to dismiss my silly actions.

"Ahhh. Chile, ya sho' ya wan dis Kevin? You haf t' be sho' cuz ya gon git wut ya ask fo', and it's aginst de saints. Are ya sho', chile?"

"Yes I am sure."

Sheesh. What didn't this woman understand? I knew asking for a man seemed frivolous, but that is what I wanted and I had said yes about six or seven times.

Marie gave a sigh. She seemed disappointed.

"Fine, chile. Take de bag and follow de instructions t' de letter 'n wear de juju on ya body. Oh, da eggs too, don fuhgit de eggs."

I snatched the bag off of the floor, and folded the top down so that Arnelle couldn't peak inside to see what it contained. I was not going to let Kevin get away, and as far as I was concerned, this bag held my future. I held it like it contained nitroglycerin.

"How much do I owe you, Marie?"

I realized we still hadn't discussed a price.

"Chile, wut-evah ya wan' t' give is fine."

What? What if I wanted to give you a dollar? How can you do business like that? You need a sign with a pricelist up in here. I went into my purse and saw I only had a bill with Benjamin Franklin's face on it. *Oh, who cares, Kevin will be mine and this woman did it for me. A hundred dollars is nothing compared to a lifetime of happiness.* I gave Marie the money and headed for the door.

"Chile," she called after me. "Ya sho' now dat ya wan dis man? I tell ya, you mus be careful."

Suddenly, I turned around to face Marie; something had just dawned on me.

"I never told you his name was Kevin." My eyes were wide with amazement. "How did you know that?"

A huge smile crept across Marie's face and she said, "Chile, I tell ya, I see deeper dan ya tink. I know mo', so much mo', and dat's why I say be careful. But ya don' lissun. Der sum tings yo' black room kint protect ya frum, 'n not Marie. Be careful. Gwon now, I leave da do' opin so ya haf light to git down dem stairs. Yeah?"

"Yes."

I smiled and turned back around, not sure why she wanted me to be careful. It was amazing that she knew about my den. Maybe she saw that Kevin was a womanizer and didn't want me to get my feelings hurt. Not only was Marie a spiritual healer, she had a soft, kind heart too. I was flattered she'd taken such an interest in my wellbeing. *But don't worry about me, Marie. "Careful" is my middle name. I just want "Walker" to be my last name.*

I walked out onto the street, and Arnelle was waiting right by the doorbell.

"Hey, girl," I said like I was surprised to see her. "How was your day?"

"It was great. I got a bite to eat over at this cute café down the street and worried myself to death over my friend who was off with some voodoo lady."

Arnelle was sarcastic. I knew she had been worried, but I didn't think she'd get herself so worked up. Arnelle took a step back and looked me up and down.

"Ooh, what happened? Your hair is all over your head and you smell like you fell in a vat of beer. Are you drunk? What went on in there?"

I tried to run my fingers through my hair. I couldn't. My roots had frizzed up.

"No. I'm not drunk and I can't tell you what happened in there."

"What? Are you joking, Channa? I've been worried sick for over an hour and you can't tell me?"

Chapter 11

I daydreamed about what life would be like once I landed in New Jersey. I imagined Kevin waiting for me at the airport, falling to one knee as soon as he saw me.

"Marry me, Channa," he would say, nervously fumbling with a small jewelry box with a hella sparkling engagement ring.

"Kevin, how did you know I was here?" I would ask him, dropping my bags and running up to him.

"My heart brought me to you, it just knew," he would say as he opened the box and revealing the glowing diamond.

I'd say yes, of course, letting a single tear fall down my cheek and into the palm of his hand. He'd stand and kiss me passionately as the crowded airport would burst into applause like the ending of a cheesy, romance movie.

How long will it take for this magic to kick in? I wondered.

I met Arnelle for lunch as promised, but I decided to let her know right away that I was leaving.

"Arnelle, I just want you to know I'm glad I came."

"I'm glad too, Channa."

"But…I'm sorry…I need to go home."

Arnelle looked like I smacked her.

"What? Why?"

"Oh, don't get mad or anything. I was just thinking that you and the kids were going to be busy with the conference and maybe I should just get home. I feel weird admitting that I'm sort of anxious to see if Marie Laveau's spell works."

Arnelle let out a long, sad sigh.

"Sure, Channa, I understand. We will be busy, but I was going to make time to see you."

I felt guilty; she seemed as though I broke her heart.

"Don't be like that, Arnelle. I didn't think you'd be upset. I was afraid of slowing you guys down and so I changed my flight. I already dragged you along on my voodoo escapades. I'm hogging up all your time. Go to your conference and have a good time with your kids. And this way, I won't be sitting around in my room watching TV shows I could see at home."

"Yeah, well, I thought you'd take a tour or something. Maybe learn a little Creole history."

"Like what? I don't know much about Creole history."

Arnelle seemed to light up at the opportunity to educate someone on this fascinating culture.

"Creoles are descendants of Haiti or the Dominican Republic."

"Really? I always thought they were slaves whose masters just happened to be French and that's why they didn't speak English."

"No...see, the Haitians who were fair-skinned, and whose hair was naturally straight were the chosen traveling companions to the slave masters. You couldn't have the traditional wide flat nose of the African. The pointier your nose, and the thinner your lips, the better. It was the look more accepted by whites."

"I never knew that."

"Don't feel bad. Not too many people do. Anyway, many Creoles had never been slaves, but they were indentured servants. The fairer a woman's skin was, the more special treatment she was treated to, because that was more desirable. They were treated like prizes."

"What? Prizes? Like trophies?"

"Yup. The slave owners took great pride in their indentured servants. It was a status symbol to have good-looking

Creole women who would answer your every beck and call. A man whose Creole woman was lusted after by every one of his slave-owning peers was a man of great notoriety in the community. These men would make their Creole servants have sex with other slave owners as payments for debt, or just for their own perversions. The Haitian and Dominican slave masters were famous for trading women back and forth amongst each other."

"Wow! Are you serious? They really took advantage of those women. How disgusting. Do you consider yourself a Creole?"

"Well, no. I do not consider myself to be a Creole. But, I can relate to keeping life trouble free and not announcing my race. I'm just trying to get what I need without the drama of everyone knowing I'm Black."

I boarded the plane and relaxed in my roomy seat. My cell phone started going off while we were waiting for the other passengers to board. *Huh? Oh, it's Deja.* I checked the number and picked up knowing I would get a much-needed, light-hearted laugh after my vacation.

"Hey, Deja."

"Hey, stranger. Where are you?"

"I'm on the plane ready to come home."

"Gurl, did you meet any nasty men?"

"No, Deja," I said feigning disgust. "It wasn't that kind of trip."

"What? What do you mean it wasn't that kind of trip? Every trip out of town and away from your man is that kind of trip. Come on, spill it, heifer!"

"No, really. I didn't meet anybody. There was a very strong looking bellboy..."

I chuckled to myself. Lusting after that young buck made me feel like a nasty old woman, which I probably was.

"See, I knew you were holdin' out on me."

"No, it's not like that. Before you interrupted me, I was going to say, 'but he was just a boy.'"

"Uggh. How old? Never mind, that's not important. He has to learn sometime. Did he at least look legal?"

"Yeah, he looked legal."

Deja is a trip.

"Well, that's all you would need to tell the cops after his mama called them on you."

I almost fell out of my seat laughing. "I'm not into robbing cradles."

"Who's talking about robbing a cradle? You just wanna borrow that baby for a little while and send him back. The young ones get too needy, gurl. Anyway, I can't wait to let you see my hair. That little fourteen year-old girl really did a hell of a job."

"How long did it take her?"

"Oh, she finished that second day. That's not bad seein' as how she wasn't trying to charge me a lot of money. I still gave her the fifty that she charged and another fifty. Shit, Channa, I couldn't have beat that with a stick."

"You're crazy."

"And I know I look good, everybody at work loves it. I style it differently every day, just because I can. I have so much freedom with this style, and it's human hair, so I can hot curl it."

"Gurl, don't talk to me about hot curling or hot combing. You know my hair got wet."

"Ah-ha-ha-ha! Buckwheat's granny."

"Shut up, Deja. It's not funny. OK, it is, but it looks horrible. Half is curly and half is straight. I had to get some cheap gel from the hotel gift shop, and you know it wasn't my usual product so I had to do my best in pulling this mess back."

"You mean half is nappy and half is not? I told you not to let it grow out like that. You got to figure out what to do with it and quick. Go find yourself a skilled hair braider and let her do you up. My braids are beautiful."

"I'll see. I'm still undecided. Hold on a sec. They're making an announcement."

The stewardess was making a broadcast over the loud speaker.

"All passengers please find your seats, place all carry-on items... smoking is prohibited on this flight."

"I have to go, Deja, I'll call you when I get home."

"OK, gurl, talk to you then."

I hung up with Deja and turned off my cell phone.

"You haf t' be sho' cuz ya gon git wut ya ask fo' but it's against de saints."

I was watching the city get more and more distant below when Marie's voice came to mind. *What exactly did that mean? Against the saints?* I guessed I should have asked more questions, said more than "yes" the whole time. All I knew was that if I followed her instructions, I would get the commitment from Kevin that I wanted. I just figured it was against the saints because of my already wonderful boyfriend, Carl. How could I throw a man away who cared for me in such an unselfish way? The saints wouldn't be pleased since this was unfair to Carl. But I hoped they'd get over it because I couldn't keep Carl around while my flesh craved Kevin's touch.

Besides, Marie said she already knew what I wanted. So it couldn't be so bad. I mean, why single me out to give me something that would hurt me? I thought back to the woman in white and her knotted scarf approaching me in the shop. She knew I needed help. She seemed drawn to me. Maybe it was meant for me to come to New Orleans and for Marie Laveau to cleanse me. I was meant to get my commitment from Kevin, so where was the danger in that? I just knew that instead of leaving before I woke up, he would be there for breakfast; possibly lunch as well as dinner, too. I drifted off to sleep, dreaming of taking Kevin home to meet my mother and grandmother. Everyone would love him. He was smart and successful and the perfect man on paper and in my life.

Once the plane landed, I went inside the airport and headed to the baggage claim area, but there was *no Kevin on bended knee.* I shrugged off the fantasy and put three dollars in the machine that held the dollies and took the next available cart. I had called a car service before I left the hotel. I was in no mood to fight other passengers for a cab. I just wanted to get my bags and go. I moved over to the turnstile and waited for it to start circling.

Once I had my bags, I made it out to the curb and the cool weather immediately reminded me I was home. New Orleans was hot, but it was winter in New Jersey. I saw a man holding a sign with my name on it: CHANNA RENÉE JONES.

I got in the car and told the driver, "We need to make a stop in Newark before going to Montclair."

"Yes, Ms. Jones," the driver nodded in his rearview mirror.

I rang the doorbell and waited for about forty-five seconds before being greeted by my grandmother, Mildred Ruth Smith. She was a strong, classy woman with eyes that were a sea of blue, courtesy of her White and Native American ancestors. Her fine salt and pepper curly hair was a gift from her Black mother; it was neatly pulled up into a bun. My grandmother she stood in the doorway and smiled and hugged me with wide open arms.

"Hi, Grandma."

I was so happy to see her, as always.

"Come on in, baby."

My mother was standing behind her, and I embraced her as well. She was a beautiful sight for sore eyes. With her flawless cinnamon complexion, she was often compared to Dorothy Dandridge. It felt good to be home. Somebody was baking and I caught a whiff of something sweet in the air.

"Mmm-mmm. Something smells gooood."

We strolled into the kitchen as I reached into my purse to pull out a bag of souvenirs. I handed my mother and grandmother each a set of Mardi Gras beads.

"Thank you, baby. I'm putting mine on now."

My grandmother put her beads around her neck and washed her hands so she could get back to mixing the batter she was working on.

"I'm making some carrot cake, Channa. Do you want a slice? You can take some home with you."

"Oh, I'm going to take a piece, Grandma. It smells delicious."

I was eyeing the cake she had cooling on the kitchen island. There was always some cooking going on in the house my mother shared with my grandmother. The walls of the kitchen were soft hues of green, with matching flour and sugar canisters. The potholders and oven mitts were all matching floral prints that coordinated with the curtains. Not particularly my taste, but it felt welcoming and cozy.

"Come on in the living room, Sunshine, and talk to me. I haven't spoken to you in days," my mother said, excited to catch up.

We sat on the plastic slipcover protecting the cream-colored couch. Grandma didn't mind that it made an annoying crunching sound when you tried to settle into a seat. The only thing that concerned her was keeping her house clean and free from permanent stains. She always said that it didn't matter how much money you had, you should still take care of, and treasure, your possessions as if they were priceless.

"So, how was your trip?" my mother asked.

"It was great, Ma. The friend I went with, Arnelle, really showed me a good time."

I had to embellish a bit—I couldn't come out and tell her what I'd done. We didn't go to voodoo priestesses in my family. It wasn't the Catholic way.

"Her kids went too, right? How was that?"

"It was OK. Kids aren't really my thing, but hers were sweet. They hugged me as if they knew me when we met at the airport."

"I can't wait until I have some grandchildren."

"Ma, please. Not now, I just got off a long flight. Besides, you have two children to harass. What about Kyle?"

I thought about my brother and how she never had these conversations with him. He was so self-absorbed and I was the only one who seemed to notice.

"Sunshine! Come here for a second," Grandma called out from the kitchen.

I signaled for my mother to follow me. I got up, making the plastic burp, and made my way to Grandma. I caught a glimpse of the various portraits of my elder family members. There were black and white photographs of my grandma's cousins, many of whom I'd never met. My grandmother had framed memories of her more youthful days when she and her siblings would dress up and pose in their Sunday best before going to church. Pictures of her children and grandchildren adorned the mantle hanging over the old, brick fireplace in the dining room.

Oh, the fireplace brought back childhood memories of Grandma toasting more than marshmallows over the open flames. Whenever she was preparing a Sunday or holiday dinner, the house was lively with my mother and Auntie scurrying back and forth through the kitchen. The fireplace would be covered in Christmas stockings stuffed with books, toy cars, and dolls; the names of all immediate family members embroidered with golden thread. With all of our family coming around for the holiday, Grandma would have more pots than she had burners on the stove. She would set up her mini grill kit and spread hickory chips on the fireplace's floor and set up a pot or two right there. *She is so amazing.* Those were great times full of carefree fun, but she knew how to make the house comforting as well. Life wasn't full of holidays.

That house held those memories because of my grandmother's flair. After I left Relsek, my mother sold her house in Brooklyn and bought the one in Newark. My medical bills wiped me out, and helping me put a financial strain on her as well. I gave up my place and moved to Newark with my grandmother and her. I was loved and cared for with a tenderness surpassing anything I could have imagined. There were times when I was overcome with my situation, and thought that suicide was the only answer. My mother and grandmother were there to restore my faith in God's strength. When food was scarce and money was low, my grandma would simply remind me, "God sees us, it will be OK. We will be OK."

Her words were an inspiration that gave me the power to carry on and know I would never be alone as God was always with me.

"So, Channa, we were debating about where we should have Thanksgiving dinner this year."

I slid into a seat at the island directly in front of the mixing bowl which held the carrot cake batter. Grandma didn't even look up from mix the cake. She was a senior but, if anyone would see how fast she was moving her arms, one would never believe that is was in her eighties.

"Oh yeah," my mother said pulling up the chair next to me, "We wanted to know if we should do dinner at your place or here."

"You know it doesn't matter to me. We can do it at my house. Who's coming, Grandma?"

"Well, of course, your Auntie June and the kids. A few of your other cousins too. You know, the usual crowd."

Grandma was done mixing her batter and began to pour the thick liquid into the awaiting cake pan.

"That's fine, I just need to know how many places to set at the table. So, what else has been going on?"

I must have asked a loaded question because my mother and grandmother both looked at each other then dropped their eyes to the floor. Something wasn't right.

"Ma, what's wrong?"

I turned to force her to look me in the eye.

She didn't answer. Instead, my grandmother interjected, "It's Uncle Jake, Sunshine. He's sick."

"Well, how sick is he? What has Auntie June said?"

Uncle Jake was my Auntie June's husband and a solid member of the family. My childhood was filled with blissful memories of my aunt and uncle, and to hear he was sick was distressing. I started to worry about my aunt. She'd been there for me through every step of the accidents. Her words of encouragement always resounded in my ears when she was not around. A memory of her visiting me in Relsek ran through my mind. Auntie June assured me that God was not punishing me, but He had a greater purpose for my life. She told me to realize just who was in control and allow Him to guide me. With the tone my mother and grandmother had taken, I became afraid that it was my turn to comfort Auntie June.

"He's got cancer."

My grandmother's words sent a shockwave of pain through my body.

"He's staying in the hospital."

I placed my elbows on the island counter, my head was spinning and I needed to hold it up. I needed to process everything I was told. The kitchen remained silent.

Uncle Jake was like a father to me. With my own dad out of the picture most of the time, Uncle Jake became the man of the family. He taught me to ride a bike, frowned at my tight clothing, and said I was a princess when I felt more like a toad. He'd done repairs around my mother's house, manned the grill at family cookouts, and I gave him ties for Father's Day for as long as I could remember. Losing Uncle Jake would be catastrophic. Just the thought of him in the hospital, and not able to cut the turkey was unbearable. Without him, Thanksgiving would be a day that no one would enjoy.

"We're just going to have to make sure all of Uncle Jake's favorites are made and take Thanksgiving to him at the hospital. Have you already decided on a menu?"

I lifted my chin an inch and threw back my shoulders. I needed to be strong.

"Your Aunt June usually makes the macaroni and cheese, but I don't want her to do any cooking this year. She needs to take care of her husband." Grandma turned away and placed the cake pan into the oven.

My mother followed suit, "I'll go ahead and make it, along with the ham and turkey. Sunshine, do you think you can help out with the pot roast and rice?"

"Sure thing, Ma. I'll make some sweet potato pie too."

"Are you sure you know how to make a sweet potato pie, Channa?"

The thought of me baking caused my grandmother to turn around so fast, I felt a breeze.

"I don't remember you ever trying your hand at dessert."

We all laughed at my grandmother's light mockery of my baking skills, and it was just what we needed after such a sobering moment. It was true, I wasn't Sara Lee and had never tried my hand at dessert, but I wanted to try something new this year and hoped it would turn out well enough to make Uncle Jake happy.

"I'll be fine, Grandma, and you'll love my pie almost as much as I'm going to love this carrot cake."

"Oh, I almost forgot about that cake. Give me a second and let me put the icing I made on it so you can take it with you. I got a box."

She hurried over to the refrigerator and pulled out a small, white, plastic container filled with her homemade cream cheese icing. It looked scrumptious as she waved her knife like a magic wand causing a layer of velvety, smoothness to cover the masterpiece she'd baked earlier. Grandma pulled a white cake box, like the ones you get from a bakery, out from the kitchen cabinet right above the sink. I watched as she carefully placed the cake inside and tied a string around the box to keep it closed.

"I can't wait to get that cake home. It is going to be demolished in two days."

"Well, as long as you enjoy it, baby. The other one I'm making is for your brother. I'm going to send it to him."

My grandmother said that with the kind of pride she got whenever she did something for my brother.

"Why are you sending Kyle a cake?"

It's not like he can't just drive by and visit like I did and pick up his own damn cake. Kyle was a staff writer for a black sitcom at the Fox Network in New York. You'd think he lived in Los Angeles the way he never visited.

"That's right, I haven't had a chance to tell you," my mother interrupted. "But Kyle isn't coming to Thanksgiving this year. He said he had to work so he's just going to stay near the job and head over to his girlfriend's house."

"Oh, well I guess that's one less place at the table," I said, as I tried not to sound disappointed.

Of course my brother will not be joining us this year. He's always putting something of less importance in front of his family. I recalled the time after my second car accident when I was waiting for him to pick me up from the emergency room. Hours had passed and there was no sign of Kyle, so I called my mother to find out what happened. My mother called him then called me back, "Just hold on, Sunshine. Kyle said he'd be there as soon as the game is over."

The game? I was just in an accident. I'm at the EMERGENCY ROOM! I wanted to yell, but there was no use. My brother could do no wrong. If his own flesh and blood wasn't more important than a game on TV, what did he care about Thanksgiving?

"Yeah, we'll miss him, but you know how busy he is. I'm so proud of my son…of both of my children."

My mother smiled at me as she patted me on one cheek and kissed the other.

"I know you do, Ma, and I love you too. OK, I'd better get going. I have a car waiting outside. Love you, Grandma."

I kissed my grandmother on the cheek and thanked her for my cake as I grabbed the box holding my sweet treat and headed for the front door.

"OK, Sunshine, we'll talk more about Thanksgiving later."

Grandma raised her hand as her goodbye wave.

I got to the car and instructed the driver to take me home to Montclair. I slid into the back seat and stared out the window watching my mother's house until I couldn't see it anymore. I wondered how my cousins were handling their father's diagnosis. With everything on my mind from Arnelle revealing the truth about her abusive ex-husband, to finding out Uncle Jake may be dying, calling Carl was one of the farthest things from my mind. When I was almost home, I remembered I should at least let him know I was back in town so he wouldn't get worried.

I pulled my cell phone from my purse and hit Carl's number on speed dial. "Hi baby. Guess who's back."

"Channa? When did you get in? Where are you?"

"Back in Jersey. I'm on my way home now."

"How are you getting home?"

"I called a car service to meet me at the airport."

"Why didn't you call me? I would've met you and driven you home. You know I worry about you."

Carl sounded a tad bit peeved.

"I know, but I knew you were probably studying and I didn't want to interrupt you. Anyway, are you coming over? I really would like to see you."

With the way my day was turning out, I needed a nice cuddle session with Carl. I always felt safe in his arms.

"Of course, I'm coming over. And you know what? I'm taking you to dinner. I know it's too late to cook, and those in-flight meals are crappy."

"All right, I'll see you in a few."

I hung up just as we were pulling into my driveway. The

driver was kind enough to put the bags inside my entranceway, and he didn't talk my ears off during the ride, so I gave him a well-deserved tip, as Ms. Channa does.

I went inside and called my neighbor who watched Tango whenever I went out of town, and she was ringing my doorbell in a matter of minutes. I welcomed her at the door, and Tango leapt on my leg begging me to pick him up.

"Hey Tango. Hey. How's my baby? Did you miss me? I missed you."

I gave him a bowl of food then got ready for my dinner with Carl.

"Carl, Carl, Carl," I said going up the stairs.

He hadn't seen me in days, and I needed to be extra pretty for our date. After I showered, I found a rosy-red, knee-length pencil skirt. It hugged my curves and accentuated all of the positive aspects. I put on a pair of black, knee-high boots and coordinated a form-fitting, thin black sweater. I put on a long, oversized necklace and let it drape over my breasts, bringing just enough attention to the girls. Then I found my matching belt and earrings to complete the outfit. I looked sleek and sexy, except for my hair. There was nothing sleek about it. I picked up my hot comb and hugged it like a long lost friend. Home sweet home. I touched up my roots and parted my hair in the center and let it fall bone straight over my shoulders. *Hot damn, Miss Chaaannnaaa! Just a little make-up and you're a complete package, girlfriend.*

Carl called when he was outside and I went to meet him in my driveway. I got inside the car and he kissed me right away.

"Baby. You look good."

He leaned back and let his eyes travel my dangerous curves and shuddered.

"Mmm-mmm."

"Thank you. You're not so bad yourself."

I secured my seatbelt and gave him a sideways glance. It

was true. He had on a black suit, a fresh haircut, and my favorite cologne.

"What do you want to eat?"

He threw the car into reverse and backed out of the driveway.

"It doesn't matter, pick a place."

"Good. I want some catfish so we're going to this new soul food restaurant in Newark."

"We can try it, but no one's soul food is better than my mother and grandmother's cooking."

I thought back to the smells coming from my grandmother's kitchen from earlier.

"Yeah, well, everyone says that. Don't worry. I've eaten there before. It's good."

Looking across the table at Carl, I found myself half listening as he described the progress he was making with his research for the high-profile case on which his firm was working. Here I was at dinner with Carl, but my mind kept drifting back to New Orleans. Thoughts of the Big Easy led to thoughts of Kevin. I was back in New Jersey with one mission, and one mission only. *I'm going to make Kevin Dean Walker mine. Marie has given me the arsenal I need and I'm determined to see it through.* Carl was laughing at one of his corny jokes, and it brought me out of my thoughts. I needed to figure out what I would do with the present relationship I was in. I smiled and nodded at Carl as if I was hanging onto every single word that came from his mouth, but I could only think about how he was going to react once he realized that I no longer wanted to be with him.

Our food arrived, and we dug right in. In between chews, Carl wanted to know if I'd spend Thanksgiving with him.

"I don't think so, Carl, " I started to say, my heart sinking at the mention of Thanksgiving.

"Come on, it'll be great. We can fly to Houston and you

can meet my family. I know they'll love you. Please?"

He looked like a sweet little kid asking to keep a stray puppy.

"I just don't think it would be good to go. My brother already said he's not going to make it and so it would be bad if I were gone too. And they want to have the dinner at my house this year, but even still, we need to take food to the hospital..."

"The hospital? What?"

"I just found out that Uncle Jake has cancer."

I couldn't believe I said it, it felt so real. Just then I wanted to cry.

"Don't worry, everything will work out for the best."

Carl put down his fork and took my hands in his, but I didn't look in his eyes. I just looked at his hands.

"I sure hope so, but I'm not too convinced. Uncle Jake smoked a pack of Newports a day for years, decades."

"Oh, I didn't realize his smoking was so serious."

"Yeah, he loved his cancer sticks more than he loved his lungs."

My nose burned, the tears were on the way.

"You don't really believe that do you?"

Carl's voice was soft, and his thumbs rubbed the tops of my hands.

"No...but Uncle Jake's been around for as long as I can remember. Losing him would be like losing a father."

My mind drifted away for a moment. I contemplated what holidays, dinners and family reunions would be like if Uncle Jake was not present. What would get-togethers be like without Uncle Jake? I dispelled the idea from my head and banished any notion of losing my favorite uncle. *He'll pull through this. He's tough.* I ate the remainder of my meal in silence, wondering what more could happen.

Chapter 10

After dinner, Carl drove me home. He walked me to my door and waited for me to find my keys. I unlocked the door and stepped inside, noticing that he didn't follow me in.

"Baby, aren't you coming in?"

I'd been gone for a few days and I knew he wanted me.

"Channa, you had a long trip, got some disturbing news, and ate all that catfish. I know you just want to go to sleep and you don't need me putting my hands all over you."

I raised my eyebrow at that. He lowered his voice and leaned closer.

"Because, you know, I'll be putting my hands all over you."

"Mmm-hmm."

I dropped my purse by the door and took hold of his hands, examining them, sliding my fingers over them. His hands were strong, not too smooth, but thankfully, not rough. His fingers were thick and it reminded me of another part that had above-average girth.

"These hands? I can't see the harm in having them on my body. Where would you put them? Here?"

I pulled him over the threshold and put his hands where my waist ended and hips began.

"Uh huh. I'd put them there."

"And would you put them here?"

I guided his hands up my sides and onto my breasts.

"I did like having them here."

"Uh huh."

Carl looked at his hands and extended his thumbs to trace the curves on the bottoms of my breasts. His breathing pattern changed.

"Well, what would I do with my hands? Should I put them here?" I left his hands where they were and put my hands inside his open jacket to rub all over his chest.

"No, I think I should put them here." I let my hands fall to his belt, slowly pulling it loose. I reached inside his pants and found a monster of a sausage waiting for me.

Carl used his foot to close the door behind him, the light from the porch no longer illuminating the foyer. We stood in the darkness, fondling each other and listening to the choppiness of our breath that was created by the physical excitement.

"Carl?" I said, breaking the silence.

"Yes?"

"Can we take this upstairs?"

I knew I was probably wrong, seducing Carl when I so clearly longed for Kevin. I could hear Marie Laveau's words bouncing around my brain as Carl picked me up and carried me to my bedroom. *Is dis da man you wan, chile?* She was talking about Kevin, and that's who I wanted, but I watched Carl rip at his suit like Superman in a phone booth. He almost pulled it off in one swoop, his shirt arms still in his jacket arms, crumbled in a pile on the floor. He jiggled his hips, sending his unbuckled pants to the floor.

My face was locked in a seductive smile, eyes focused on the stiff soldier standing at attention between Carl's legs. My mind, however, wondered where Kevin was. There was no way he'd ever drop one of his expensive suits to the floor, no matter how hot I'd gotten him.

Chile, are ya sure?

Carl crawled onto the bed. He reached for my boot and hesitated at the zipper. *I bet Kevin would say to keep them on.* He unzipped my left boot and pulled it off slowly, and he let his hand stroke the side of my calf. I enjoyed the touch and the thrust of his hand. He repeated the process on the other side. My boots, probably in a crumpled mess with his suit, hit the floor as his hands were under my skirt. He pulled off my panties, then pulled off my skirt, and looked at my honey hive like an unwrapped present that Santa had given him for Christmas. *Open your pussy for me, Channa Renée Jones.* I felt woozy. Kevin wasn't in the room, but he was in my head. And I wanted Kevin's head in me. My juices started to flow and I parted my knees, desperate for *somebody's* love rod to penetrate.

Carl pulled my top off of my belly, and he bent his head and kissed my stomach. I raised my ass off the bed, eagerly waiting for his kisses to go south. My rum drop rubbed against his chest. He continued north. He pulled my turtleneck as far up as it could go with me on my back. I sat up, hoping to hurry him along. I pulled the top the rest of the way, shaking my hair until it all fell back to my shoulders. He kissed me, his warm lips pressed against mine, parting ways, our tongues colliding. All the while, he fumbled with the hooks of my bra, sighing with relief once my breasts were free and hardening with the cool air.

Carl's the type that likes to look at all the food on his plate and rub his hands together in anticipation for a really good meal. It's very sweet, especially when I've gone through all the trouble of cooking, but this was sex. He was up on his knees, his knees between my legs, and he scanned my body as if he didn't know which dish to dig into first. Kevin always looked at me that way, so by the time he got me naked, he knew exactly where to go.

You know it's yours. Fuck me, baby.

I pulled my hips up, in a desperate invitation. He met my hips and pulled me higher as he slid his throbbing sausage deep into my honey hive.

"Unh!" I gasped, pulling at the sheets around me as I felt an ecstatic relief come over me.

I'd wanted it so bad. Kevin's love rod inside me where I'd

take it, hold it, taste it, and keep it. I didn't let it phase me that it was really Carl in the room.

"Oh, Channa," Carl moaned.

I shut my eyes as tight as I could and told myself it was Kevin speaking.

Ooh, Channa. He pried my hands away from the sheets. His fingers interlocked with mine, and forced my arms over head, pressed down at the sides of my head. My hair caught beneath, the pain heightening my senses. Ooh, Channa. Ooh, Channa.

"Go deeper. Faster."

I swayed my hips to set the pace.

He let go of my hands and reached just below my knees, lifting my legs higher until my ankles rested on his shoulders. I welcomed him in, digging deeper, going faster, his tool a piston on a well-oiled machine. His sack swung to my rhythm, slapping at my ass and the bed slamming hard into the headboard. I thought, "For sure, we'll break the box spring this time, Kevin."

"Oh, yes! Oh God!" I screamed out.

"Oh, Channa! Oh-oh, Channa!"

My body started to shudder. Kevin was hitting the right spot, over and over again, pounding at it like a punching bag. My words started to stutter, feeling his swollen dick stretch the walls of my honey hive, rubbing against my rum drop as he went. I leaned up, arching my bare back, forcing my breasts to press into my thighs. He couldn't get any deeper, but I was trying to get him in farther. It was too good, it was what I needed, it was about to happen.

"Oh God! Oh God! I'm cumming! Kevin, I'm cumming!"

The pitch of my voice was higher than ever, probably sending Tango to bury his head under his doggie pillow. The dam broke, spilling my juices all over the sheets. I fell back into the pillows, satisfied. Breathing heavy and sweating.

"Oh God. Whew. Baby. You put a hurtin' on me tonight. Baby?"

When I opened my eyes, I saw Carl still on his knees between my legs. His manhood looked like a deflated sausage. He was glaring at me.

"What? What's wrong? Did you cum?"

"Channa, who's Kevin?"

Oh shit. Did I say Kevin's name?

"What?"

"You just said, Kevin. Who is he?"

"I don't know what you're talking about."

Men say that type of thing all the time when they get busted. I've heard it, and I said it. It was the cheater's reflex.

"I know what I heard."

Carl looked so hurt. Having your woman call out another man's name at the height of her climax had to shatter the ego. As my senses came back to me, I thought that maybe Carl didn't suspect I was cheating on him. Maybe he thought I was just reminiscing about an ex.

"Carl, if I said what you say I did. Then I'm sorry. I didn't mean anything by it. Kevin is an old boyfriend, but I don't know why I said his name."

"Channa, I'm going home."

Carl pushed himself backwards until he was off the bed.

"I know that I'm not the first man you've been with. But, if you've got some unfinished business with this Kevin dude, you need to let me know."

This was it, Carl was giving me an out and I'd be free to pursue Kevin, guilt-free. But, I've been free for Kevin before and he didn't commit to me then. I had a lot of faith in Marie Laveau's spell, but I still didn't want to take the chance of being alone.

"There's no unfinished business. I haven't spoken to Kevin in years."

I got up and stood in front of Carl.

"I'm telling you the truth. I love you."

Then I felt the guilt. It was true that I loved Carl, but Kevin was who I really wanted to be with. I wasn't being any more honest or sincere than Kevin was with me. I needed to talk to Kevin, to find out where he stood before working any voodoo and breaking any hearts.

"Why don't you come back to bed and let me make it up to you?"

He resisted for a while, but I broke him down. I proved my love for him over and over again. Then I fondled him, suckled him, and rode him. I'd let him sleep for a short time before seducing him again.

"Oh Carl," I'd say, hoping the fucking would make him forget what I had said.

Carl left earlier than usual. He tried to smile and be happy. But I could tell he just wasn't into it. I did a lot of damage just by uttering Kevin's name. So Kevin was going to have to make me believe it was worth it. But it wouldn't matter. I already knew he was.

The man I was seeing before I woke up in the physical rehabilitation center Relsek let go of me like I was a "hot potato." He was the one I thought would've stood by my side. Yet Kevin the player, the one I expected to say, "Well, it was good while it lasted, but I'm out," stayed. He supported me when I couldn't roll to the other side of a hospital bed. Kevin the player, walked with me while I was using a walker on Rodeo Drive in Beverly Hills. He kept his head high. He never let me feel like a victim, and he never let me forget that I was still a woman. He showed me compassion, empathy, passion and most of all, he was there. At the time, I thought I was in love with him because of that, but that subsided and my eyes were open to so much more. Kevin was all I wanted in a man. He was handsome, successful, and I knew that he was going to stay with me no matter what.

So, I'd been single before. Kevin had chances to commit

to me many times. But he didn't. That was what I worried about. I wanted to give up all other men and spend my life with just Kevin, and right now, I had a really good guy that didn't deserve the heartbreak. I just wanted Kevin to tell me, *what's in it for me if I let Carl go for you?*

I tried to call him at work and only got his voicemail. I thought maybe he'd taken the day off and was at home, but I only got the machine. I called him on his cell phone, knowing surely he wouldn't leave that behind. But he didn't answer. His wireless service gave me the option to page him, and I did, but he never called back.

"That's all right, Kevin Dean Walker," I said, clutching the bag Marie Laveau had given me. "I got somethin" for you."

Chapter 9

Marie instructed me to place an egg in every room of my house, and to dispose of them nine days later. Putting the eggs around my house was the easy part. I went from room to room, leaving eggs in vases and cabinet drawers, behind pictures and under long drapes

Nine days later, I knew I had to find the eggs and get them out of my house, the evil and negativity soaked behind the shell. Then I'd have to find a crossroad with a four-way stop and throw the eggs down in the middle. Of course, this was Montclair and I wasn't trying to be throwing eggs in front of my neighbors. I waited until it had gotten late and drove down the street from the Elementary School where there was a four-way stop at the intersection. Once I was sure no one was looking, I rushed to the nearest corner and started lobbing the eggs toward the middle of the road.

I felt like a mischievous teenager, looking around for witnesses before winding up a fastball. SNAP! The egg hit the ground, oozing yolky yellow. CRUNCH! Another egg was shattered, with more white shell chips splattering out like fireworks. By the time I threw my last egg, I was shaking more from my belly laugh than I was from the chilly temperature.

"So long, suckers," I said to the curse-filled eggs.

That'll teach you to mess with me. Ha-ha. Just then, I caught a glimpse of headlights a good distance up the street.

"Oh shit!" I said like any teenaged deviant who was in

danger of being busted.

And then I broke out for my car like a roach when the lights come on. When the car reached the intersection, I was huddled by the left rear wheel of my car, with an extreme case of the giggles. The car rolled over the scattered shells, the sound lingered in the quiet of the night.

I was free. I sucked the evil right out of my house and smashed it to bits, finished off by a Good Samaritan's car. I still had no idea of who wanted to put a spell on me in the first place, but at that moment, I didn't care. No one could touch me. My path to Kevin was wide open.

It was time to get back to Marie's bag and start on the spell. Sitting Indian style on my kitchen floor, I opened the bag slowly, and anticipated a spirit or two to rise from its contents. My palms became drenched in sweat as my nerves began to rattle just a little. I could feel my full bladder was ready to relieve itself, but I was not going to move until I was finished with the task at hand.

"No, squeeze it back in. Just relax, Channa," I whispered to myself. "You can hold it. Bladder, you're gonna have to hold it for now."

I crossed my legs tight, as if they were barriers stopping the flow of fluids from my body.

"Now, let's see what Marie gave me."

I reached inside and pulled out two red candles. The first candle was fashioned into a male figure. Attached to the molded wax man was a note with Marie's instructions. The ends of the pages were frayed as if they were torn from a loose-leaf notebook. I took the note, and my urge to tinkle subsided as I began to read.

I would need something that belonged to Kevin, and some of his hair. It could be anything, but a piece of clothing was best. Then I needed to take something of mine, preferably something I liked to wear, and some of my hair. I needed to entwine Kevin's hair into mine and make something like a rope or string. I was to use it to wrap our items together saying, "the ties that bind, he will be mine," until I ran out of hair. Then I'd have to place it under his side of the bed.

It didn't seem too hard. *I'm just glad I don't have to dance around with a chicken or something.* Of course, the hardest part would be finding something Kevin left behind.

My mind began to race as I tried to remember if Kevin had ever left anything at my house. A shirt? A tie? A sock? I got up and began a frantic dash from room to room, hoping to find one of Kevin's possessions. I talked to myself the whole time.

I went upstairs to check my medicine cabinet. "Nope. It wouldn't be in here."

I closed the cabinet door and looked at myself in the mirror.

"Come on, think, Channa. Where could it be? Oh. Your closet."

I pointed at myself, but I was sure something had to be there. I headed to my closet.

"Come on. Gimme something."

I tossed the contents of the drawers from one side to another, but came up with nothing.

"Nada! That man never spends the night. There's nothing here that even smells like him."

I thought about the times I'd wake up alone, the scent of Kevin lingering in my sheets, the way I felt cheap, and how I'd race to throw the linens in the wash to cleanse away the experience. After ten years, I couldn't find anything to prove Kevin had been in my life. And then, "Oh, wait a minute. I know."

I went back downstairs, banging my hand on the railing as I made grand declarations, "I know something's gotta be there. I know it. That man hasn't been a ghost, materializing in and out at a whim."

I grabbed a coat from the closet in the entranceway and headed out to the garage. There, I took down old boxes once neatly stacked on a five-tier shelf. I'd been storing things I didn't need, but couldn't part with for some time, and brought them over to my new house from my old Jersey City apartment.

"I know something of yours is in there, Kevin. And I'm coming to get ya."

Forcefully, I moved from box to box throwing around old sweaters and jackets that no longer fit. I dumped my old curling and flat irons from a box that also had magazine clippings of hairstyles I'd instructed Ms. Claire, my old beautician, to recreate on my locks. *Ooh, Kevin loved me in that one.* I smiled at the sexy, Veronica Lake classic style a model wore. But still, nothing in that box belonged to Kev. I even looked in the dusty box of old school textbooks.

"Not in here."

I moved on to the box of old pots and pans that did not match my new kitchen décor.

"Nope."

I was frustrated and exhausted after my search effort proved fruitless. I'd searched every box on those shelves and found nothing of Kevin's.

"Ten years, Kev! Are you kidding me?"

Irritated beyond belief, I turned and saw a box on the floor of the opposite wall lying next to the garden tools. I rushed over to it, my last vestige of hope. I turned the box over searching for the label and spotted it on the side of the box. It read, "Bedroom Drawers." *Of course.*

"Bingo! Ha, ha, ha! Now, what do we have here, Mr. Walker?"

I discovered an attaché case with the initials, K.D.W. emblazoned in gold lettering in the top right corner. This was Kevin's old case. I remembered the night I gave him a new one like it happened yesterday.

Kevin had tried really hard to recruit Nelson Michaels, a starting sophomore at Syracuse. Nelson had gotten very arrogant with all of the attention he was getting and wanted Kevin to jump through hoops like all of the other recruiters. Kevin finally said, "Forget it, once you trip over that big head of yours, nobody is gonna want you. I was trying to give you a career and a home, but all you want are trinkets and yes-men."

Kevin confided his career worries; he felt that signing Nelson would be a pivotal point to his future.

"Oh, trust me baby, you can sweet talk a nun out of her panties. He'll sign with you."

I gave him a wink and a devilish grin. Kevin looked away, showing modesty and flattery. But then, he *looked at me*, I mean, in a way he never seemed to do before. His voice got really soft and he told me, "Thanks Channa. It helps having you in my corner."

My heart did a pole vault. Two weeks later, when Nelson Michaels, the Knicks' newbie, was splashed in the papers, I took Kevin out to celebrate and gave him a new, top-of-the-line briefcase. He left the old one in my car and never asked for it back.

All these years later, I still had it. Inside the case was a bottle of cologne, a pair of his socks, a toothbrush, and a hairbrush with some hair tangled in the bristles.

"Jackpot!"

I went back to the kitchen, holding the case like the treasure it was, almost missing the ringing telephone. I answered, breathing heavy from the strenuous activity, "Hello?"

"Hey gurl, it's Deja."

Shit, I should've checked the caller ID.

"Oh, hey Deja. What are you up to?"

"Gurl. Why you breathing so hard? Don't tell me I interrupted one of your nasty sex sessions."

"Deja please. Now you know I wouldn't answer the phone if I was doing my thang. I just had to carry some things in from the garage."

"In this weather? What could be that serious that your diva ass needs to freeze for it?"

"Blankets."

I went with her theme. Anything not to talk about what I was really doing in there.

"I needed to get some blankets so I can stay warm tonight."

"Gurl, please. You have two men to keep you warm at night. Anyway, I'm going to take a picture of my hair and e-mail it to you. You've got to see how good it looks. It'll help you make your mind up on what to do with yours."

Hair? More talk about those braids?

"I don't know about all of that, but I would like to see what the hell you've been raving about."

"Well, let me rant and rave about these wedding plans then. *Guurrrrllll*, my head is spinning. I see why people hire wedding planners."

"I told you I'd help out if you needed it."

"I know, and I don't mind imposing on my friends, but I pretty much have everything under control now. So, what's been going on with you?"

"Oh, not too much. Hey, Deja, can I ask you something?"

"Of course, shoot."

"What do you know about magic...you know...voodoo?"

Almost as quickly as I asked, I wanted to take the question back. When we were attending Columbia in pursuit of our MBAs, Deja and I would go to a Monday Bible study class at Abssynian Baptist Church in Harlem. It gave us the stimulation and confidence needed before we faced the grilling courses waiting for us on campus. Deja constantly shared childhood stories of being raised by her grandfather, the Baptist Minister, and her grandmother. Deja spent every other day in church growing up, and whenever a situation ever became too much for Deja to handle, she always turned to God to keep her grounded. So, asking her opinion about voodoo was dangerous. *Damn, I should've said something else about hair.*

"Hahahaha, I didn't know there was a difference between the two. You just hold on a second. I know how your ass thinks, and you don't ask a question like that unless you are contemplating doing whatever it is you want to know about. I'll be right back, I'm going to look something up, just give me a minute."

I waited in silence wondering what the hell Deja was up to. What did she mean by, "look something up?" She came back in about two minutes. I heard the static on the line crackle as she picked the phone up to talk to me.

"OK, here it is. I know you're Catholic and we went to Bible study together, but I think you forgot something along the way. I want to read Deuteronomy: Chapter 18, verses 10 through 12."

'There shall not be found among you anyone that maketh his son or his daughter to pass through the fire or that useth divination or an observer of times, or an enchanter, or a witch.

Or a charmer, or a consulter, or consultant with familiar spirits, or a wizard, or a necromancer.

For all that do these things are abominations unto the LORD: and because of these abominations the LORD thy God doth drive them out from before thee.'

"So, Channa, what's up? Really?"

I should've known Deja was going to go and get all religious on me. I didn't need anyone to preach to me.

"Well, you know I was thinking about maybe looking into it a little, just for a small love potion to give Kevin."

"Oh, Channa, God has done so much for you. Look at how blessed you are. You have your health, a nice home, security, and God gave all that to you. He will continue to bless you if you keep your faith and desires with the Lord, and you will be lead in the right direction. You mustn't let your faith be led by 'man.' You owe your life to God and you cannot ever forget what he has done for you."

Deja was serious and concerned.

"I know the strength God possesses, and how he has carried me through rough times, and I have been rewarded for believing in Him. But Deja, I'm only a human being who is weak, with flaws and imperfections. I just want to have a happy life while I'm on this earth. I'm fighting a losing battle with true love, and I want to win for a change."

Hearing Deja's reaction to my feeling, I could not inform her of my true intention. I just couldn't share with her about my thoughts and my actions with voodoo. *She would've had a heart attack, then grab a priest, and be on the first thing moving toward Jersey to stop me.*

"Deja, God has given me everything I've ever needed and asked for except for Kevin."

"Yes, God gave you the answer to all of your prayers. I know you know that, because you told me yourself after you recovered from being paralyzed from your breasts down. You said something though, and it has stuck with me. You said, 'God answers all prayers but sometimes He just says, no.' Remember gurl?"

"Yes, I know what I said, but I'm just so tired. I'm tired Deja."

Deja took a long pause, the words that broke the silence sounded forced. "Well, what are you tired about?"

"Nothing, I have to go. Someone is at the door."

I lied. I didn't want to hear anymore.

"Wait. I just want you to remember that I'm your friend and I love you. I told you, I'm here for you and I mean that. Please, don't do anything that goes against what God has willed. Remember your own words: 'God answers all prayers but sometimes He says no.' OK, gurl, I'll let you go. Love ya and call me later."

Chapter 8

One Month Later

I decided it was time to find out if Marie Laveau was the real thing or just another snake-oil salesman preying on misfortune and desperation. I had followed her instructions. I had to play my hand swiftly and intelligently so Kevin wouldn't have a clue what I was up to for the New Year. *He's going to be spending the night at my place. I won't be taking "No, I have an early meeting" for an answer.* I planned to be sweet, but also stubborn as a mule.

I glanced at the calendar on my wall next to the phone in my kitchen. It was 2004, a few days away from being history, and bowing out gracefully for 2005. I know none of my friends or family would have ever imagined that Miss Channa I-Have-My-Act-Together Renée Jones would settle for the undeclared love of a man who was dating many others. But I hadn't only settled for this love, I craved it. Tango was at my feet and cocked his head to the side, probably wondering why I was so frustrated with a calendar.

"If you only knew, baby," I said, reaching down to pet his fuzzy little head.

I'd been engaged before, so commitment was definitely something I was looking for. Andre was able to see that right away. Only a year and a few months passed before he was bent down on one knee. Andre bought a stunning one and a half carat canary diamond set in a platinum band, dotted with tiny, sparkling freckles as a symbol of his devotion. Kevin was twice the man that Andre was - couldn't he see I was ready? With Andre, I had the key to his apartment, his voicemail pass-code for his phones, and I knew that if I called, Andre would answer the phone right away. Kevin programmed his phone to vibrate and wouldn't even let me stay the night at his place, let alone give me the keys and codes to anything. I mean, Andre and I talked for hours, it was still a mystery to me that I hadn't found out about Erica. If the thought of Andre didn't infuriate me so much, I'd call him and ask him for his side of the story. I wanted the answers to the "why's" and "when's" about him that plagued my mind. However, I knew some things were better left alone, and didn't need to be probed any further. Besides, I really didn't want to speak to Andre ever again.

Maybe that was the problem. With Andre, I had trust and honesty, and it made me blind to a lie. Perhaps, this mystery and distrust of Kevin kept me safe from hurt. I didn't know. What I did know was that I was ready for the next level with Kevin. I'd been to hell and back and he stuck around the whole time. I'd grown up and counted my blessings, and Kevin had been one of them. I'd held his hand through some of his struggles and worries, and I knew he loved me for it.

So, maybe Kevin knew I wasn't ready THEN and maybe even Kevin wasn't ready THEN. But he was at the height of his career, and I had everything I needed. What was missing was a real relationship; the kind of relationship where you had someone to go home to. We were both ready to hold each other's hands and look to our future. Together. And if he needed a little nudge to get my point, then Marie Laveau had what it took to give him the push.

I made up my mind to call Kevin. I was going to ask him out for a date. He answered his phone on the first ring so I knew it was a good sign.

"Hello?"

"Well if it isn't Channa Renée Jones."

Kevin sounded happy to hear from me, another good

sign.

"Hi, Kev, whatcha doing?"

I was speaking in a low, soft tone to Kev so I would sound normal, but my body was shaking loud enough for him to hear through the phone.

"Nothing much, just sitting around, catching up on the game highlights I missed last night."

Good. At least he wasn't there with a woman, a really great sign.

"Well, I was wondering, when you aren't watching ESPN or whatever, if you wanted to go see *The Producers* on Broadway?"

"Uhh, wait a minute, is that the new Mel Brooks musical?"

"Yes it is Mr. Theater buff. I was going to pick up tickets and figured I'd ring you up and see if you were free to go."

"Oh, definitely. I heard that thing was hilarious. It's about two guys who try to run a scam by having this play that's supposed to be a flop over-financed, so that they could pocket the difference and head out of town when the show fails. Only the play turns out to be a hit."

"It should be good. It won a Tony Award for the best musical."

"Yeah, that sounds good; we can definitely check that out."

Ah, no resistance.

"And don't worry about paying for parking, I'll drive, Mr. Walker. As a matter of fact, the entire evening will be my treat. I'll even take you to dinner at *Jezebel's* over on 10th Avenue afterward."

"Well, hey now. What did I do to deserve all of this? You know what, don't even answer that, I'll just take it as it comes."

"OK, it's a date then. Make sure you dress appropriately for the evening."

"Oh, hahaha. You got jokes. You're too much Ms. Jones. You know you don't have to tell me about style. What date shall I mark my calendar for?"

"December 28th."

"Great. I'll mark my calendar for the 28th. And don't be late picking me up."

Oh, I wouldn't be one millisecond late.

"I won't, baby. See you soon."

I disconnected my call knowing I left Kevin with a smile on his face from my sassiness, and from the anticipation for our date. *But you won't know what hit you, Mr. Walker.* I giggled and looked at Tango, who had fallen asleep at my feet by that time. Without having anyone to share my excitement with, my mind wandered on to Carl, who also liked to hear good news. But this wasn't what he'd call good news. It was time for me to sit down and have a discussion with him. I didn't want to hurt him any longer, so it was time to set him free. Carl was a good, decent, honest, and hard-working man, but I wasn't in love with him. It wasn't fair to string him along the way I'd been doing for the past couple of years. I liked him very much, but his lack of style along with those corny phrases were traits I couldn't settle down with for a long period of time.

Life with Carl would be plain and uninteresting. I imagined it all; after long days of school and working as a paralegal, he'd come home wearing his suit from Sears, and bore me with one dry story after another about the cases he was working on. Then we'd curl up for an exciting night of *Law and Order* or *CSI*. He was just a creature of habit who never strayed from his normal routine. He would keep ordering the same "cup of Joe" from Starbucks everyday, and order the same food from the same restaurant on the day of the week he had scheduled for that particular meal.

"Plain and uninteresting."

I looked down and spoke to the top of Tango's head. He stirred around and opened an eye, but drifted off to sleep again.

"Tango. I know Carl is a good guy, but I have needs. Having sex with a man who sticks to routines is no better than dry humping a broom handle. I don't get how a man with *so much equipment* never learned how to use it! No, really, Tango, sure he's average in height, which would make you think his dick size was average too, but it's not. Carl is like a secret sale. You know. You go to the counter of your favorite store to purchase the expensive dress you just convinced yourself to buy, and then you find out at the register that it rings up for half price."

Tango didn't care, of course, but I remembered the first time I saw Carl naked. I knew he had a solid build and should be packing something in his pants that could make me holler. My eyes damn near jumped out of their sockets once they feasted on his huge overgrown sausage. But, Carl didn't know what to do with the length or girth he was blessed with. He thought he could just stick it in and wiggle it around and everything would be OK. Uh, no. He just didn't know how to screw. Lawd knows I tried to work with him, but it was a fruitless effort. I'd ride his dick, putting his hands on my hips so he could learn the rhythm. I was like a dance instructor teaching a hopeless man with two left feet. Ugh, and try to teach a guy like that how to dance to "Super Freak." It just wasn't happening!

"Nope Tango. Carl just can't be in my life. No way! This can't be it, Tango. There has to be more in store for me. I'm going after the exciting lifestyle I deserve to live. You hear me, Tango? I'm gonna get my Kevin. Get used to seeing him in the morning.

"Kevin will surely keep me on my toes for a lifetime. He's done it for almost ten years. And sure, his life is routine, but the faces and places consistently change. He's always scouting for new recruits and introducing me to new players. I'll probably meet that Tyshawn Morris guy he keeps raving about real soon."

I leaned back into my kitchen counter and daydreamed about Kevin and his scouting missions that carried him off to strange, exotic places around the world. The thought of what could happen made the prospect of an exciting redundant life with Kevin much more appealing than a boring redundant one with Carl.

"Kevin's repetitive lifestyle was known to bash every basketball game at Madison Square Garden in the sky box. He would watch the Knicks kick butt, and then jet-set around the world all on the Knick's dime."

I threw my head back and laughed thinking about the games, the endless amounts of shrimp, and the fun of sipping glasses of *Moet* with the team member's wives. Kevin would be on the floor watching his recruits go on to make their mark as fierce sports icons.

"It's gonna be perfect."

Tango looked up at me as if he was going to speak. My hands stretched out to both sides as if my arms were trying to embrace the wonderful future I was imagining. He wagged his tail.

"A-ha! You can see it too, huh?"

I scooped him up into my arms, went to the den, and plopped down into the comfy couch. I looked around at my black walls, and wondered if I needed them anymore, after Marie Laveau's cleansing. I knew I didn't feel like something was lurking out there to get me anymore. I gave Tango a big squeeze and put him beside me.

"And Tango, when we're not at The Garden, we'll be at a movie premiere. You know I love movie premieres and so does, Kevin! We are perfect for each other, right? With my MBA in marketing and Kev's penchant for advertising and making things move, we both enjoy tearing apart the human psyche by watching how others react to movie scenes. And we both love Asian food, Japanese sushi, Korean CYMK jigae, Chinese Chilean sea bass, Thai green curry chicken, and Vietnamese bun ba mau. Oh, I'm getting hungry just thinking about it all. Our taste buds alone could take us for trips across the globe.

"And there's no double guessing—sex with Kevin is earth shattering, back-breaking, toe-curling sinful pleasure. Mmm-hmmm! When I'm on I-95, I forget that the ride ends the same way each time...Kevin leaving before I wake up. But his big, fat, juicy helmet-head would still transport me to another world even after ten years. When he makes love to me with that hearty cucumber, and those robust, succulent, black plum balls tapping my soft ass, making my voice moan with each stroke. I want him all over again as if it's our first time. Mmmm-hmmmmm!"

I was getting hot and moist just thinking about it. Kevin just had that effect on me. I sighed, "And so, you can see, with me feeling this way about Kevin, it's completely unjust to keep Carl around. I'm going to talk to him soon, Tango, I promise."

The weight of breaking Carl's heart felt too heavy, so I changed the subject.

"Well, in the meantime, I have to make sure Marie's magic works."

I went back into Marie's bag to make sure I didn't miss anything. Inside the bag was a small note from Marie unveiling one further instruction:

"If u want to bring de bees to hunny u hav to becom sweet. Put a scoop of hunny deep in ur private hole. It wil draw de bee u seek."

"Ahhh. Marie Laveau's a freak," I exclaimed out loud, scaring Tango, who jumped off the couch and left the room.

"First, this woman pours beer over my head while I'm naked almost giving me pneumonia. Now she wants me to put honey in my honey hive? For what? So I can get a yeast infection?"

I was sort of discouraged about what I'd gotten myself into. But I'd come too far to stop, so being the nut I am, what was a little honey going to hurt?

"Hmph, Kevin and his freaky self will probably like it."

I flashed back to the time I was on my period - how he pulled out my tampon and went down on me. And then how he came on the side of my face and LICKED IT OFF! *Oh, see, I got me a freak. This honey won't faze him at all.*

I had a big date that was more important than any I'd ever had. I had to find something extra sexy and special to wear. I hadn't bought any designer clothes in quite sometime. I was going out with Kevin, and he did have style, so I couldn't show up looking frumpy. I sure as hell wasn't going to sport my brown suede sneakers I got on sale at *Payless*. I wasn't going to wear the boots from our last date that suffocated my toes either, and I for damn sure wasn't going to wear the white sandals from New Orleans. I had to go shopping, but it was for a good cause. I considered it to be my last shot to make Kevin mine. I needed to unleash every magical weapon Marie had given me, and find something to wear that was worthy of a femme fatale.

The moment had finally come, and I was sitting outside Kevin's building waiting for him to come down. Driving over the speed limit with excitement in my heart, I arrived a little early to see Kev in the city.

Kevin's doorman greeted me as I rolled down the driver's side window. "I'm here to pick up Mr. Walker."

I smiled. I'd been to Kevin's building plenty of times before and the doorman was familiar with me, as I was with him.

"Yes. I will ring Mr. Walker for you."

The doorman was Latin, his hair slicked back with my grandmother's pomade. That old-fashioned *DAX* grease was obviously still a big seller in some markets. He spoke with so much class, it was shameful he couldn't let go of that 1950's Ricky Ricardo look. Through the glass doors, I could see him pick up the phone, say something, and hang up. He returned to the car seconds later.

"Mr. Walker will be down shortly."

He bowed his head slightly and returned to the building.

I rolled my window up, and as I waited, I reminisced on how far Kevin and I had come. When he graduated from NYU Law School, he moved into a basement apartment in Queens. Talk about a bachelor bad. That place was always damp, and where there was dampness, there were water bugs or any bug for that matter. He didn't help his infestation problem by leaving filthy dishes lying around. I would stop by one week and the sink would be full of dishes. The next week, the same dishes would be in the sink. Plates of discarded food littered his humble abode, as mold from bread, uneaten eggs, or any other treat Kevin didn't throw away seemed to greet me at the door with a pungent, "Hello!" Kevin + neat freak = oxymoron. At that point, we hadn't had sex yet, and the smell of his apartment may have had something to do with that.

The only items in his apartment that had any order were the photographs of his family he had arranged so neatly. Most women would have been turned off, but not Channa! I knew the man was filthy and didn't care. I was more intrigued by the incessant drive Kevin possessed that seemed lacking in most men. It made me overlook what I saw to be a minute flaw born from the sleepless nights spent studying and busy days filled with classes and internships.

Kevin had only been working with the Knicks for a few months when we met.

"Once I get my finances under control, I'm going to move out of this hole and into an apartment in Manhattan. I'll be closer to Madison Square Garden and gettin' paaaaaiddd!" He had said to me.

Isn't life funny? Not only did he get an apartment in the city, but he bought an especially expensive piece of New York realty. Talk about moving on up. He moved right into the Parkview Towers.

The Towers sat directly next to Trump Plaza off of 5th Avenue and 67th Street. Now I watched as Kevin's *doorman* walked back into the brightly lit hallway, thinking that only in America could you go from living in a basement with water bugs, to owning a condo worth 2.8 million dollars. Ouch! I knew his maintenance fees had to be through the roof.

As I giggled to myself at the thoughts I had, I turned my head just in time to see Mr. Kevin Dean Walker take full, determined strides toward the passenger side of my car. Good Lord! That man looked good enough to eat. His frame was immaculately fitted with a long black wool trench coat. His hands were shielded from the cold in his fitted, sleek leather gloves that matched his coat. I felt my pussy tense up at the sight of this man and hoped the honey wouldn't drain into my panties. *I should've put on a panty liner.* I hoped I wouldn't leak and ruin my brand new outfit.

I had purchased a gray wool skirt with thick burnt orange trim cords. It came just below my knees and had splits on the right and left sides, which were mid-thigh high. It was figure hugging. It clung to my ample and round booty like white on rice. My gray silk blouse tucked in snugly to contour my tiny waist, and exceptionally flat tummy. I'd gotten some hooker boots that came knee high and had a two-inch heel with medium thickness. I felt like a million bucks. I had forgotten just how much I enjoyed dressing up. Since my injury I hadn't dressed-up the way I used to. I just hated the whole clothing process—you know, searching for the right store. Then trying on the clothes, and worrying about if I could find the right shoes to wear with the outfit. Shopping was a chore.

After the whole process of getting the "right" outfit, I felt like it didn't tell the viewer who I was and who I am now. But right now, I wasn't thinking about any of this, I was enjoying the moment and loving it to the tenth power.

With a push of a button, I unlocked the car doors as Kevin got closer. He opened passenger's door and slid in, planting kisses on my nose, right then left cheek and forehead. *Oooh, he makes my nipples hard when he does that.*

"Damn, Channa baby, you look good sitting right where

you are. I can't wait to hug you."

His eyes scanned my body in such a way that I could almost feel it.

"Thanks for the kisses, baby. I knew you'd like my outfit, but I bought it just for you."

I gave him a sexy little smirk, just enough to get his imagination going. I had to add some dramatic moves. I sped out of the parking space and let my head lay on my car's headrest. There was no traffic, so we'd be on 42nd and Broadway in about seven minutes or so.

"So, this is the new ride? Very nice, Ms. Jones, very nice. Yeah, talk about keeping up with the Joneses."

Kevin surveyed the soft leather interior of the car as he ran his hand over the wood grain dashboard.

"Ow, I'm scared of you."

"Hahaha. You are so witty, Kev. I guess that means you like it, huh?"

"Yeah, I love it. This is my first time in it since you bought it. Very nice choice."

"Well, thank you. I always make good decisions."

I wished what I just said was true. My whole purpose for this evening was to make Marie's magic work on Kevin. I could only hope I was doing the right thing to get my man.

"Yes, and going to see *The Producers* is definitely one of your better ones."

"So, what's going on in the wide world of sports?"

"Ah, the same. Well, actually, this is an exciting time for Tyshawn. He's been playing really well every night; scoring, getting those boards, and staying out of foul trouble."

"Well, that sounds good."

"Yeah, it's made him one of our more valuable starters in only a few months. He's consistent which is what we need. His play is also getting him a lot of recognition now. We've got clothing endorsements lined up, as well as fast food commercials."

"Wow. That's really great, Kev. He's on his way to becoming a superstar. So, when do I get to meet the incomparable

Mr. Morris?"

I glanced over to catch his reaction as I asked the question, before focusing back on the road. The last time I mentioned meeting Tyshawn Morris, Kevin grew very defensive and questioned my intentions. This time, his face did not frown up.

"Don't worry. You get to meet him soon."

Wow! That's a welcoming response.

We pulled up to the theater, and I got out of the car to hand my keys to the valet. Kevin was waiting for me on the other side with his slightly bent arm extended. This was completely new. Kevin gave me his arm as we waltzed into the playhouse holding each other closely as we waited on line. I didn't know which kicked in first, the cleansing or the spell, but something was causing Mr. Walker to act out of character. He was affectionate and seemed open tonight. I loved every last second of it.

Just as I was reveling in my moment, I heard a cell phone ring. I let go of Kevin to check my purse, then realized it wasn't my phone. Kevin reached in his pocket and pulled out his cell phone to answer it. *Well, it isn't on vibrate, but here we go. Probably a woman.*

"Hello?" Kevin said into his sleek, silver phone.

"Oh, hi Tonya, how are you?"

I knew it. Sure, have a conversation like I'm not even here.

"Yes, I know and I've been meaning to call you back, but I have been a little tied up. In fact, I'm on a date now so can I speak to you another time? OK, thanks."

Kevin flipped his phone shut and gave me a wink.

I stood there in disbelief as my mind raced to process all the new firsts that were taking place. This was the first night I have ever heard Kevin's phone ring, it was the first night he answered his in my presence. It was also the first night I'd seen him have a conversation with another woman, and tell her he was on a date with me. What the hell was going on? There had to be a reasonable explanation, like he just bought a new phone and doesn't know how to put on vibrate mode yet. Maybe he forgot he had the ringer on all together. Maybe hell was freezing over and the play's leading role would be played by a penguin. None of that would explain why he didn't just ignore the call like he'd done so many times before. No, he actually answered it. I needed to sit down, but I had to find out how real this was. I just knew I was on Fantasy Island, and a little man would be running out soon shouting, "The plane, boss, the plane!"

No man likes to be questioned about who he was on the phone with, especially not by a woman he doesn't consider to be his girl. So I tested him.

"Kev, who was that you were speaking to?"

"Just some woman who likes me."

"Oh, just some woman who likes you *and* calls you, huh?"

"Ha, ha. Don't tell me you're jealous, Channa. Look, if you must know, I haven't returned her last three messages and she wanted to know why."

"Oh, and why haven't you, Mr. Walker?"

Before he spoke, he came close, taking both of my hands; his sugar bear brown eyes deeply penetrating mine.

"Channa, I want a change in my life. I'm so tired of playing the field. I just want to relax and see what it feels like to be with one woman."

I think my heart stopped beating.

"What are you talking about, Kevin?"

This was all coming out of left field for me. I loved him, and I wanted to hear those words for so long, but they may be followed by him saying, "But I don't want to relax right now, maybe in about ten years." I wasn't going to say anything until he clarified exactly what he was trying to say.

"I know you're an attractive woman who could have any man that you want, but do you think you could have one man in your life? Do you think you would be able to stay committed to only him and learn to love again? I know when we met, you were going through a bad break up and it was hard for you to trust anyone, but we've made it this long. So why not give it a shot?"

Now the cat had my tongue. All of this time, the moment I had dreamt of for years had come, and I was speechless. My knight had come down off of his high horse and declared he wanted to be true. With my hands still in his, I used him to support my weight as I stood on my tiptoes and gave Kevin a scene-stealing movie kiss, equipped with tongue action, heavy smacking, and head rotation. The other people in line watched our public display of affection and I overheard one patron say, "Only in New York do you see this stuff."

Time stood still for a little while and allowed me to appreciate all that I had in life. I was able to add Kevin Dean Walker to that list, and I couldn't wait to get him out of those clothes and into bed. It didn't matter if we went to his place or mine because soon we would be calling both places, "ours."

The night ended in Montclair. We made love passionately. We both must have kept bottled up for ten years. Sex with Kevin was always good, but now that we knew how each other felt, sex took on a much deeper meaning. He held me closer and squeezed me tighter than he'd ever done before. We consummated our newfound relationship. He gazed deeply into my soul as I-95 penetrated all roadblocks and barriers. He dove head first into my pool of wetness, over and over until we became one. I had to keep composure as he licked my rum drop and whispered how it was sweet like honey. I didn't want to laugh as I thought of Marie's note. Once we both climaxed, we collapsed in a pool of sweat as our naked bodies embraced. I watched him fall asleep and knew he was out cold when he began snoring lightly.

I took in all of his dark chocolate beauty as he contrasted beautifully with my starched white sheets. His large sturdy hands had fallen to his sides and I ran my fingertips through the tiny, soft, dark curls of hair on his chest that snapped back into place when tugged at slightly. The seemingly elastic curls also draped themselves over Kevin's long, six foot six inch frame legs. My eyes followed his manly hairiness from his ankle right up to the sweet magic wand that made all of my worries disappear. His dick was resting peacefully on his right leg, begging for me to stroke it. I loved seeing it when it wasn't too hard, and not too soft, but right in between. I knew that the slightest touch of my hand or brush of my lips would cause a rock-hard formation, with a mountain leading me to the pinnacle of rapture.

I could have stared at Kevin all night, but I had to finish executing the plan. I carefully slid out of bed, trying not to make a sound. Tango was sleeping on the floor by my side of the bed and started yelping once he saw me getting up. *Shhh.* Startled, my face cringed as I quickly lifted Tango into my arms to quiet him down. I stood and froze, slowly turning back to see if Tango's outburst disturbed Kevin's peaceful rest. He was in the same position, undisturbed.

"You're lucky, Tango," I chastised him in a whisper.

I took the *juju bag* out of the nightstand, keeping my eyes on Kevin as I made my way over to his side of the bed. I knelt and gently pushed the packet under Kevin's side of the mattress. *Whew*, I let out a big sigh, *now everything was complete.* I'd done everything Marie told me to, exactly how she told me to do it. Living happily ever after with Kevin was now a certainty.

I eased my body back into the bed using the same smoothness with which I'd gotten out. I snuggled up next to my man, putting my head on his chest as my hand gripped his dick firmly. I stroked and gingerly held him in the palm of my hands. His manhood was my stress toy, one of those balls or cubes you get at work or at a business convention, that no matter how much you squeeze, it never loses its shape as it absorbs any stress you may be feeling. The weight and smooth feel of his manhood begged for me to hold on to it forever, and I would.

Chapter 7

A strong hand squeezing my left breast awakened me. There was a subtle humming behind my right ear, and hot air synchronized with the sound on my bare shoulder. It was morning and a man was in my bed. I looked down at the arm draped across my naked chest. I would know that arm anywhere. Kevin had spent the night. My heart skipped a beat and I momentarily lost my breath, causing what I could only describe as an out-of-body experience. A ray of sunshine beamed through the window, basking my bed with glowing morning light. We were illuminated like a Da Vinci masterpiece, deified. The birds chirping outside sounded like the Hallelujah Choir. Tweets and coos scored to Mendelssohn. I saw colors, all colors, as if for the first time. The same trinkets and bric-a-brac that had been in my bedroom became the rainbow. And the room smelled like roses, sweet from morning dew.

I wasn't dreaming. Everything from the night before really happened, but still, I moved through the morning in a dreamlike state as my astonishment in Kevin's 180-degree turn took on a new meaning. Not only did I NOT have to coax him into spending the night, but Kevin also took me to breakfast, as I had fantasized about for so long. We ate at a diner on Route 3, a local highway full of shopping plazas and restaurants, which was about fifteen minutes from my house.

During our meal with bacon and eggs, I sat stunned, listening to Kevin's discussion on how a one-on-one relationship should be.

"Channa, I'm dead serious. I know you have your little boyfriends but it's time to clean house and cut them off."

Aw, Kev. Don't bring up Carl while I'm still feeling the aftereffect of riding I-95.

"Well, if we are one-on-one, of course I would."

"Good, because I'm doing the same thing with my friends. Are you sure you're ready for this? Are you ready for all of me?"

I just didn't get it. Why was I always being questioned if I was sure about Kevin? Marie did it over and over, and now Kevin was asking me too. *If I wasn't, I wouldn't have gone through such lengths to make it happen.*

"Kevin, I think I know what I'm getting. I'm ready for all of it."

"OK, I just want to be sure."

We finished eating, and I took him back over the bridge, dropping him off in front of his condo. As I drove back home, I thought about our conversation at the diner. What did he mean by, *all of him*? Didn't I know all I needed to know to be committed to him? Maybe he was nervous about being with one woman after a life of bed hopping, and wasn't sure if he would be a good boyfriend. I had to call Deja and see what she thought about all of the new developments.

I pulled into my driveway, and once I became settled in the house, I picked up the phone to dial Deja.

"Hey Deja."

"Hey! Wow, you sound all bright and cheery. What did Santa put in *your* stocking?"

"Deja, you will never believe where I just came from."

"Ooh. Where?"

"Dropping Kevin off at home...after he spent the night here."

"Whaaaat?! You finally got that man to sleep over?"

"Yup."

"Well, isn't that sweet? Now, get to the juicy stuff. What

did you do to make that man stay all night? I know it can't be the sex. He's been hittin' that for years."

"You know you can't get a man with just sex, Deja."

"Hold up. You can get an *ugly* man with just sex. He'd be so happy somebody would ride his ugly ass, he'd give you anything you want and follow you around all day like a stray dog. But that's another story. Now tell me about Kevin."

"Well, last night we went to see *The Producers* on Broadway, and while we were in line waiting for our seats, Kevin told me he wanted to commit."

"What? Just like that? Damn!"

"Yup, just like that. Even at breakfast this morning…"

"Breakfast?!"

"Yes, breakfast, gurl. We went to breakfast and he told me I needed to cut off my other men, and he would cut off his friends for me."

"Well, well, well…Kevin finally got off the pot. I never thought I'd live to see the day. I guess Santa gave you everything you asked for."

"Anything and everything I could've wanted was given to me."

"Good, that's real good. And hey, I didn't get a chance to wish you a Merry Christmas. I told myself I would call, but I had to juggle time between my family and the in-laws to be. What did you do for Christmas?"

"Well, we had dinner here, and my mother and grandmother still took over instead of sitting back and letting me play hostess. Ugh, and gurl, you know Kyle and his triflin' ass didn't show up. He had the nerve to send my mother the DVD collection of his TV show's first season along with a brand new DVD player. You know, all my mother did was brag about it all day. I swear, he gets away with murder, and she never says anything."

"That sounds familiar."

"What does?"

"Oh, nothing. Just that you've been letting Kevin get

away with murder and you forgive him every time."

Did I?

"Hey, how'd we make this about me? There's a big difference here. Kyle is my mother's son, he's the baby and always will be, so she coochie-coos over him. He just walks all over her. Kevin has a really big dick and knows how to use it, and you'd be coochie-cooing over it too."

We burst out laughing.

Of course, Deja always brings it back to serious stuff saying, "So, where was Carl this Christmas?"

"Houston. Gosh, why'd you bring him up? I guess I'm glad you did, I have to deal with the sticky business of telling Carl it's over. Got any ideas?"

"Channa! Why would you want to do that? Because Kevin told you to?"

"No, Deja. I do have a mind of my own. You've always known how I felt, or didn't feel about Carl. I never really wanted Carl as my man, and now that Kevin is mine, I'm not going to let anyone rain on my parade."

"I know, but he's a good and fair man. You know he'll be there for you so maybe you should give yourself some time to really think this through."

"Give myself some time? Deja, I'm not wasting any more time. I know what I want. Now it's available and I'm taking it."

"OK, Channa. OK."

Deja fell silent on her end. I knew she had something on her chest to talk about, and needed to get her thoughts together to vocalize it.

A few seconds later, she sighed and said, "I want you to be honest with me. You know, I know you, and we go way back. The other day when you were asking about magic, were you really just asking, or were you trying to tell me that you'd already done some voodoo trick to get Kevin? This all seems very sudden."

"What? Not at all, Deja."

I hated to lie to her, but it was evident from the last conversation that this was something she couldn't understand.

"I had just come back from New Orleans, and I admit the city made me a little curious, but out of sight, out of mind. I haven't thought about that stuff since."

I hoped she would buy what I was selling, but I knew I could change the subject and take her mind off it all.

"So, you spent time with the in-laws-to-be, huh? How are those wedding plans coming?"

"Oh, they're coming. I'm just about done with all of the planning. I'm just ready for the day to get here."

Deja sighed again, but this was all from wedding worries.

"I can't wait to see you in your dress. Anyway, I'd better get moving. I'm supposed to put in some time today at the Gay Men's Health Crisis over in New York."

Thank you, Lucky Stars. I'm so glad I have someplace to be; otherwise Deja would keep me on the phone all day.

"OK, gurl, I'll be talking to you."

After ending the conversation with Deja, I made a mental note to give Arnelle a call once I got back from volunteering my time at GMHC. She'd left a few messages, but I'd been so preoccupied with my little "dating game" that I'd completely forgotten to get back to her.

I hopped in my car and started back over the bridge into the city. After parking in the nearby garage, I stopped at the hotdog stand before heading inside the center. I hadn't had a bite to eat since breakfast and my tummy was growling. I figured a good old-fashioned, fat-riddled chili cheese dog would hold me over. I polished my dog off, and was greeted by a familiar voice as I walked through the center's long, glass doors.

"Oooh, Miss Chaaaaannnnaaa. How you doooooin'?"

Tyrone was passing by the doors and stopped dead in his tracks once he saw me.

"I'm doing very well, Tyrone. How about you?"

"Well, I can see you are. You glowing like my hot pink dildo on a dark, naughty night."

"Tyrone. Hahaha, you're too much."

"Puh-leeze, Miss Chaaanaa, if you don't have you a good toy, you'd better get one. OK?"

Tyrone floated a couple of snaps in the air before placing his hand firmly on his hip.

"I don't need to get a toy, thank you. I have too much of the real thing."

"Huh! You think I don't?" Tyrone gasped like I'd given him a good *Dynasty* slap, "I'm just insatiable, and when left alone, what else is a girl to do?"

"Well, maybe you should tell your men to stop leaving *you* all alone."

I mirrored Tyrone with my hands on my hips. We probably looked like we were about to have a diva showdown.

"Gurl, please. In my heyday, I had to kick them out, and make them go back to their homes, and even some to their wives. They never wanted to leave all of this."

Tyrone turned around and dropped it like it was hot. *Uh-uh, no he didn't!* He straightened up and turned back to face me. He put his hands back on his hips and sucked his teeth, "Tch. It's such a shame, but the good ones are always taken."

"Tyrone! You were sleeping with married men?"

"Shoo, haven't we all at some point? Haahaa, listen, Miss Thang, those married men weren't getting what they needed at home. So, yes, they came to see Tyrone. I was very well taken care of. They had to make sure I kept their nasty secrets. Yes, child, I got clothes, cars, trips, anything I wanted. Okaaaayyyy?"

"Get out of here! Where did you find these men? I mean, there must be some club or something you can meet them at."

For some reason, I was extremely interested in what Tyrone was saying. There had been a lot of talk going around lately about so-called "brothers on the down-low." The local news station in Jersey had a week-long segment in which they followed a young black man around as he entered the seedy underworld of African-American homosexuals. They attached a hidden camera to the young man, whose face was blocked out by a blurry spot that moved as he did. You could see and hear him be one person when he hung around with his straight friends during the day, and when he went home to his girlfriend and baby. Then, when he went out to "chill with his boys," as he put it, he engaged in homosexual acts. He kept his desires for other men hidden from everyone. Ever since I had seen that story, it made me want to know more about these men. I studied people for reactions as a hobby, and needed to find out what facial responses or body language would give a down-low brother away. Who better to answer my question than a man who had sex with them?

"Child, please! Clubs? No, I didn't go to clubs like that. I always met my men when I was out shopping, or in the supermarket. Just the same way you meet your men, honey-gurrll."

"And they would just approach you? Just like that? In the open?"

"No, they wouldn't always be so obvious. They might slip me a note just like they might slip you one."

I couldn't believe what I was hearing. These men were deceitful, and Tyrone was helping them to keep this horrible secret that could ruin the lives of so many.

"Well, I certainly know none of my men would have ever—"

"Uh, uh, uh, Miss Channa," Tyrone cut me off, waving a manicured finger in my face. "I know what you're gonna say and you wrong. The woman never knows. Please, gurl, if I would've shown up at any of those prissy women's houses telling them I was their husband's lover, they wouldn't have believed me. Please, look at me. I'm a queen!"

Tyrone flung his hands out like Kiki Shepard from *Showtime at the Apollo*. And he wasn't lying; today he had on a pair of women's boot-cut jeans that hugged his little booty, and a bright yellow tube top. *Hello, Tyrone. It's December. Get yourself a turtleneck.*

"I dress the part, but those women are only afraid of their hubbies trading them in for a younger model. They'd never wrap their heads around the fact that the other woman has a penis, OK? OK!"

"Well, I think there are signs the wives may be missing."

"Maybe...anyway, what is this glow about? You came in here just smiling and swinging the door open wide...you know, you almost hit me, that's why I had to stop and look at you."

"I'm sorry. I didn't see you when I came in. I'm still high from last night."

"Well, I know you didn't smoke a joint, so it must be love that's got your head in the clouds. Did you meet someone new?"

"No, actually, it's an old flame. This guy I've been seeing for ten years told me last night that he finally wants an exclusive, one-on-one relationship."

"Oh, that's all? Shit, I thought you were gonna say that after ten years, he asked you to marry him. I was about to ask to see the bling, honey."

"Tyrone, I've been waiting a long time for this. Ten years I've been trying to get this man to commit, and he finally did. It took me this long to get him to want to be exclusive. I'm not going to scare him off with marriage talk."

"Oooooh! Oooooh! Miss Chaaannnnaa, oooh!"

Tyrone stood there with his elbows bent as if his arms were chicken wings, while his loose wrists allowed his hands to droop downward. He began jumping up and down, flailing his arms as he turned in a full circle about three times.

I couldn't understand what he was so excited about.

"What? What is it Tyrone?"

Tyrone stopped twirling and stood facing me with his head cocked to one side as he gave me the sad puppy dog look. His right forefinger was pressed against his lips as if he was stopping himself from speaking. Then he dramatically flung his finger away from his face and tossed his hand to the side, letting out a heavy sigh.

"I shouldn't tell you, but since you help me so much…this man you have sounds like a true 21st century down-low brothaaa."

"Uh-uh, don't go there, Tyrone. You don't know what you're talking about. You don't even know him."

It seemed like gay men were always trying to tell the world that straight men were gay. A celebrity's on the cover of a tabloid…GAY! A new love song comes on the radio by some sexy, young crooner….GAY! I say I have a man…. GAY!

"No, but I know the signs. Let me guess, he never spent the night, right?"

Tyrone really hit a nerve on that one, but I wasn't going to let him know it. Kevin Dean Walker was 100% man, and he loved pussy. There was no way I was going to feed into Tyrone's bullshit.

"Of course he did," I lied to save face, "Have you been taking your meds?"

"Yeah, yeah, I took one an hour ago. Listen, I have a young friend who is a bit confused about coming out. I'm not sleeping with him, but I talk to him from time to time, you know, just listen to his problems. Well, hon-ey, this man is in some shit. He's been seeing this woman for about five years now, and she's starting to drop hints about marriage. He's told me he tries to change the subject, but then she thinks it's because he's a gigolo or something and don't wanna settle down. The truth is he likes men and doesn't want to commit himself to a woman when he knows he won't be faithful. Why should he be selfish and marry her knowing his heart isn't really in it? You know what I mean?"

I could feel the chili cheese dog I had earlier turn in my stomach as Tyrone's words caused my gut to tighten into a knot. I thought about Kevin and the excuses he always gave for not staying over, but hell, he couldn't be gay. He was seeing half a dozen other women.

"Oh, is that what you tell him? It's OK then for him to keep stringing her along for five years?"

"Oh no, honey, that's not good either. He's torturing that poor girl. He never stays over her house because he feels guilty about sleeping next to her knowing he's living a lie. He doesn't want to make her a part of that lie, so he sneaks off with his 'boys' and has his fun. I told him he should tell her and let her make the decision. Some women go for it as long as it's not another woman. Staying on the down-low ain't the answer."

"I don't get it though, why when it's a black man who enjoys both sexes, he's said to be on the down-low. When it's a white guy, he's just cheating on his woman or is bisexual."

"Child, why is the sky blue? Why is the grass green? Why does my ass look so good in these jeans that it makes yours look like two volleyballs in a bag, just losing air? I don't know, Miss Channa! Maybe it's because as black people, we always have to put our own spin on things and be coined the way we want to be. Maybe white folks weren't clever enough to come up with their own hip way of saying it. You're focusing on the wrong things. Who knows? The point is you have to be careful and you can't trust anybody."

"I hear you, Tyrone. I just think you're off when it comes to my Kevin."

"I hope so. Shit, if he has you glowing like this I want to be wrong. And you right, I don't know him, so it's very possible that my signals are off. But just from what you've said about him not committing for ten years made a bell go off in my head. I've heard that story so many times before, and I'm just trying to look out for Miss Chaaaaannnnaaa like she looks out for meeeee."

He fluttered his lengthy eyelashes at me and pouted to say, "I'm sorry."

I couldn't stay upset with Tyrone. I knew his intentions weren't malicious. I thanked him and gave him a hug just to let him know I wasn't upset about anything he'd said. I then went to fulfill the duties I originally showed up to complete. My work at the center required me to help HIV-positive males find support groups and testing sites in their area. A few of the tests were for new trial drugs, and the connections I made while working at Morgan Pharmaceuticals ensured that I would be able to get many of those who needed the medication into these testing sites. Being in charge of marketing drugs to the HIV community while at Morgan, I'd become familiar with many of the different testing facilities and had known the right names to drop to get my men the finest help possible. I knew my assistance was appreciated by the warm "Hellos" I received when I walked in. Even Tyrone, in his own twisted way, thought he was looking out for me by telling me Kevin was on the down-low. I knew the men cared a great deal for me, and in turn I gave them all the medical assistance I was capable of providing.

I left GMHC and walked up the block to Starbucks. I needed to sit and clear my head over a cup of coffee. Tyrone really had my mind working overtime, comparing the information he'd shared with me with what I knew of both Carl and Kevin. I ordered my coffee, and took a seat near the window as I stared into the busy street, wondering if Tyrone could be right. Nah. I thought back to Kevin's manly body stretched across my bed and the pleasure he took in making love to me. The statement Tyrone made about Kevin never spending the night was purely coincidental. Lots of men hated to spend the night after sex was over, so that didn't make Kev gay.

Oh, my good Carl, he was so sweet and kind. Sex was dry and mediocre, but that didn't mean he was gay. First of all, he had absolutely no fashion sense. I wasn't saying that

Tyrone's sequined tube tops and spandex pants were high fashion, but he had a fashion style. This was not my Carl. Carl was just a regular guy, with a regular job, and regular sexual habits. Thinking of Carl reminded me that I needed to call him and it was time to tell him how I felt. I needed to get it over with so I could have my fresh start with Kevin.

Back on the road and not far from home, I decided I couldn't wait any longer and needed to call Carl now.

"Hey, Channa. Where are you?"

Carl sounded sweet and concerned, like he'd been waiting the whole day just to talk to me.

I kept an even tone. "I'm on the road, just getting back from GMHC."

"Oh, how are the guys doing?"

Good old Carl, even interested in my work.

"Oh, they're fine. Listen, I called because...well, we really need to talk."

There was a silence.

"Are you there? Did you hear me?"

I started to think I'd lost the connection.

"Yeah...I'm here." Carl's voice was sullen. "It's just that I know what it means when your girlfriend says, 'we need to talk.' It's never a good thing."

"Carl, can you just come over after work?"

"Sure, but you can say whatever is on your mind, right now."

It was defeat. Carl sounded defeated. It was so out of character for him. He was always so positive and chipper.

"No, we need to talk in person, Carl."

I couldn't break someone's heart over the phone, or through some impersonal e-mail or text message. I needed to be a woman and face him as I gave him the news that I could no longer be with him.

"Fine, I'll see you soon."

Carl hung up abruptly.

It took me about fifteen minutes to get home from the time

I hung up with Carl. I entered my house and performed my ritual of kissing my hand to the Bible. I said a small prayer for strength to be able to tell Carl how I really felt about him and understanding for Carl to accept my feelings.

I sat in my living room listening to the tick-tock of the wall-mounted clock when the doorbell sliced through the quiet.

"OK, here we go," I said to myself as I slowly rose and ran my sweaty palms over my pant legs. "I need to tell Carl the truth."

It wasn't going to be easy for me, but I wanted Kevin. I would gain no pleasure from hurting the man who had cared for me unconditionally for the past few years.

I reached the door and turned the knob with my greasy palm to open it. Carl stood with a solemn look on his face. He wasn't wearing the usual broad grin that welcomed me when I'd open my front door. I stepped aside to allow Carl to pass.

He stood as I sat on the couch.

"Please, have a seat, Carl."

I tapped the sofa cushion next to me. Carl chose the recliner opposite the couch instead.

"You know that I care very much for you—"

"Can you just get this over with?" Carl interrupted.

He wouldn't recline in the chair; instead, he leaned forward with his forearms resting on his knees. He wouldn't make eye contact. He only looked at his hands or his shoes.

"Wait, listen to me, Carl. There's a lot I need to say to you."

"Why? Channa, why?"

At that point, Carl looked at me. His eyes were filled with hurt and anger.

"Here I am walking around thinking everything is great.... like a damn fool. Then you call me and say we need to talk?

I know what's going on. You made me drive out of *my* way so you can give me some Dear John speech. You don't want to see me anymore."

"It's not just that—"

"Oh no? Then what is it? You want to talk about the weather? Uh...what about the stock market? Maybe make some dinner plans? Hey, pass the salt Carl, and I don't want to see you anymore."

"Carl..."

"No, Channa!" Carl raised his voice with me for the first time. "What did I do to deserve this? Huh? What?!"

Carl's eyes were wide. His fists were clenched.

I'd never seen Carl like that before, and it threw me off. I took a second to regroup my thoughts and tried to start all over again.

"Carl," I said calmly. It was me looking at my hands then. "It's just that I need to be honest with you. There's this man I'd been seeing off and on for ten years. He came into town last night and said he finally wants to be exclusive, just me and him."

Carl gave a little groan. I looked into his eyes. I had to make him understand.

"I can't lie to you. I love him. I've been with him for a long time. Long before I met you, and I've been waiting for him to say everything he said last night."

"So, somebody shows up out of thin air and claims to love you and it's suddenly *bye-bye Carl*? Just like that Channa? I've been here! Is he going to love you like I do?"

Carl's eyes were glassy. I was smashing his heart into little pieces, and it was killing me.

"This is difficult for me. Please don't make it any harder. This has been on my mind for a very long time. I wanted to tell you about him, but I wasn't sure where our relationship was going, or how you would react. I love you, Carl, and you will always be special to me."

Carl sucked his teeth and leaned back into the recliner.

He looked at the ceiling like he was trying to make sense of it all.

"You've been here loving me, taking care of me, putting up with me, and that is not something I can forget. I just feel I owe it to myself to see if I can make it work with him after ten years."

Carl didn't say a word for at least two excruciating minutes.

"Carl, please say something, anything."

Finally, he sighed and leaned forward again. He closed his eyes and raised his prayer-clasped hands to the spot between his eyes.

"It's Kevin, isn't it? You called out his name that night and lied to my face about why. He's the one. So, you really love this guy?"

"Yes, I do. I always have since he and I first met. But..."

"OK then."

"OK then what?"

Carl dropped his hands to his knees again and looked at me. He looked exhausted.

"I love you. I love you enough that I know I have to let you go right now. Like they say, if you love something, let it go, if it loves you it will come back to stay."

It was just like Carl to come up with some corny quote for the moment, but this time I didn't mind. He had calmed down, and if his clichés kept him calm, then he could keep quoting them.

"Carl, I want you to know that if you ever need anything, anything at all, please let me know."

"I'll be OK, Channa, just take care of yourself. Any guy that can wait ten years to commit to you has to be an asshole. Be careful."

Carl pushed himself up out of the chair. He bit his lower lip, closed his eyes then said, "Damn it! Just when I think everything is good between us, you do this. I know, I may not have much right now, but I wanted to take care of you. I really did."

His words sent tears to my eyes. I felt his pain and knew it was true because I felt the same way about Kevin.

"I'm sorry, Carl. I'm really sorry. I just didn't know what else to do. I didn't want to hurt you, but I couldn't lead you on either."

"Ahh, I guess it was too good to be true."

Carl began to head to the front door as I sat on the couch letting the tears fall into my lap. I couldn't even get up to face Carl as he left. I knew I'd broken his heart, and he did nothing to deserve it. The sound of the front door slamming shut jolted me from the sofa. Carl seemed calm considering what I'd just said to him, but that violent closing of my door told me that he wasn't at all pleased. My hard-working paralegal had given me his last corny cliché as I sent him back into the world with every reason to become a man who hated and mistrusted women.

Chapter 6

After Carl left my house, I went to bed and cried myself to sleep. I mourned the ending of a chapter in my life, even though I had other pages to look forward to. Some time later, my phone rang, and I rolled my head over the tear-soaked pillow to face the phone on my nightstand.

"Hello?" I said hoarsely.

"Hey baby, you 'sleep?"

It was Kevin, already calling me like I was a permanent fixture in his life.

"Yeah."

"This early? Damn, I must-a worn that out last night," Kevin laughed into the phone.

"No. Well yeah, but that's not why I'm sleeping. I broke it off with Carl and it didn't go well. I just needed to get my head together," I sighed.

I thought about all that had just happened.

"Look. It's you and me now. It had to be done. I'm sorry it was rough for you, but I'll be over to make it better."

What's this? Kevin is coming over? This soon?

"Oh, OK, baby. Can you bring me something to eat?"

I didn't feel too much like eating, but I knew I'd gone too long without food. Besides, bringing food sounded like the perfect boyfriend task, and he was starting to fit the bill.

"Sure, no problem. What are you in the mood for?"

What? Hold up. Kevin Dean Walker was asking me... me...what I wanted to eat?

"I don't know. I just need some food in my stomach. Whatever you want is fine with me."

I sat up in the bed, feeling a bit giddy.

"OK, I'll be over with some dinner. You'll be my dessert. Wear that red number, you know, the one with the matching thong."

And just like that, the smile was restored to my face.

"Mr. Walker. Are you trying to seduce me?" I said and giggled.

"Oh, you know it. Ha-haaa! And, Channa, I love you, baby."

WHAT?!

"And I love you too."

We disconnected our call and I held the cordless to my chest for a while. Kevin just laid a whopper on me. He never told me he loved me, at least, not like that. It was always in some joking way. Like, I'd be mad that we'd have sex in his office and go our separate ways and he'd say, "Come on, you know I love you." That stuff didn't count.

Once the initial shellshock was over, I got out of bed, and jumped in the shower. I got all fresh and clean and put on the sexy red lingerie Kevin requested. I checked my hair, put on a little make-up, and made the bed. You would have thought Kevin said he was around the corner with the way I raced around. All I knew was he said he loved me, so I wanted to make the night perfect. I was all his and he was all mine.

I went downstairs to the dining room. I dimmed the lights and set the table for two, complete with candlelight.

"Music, we need some music."

I glided through the house like a Hollywood Hottie from the 40's, with the long robe that matched my chemise flowing behind me in the breeze I caused. I made my way to the stereo in the den and skimmed through my CD collection. I wanted to set the mood. It had to be mellow and sexy, soulful and fresh.

"Neo Soul!"

I picked out five of my favorite artists and put the CDs into my disc changer and set it to shuffle.

"Perfect."

A short time afterwards, the doorbell rang. I flowed to the door and opened it. Kevin stood there with a big brown paper bag, a bottle of wine, and a bouquet of red roses.

"Mmmm-mmmm! If it isn't Channa Renée Jones! Damn, you look good."

"Mr. Walker."

I stepped back from the door and curtsied, making way for him to enter.

Kevin walked in and handed me the roses saying, "These are for you. You love red roses."

Kevin smirked at me devilishly. He was undressing me with his eyes, but with the sheer lingerie I had on, it wasn't necessary.

"I do love red roses. Thank you."

I puckered my lips and he leaned down to kiss me. I only meant to give him a grateful peck, but Kevin slid his arm under my robe and around my waist. His hand, still clutching the bottle, rested on my ass, and the weight of it pulled me in close. Kevin's knee separated mine, and his thigh pressed into my groin. All the while, our tongues were swirling around in our mouths with lust-filled fervor. The heat from the food in the brown bag seeped in through my side, and the coldness of the bottle sunk into the flesh on the back of my thigh.

Kevin managed to pull away at first. I still felt him harden against my belly before he moved back.

"Whew, if you don't stop kissing me like that, you won't get your food. I'm fighting the urge to just throw you up against the wall and take you right here."

I was fighting the urge too. He hadn't seen the table with the candles. And with his tongue in my mouth and I-95 pressed up against me, even I lost the ability to hear the romantic music on the stereo.

"Yeah, you're probably right, Kev. But I'm sure there isn't

anything in that bag to satisfy what I'm hungry for."

Kevin couldn't keep his eyes off of me as I ate. As much as I enjoyed the attention, I also felt a little uneasy. He'd never been so attentive, even though he was the type of guy who never missed a thing.

"So, how was your day?"

"My day was great. I woke up next to a beautiful woman and took her to breakfast, and then I got a tip that this kid we're watching was home for winter break and had been playing hoops at the rec center where he grew up. So I went out there and played some ball."

"Is he good?"

"Hell yeah. He's got some game. The funny thing is, he's a good kid. He goes to the rec center for the kids. And he's good with them. I really don't want to take him out of college before he graduates. I can't explain it, but he's already a role model. If he drops out, what's that going to say to those kids?"

"Well, listen to Mr. Walker. You love the kids."

"Yeah," Kevin moved his food around with his chopsticks, "But, if I don't sign him, somebody else will. This kid can play some serious defense. The Knicks could use him."

"Oh. I see. Who knew there'd be such moral dilemmas in b-ball?"

"Baby. You have no idea."

I'd like to say that I most remembered the mind-blowing, toe-curling sex we had. The sexual-Olympics were *very* memorable. I'd medaled in the 69 Meter Suck, maintaining my composure as Kevin licked every crevice of my honey hive like the hungry bear he was. I gained the lead, using my tongue to trace the dark vein that ran from the chocolate mushroom head, down to the base of his shaft, and followed in between the smoothness of his balls. He had been the first to get a score on the board for the High Hump, taking me up against my closed bedroom door, unable to wait another second. His hands placed firmly behind my thighs lifted me up to meet the huge lump in his pants effortlessly. I reached down for his zipper, freeing I-95 from the gridlock, but it quickly entered my slippery tunnel. Kevin exhaled relief. My expert performance was in The Hurdles. My legs spread above him, sliding, gliding, riding on his throbbing pole, yet he was the one left sweaty and breathless. But he really brought home the gold on The Vault, bracing my hips from behind and rushing inside me at full speed. All of it was enough to fill my mind, and my hive, but it was not what I remembered most. It was all that had happened *after the act,* which stood out, so new, and so fresh.

Kevin was falling asleep on top of me.

"Oh baby, you've got the GP, I'm here to tell ya."

He rolled off of me and onto his back. He was winded, and he stared at the ceiling like he was recovering from the most exhilarating time he'd ever had.

I rolled over to my side as I watched him. I was proud to have satisfied him, and admired my work. I traced my fingers along the ripples of his abs and couldn't stop myself from saying, "Kev, I love you."

Kevin stretched his arm out over my pillow. "C'mere."

I put my head on his chest and listened to his heart racing.

"Channa, I love you. Come on, let's get some sleep."

Seconds later, Kevin was knocked out. I was nestled in his arms, in my bed, and he was sleeping. The outcome of the night before was a surprise, but now, I knew he would be by my side in the morning. There was no question in my mind. I slept soundly after that, safe in my man's arms. Finally.

In the morning, Kevin was still there. I gave him a quick kiss on his lips and sat up in the bed. Internally, I had so much excitement bottled up that I just wanted to get up and start dancing like I won the lottery. I had it all. But how was that going to look to my man if he woke up and saw me dancing naked with no music? So, I did the next best thing, I made a celebratory breakfast.

By the time Kevin wiped the sleep out of his eyes, I had showered, gotten dressed, and prepared a feast fit for a king. He stumbled down the stairs and into the kitchen, groggy but smiling.

"What smells so good?"

"Oh, I'm just making some breakfast," I said, nonchalantly. "I woke up with a big appetite."

I gave him an exaggerated wink and burst into laughter.

"Mmm-hmm. I'm feeling pretty hungry too. I think you drained all my fluids last night. Oh boy, you put something on me."

Kevin slid into a kitchen chair. He looked worn out.

Of course, all I heard was the "*you put something on me*" part and almost dropped the pitcher of orange juice. I thought he was talking about the spell.

"Huh? What? I…I put something on you? What?"

So much for keeping my cool. I guess I just should've danced naked after all.

Kevin leaned back into the chair—he only had on his boxer briefs, and he ran his hand over his abs, "Whew yeah. You worked it last night, baby. What are you cooking?"

Oh, he's talking about the sex. Of course, there's no way he'd know about Marie Laveau's voodoo.

"Not much. Some veggie omelettes, sausages, biscuits, French toast, and orange juice. If it isn't enough, I have some fruit too."

Kevin smiled and looked me up and down as I poured some orange juice into his glass and placed it in front of him.

"Look at you, Channa Renée Jones. You can work it in the bedroom AND in the kitchen. And you look good doing it. I'm a lucky man."

"Yes, you sure are," I said.

He pulled me down to sit on his lap and started playing with the buttons on my blouse.

"Uh-uh, breakfast will burn, and with you looking so good in your underwear, I think you're going to need your strength."

I kissed him on his forehead and got up to set the food on the table.

"What's on your agenda today, baby?"

It felt like we'd been like that for years. It was so natural, so right, so perfect.

"I don't really have to work today since the guys have a few days off, but I'm still going in to tie some things up. You know a brotha's got to stay five steps ahead."

He sipped his orange juice and watched the plate of food as it traveled across the kitchen. I set it down before him and his eyes lit up like it was a Christmas present.

"Yeah, I know how it is. Are the Knicks playing on New Year's Day again this year?"

"Yup. They're playing the Nets actually. Everybody is home for the New Year."

He forked a heaping helping of egg into his mouth. I watched him chew, half hoping to get a rave review, half enjoying the site of a sexy man chewing.

"Oh, this is good, baby."

Kevin got lost in his plate, and I dug into mine as well. I only got a few bites in when the phone rang. I went over to the phone and answered.

"Heelllooo!"

"Hey Sunshine!" It was my mother. "You sound all chipper today."

"How are you today?"

"Oh, I can't complain. Listen, I called to see if you and Carl are going with us to church on New Year's Eve. Your grandmother wants us all together for June and your cousins."

"Uh, can I call you back about it?"

I didn't even tell my mother I was thinking about breaking up with Carl, so she would be shocked to know I did it last night. Well, not as shocked to know that I already had another half-naked man in my kitchen first thing in the morning. I didn't want to go into it with Kevin in the room.

"What's wrong?"

"Nothing, I just need to check my schedule," I lied.

"Umm-hmmm," she said suspiciously.

The truth of the matter was that we'd been in church every New Year since my accident. It was becoming a ritual.

"You'd think this was already on your schedule."

"Is Kyle going?"

I hated to be harsh, but I had to end this conversation fast.

"No," my mother got quiet.

I imagined she had straightened up and thrown her shoulders back, proudly conceding defeat.

"He has to work. He's very busy."

"Well, I'll definitely try to make it, Ma," I said.

What I wanted to say was, *Kyle isn't working. They get time off for the holidays. His show has aired reruns for two weeks straight.* But I didn't say anything.

"OK, we'll talk later. I love you."

She disconnected before I could say I loved her.

I went back to the table and ate in silence. Kevin looked up for a second, but he must've sensed I didn't want to talk about it. He finished his food, and said he'd be in the shower. I cleaned up the breakfast dishes, feeling guilty again for hurting Carl, and anticipating guilt because my mother seemed to like him. Everybody did.

"Well, what's done is done. Everybody has to find out sooner or later, it may as well come from me...today."

I made up my mind that I would visit my mother and grandmother and let them know about the big change in my life.

Kevin came down wearing his clothes from the night before.

"What do you want to do tonight? You want to catch a movie and some dinner?"

"Sure. Sounds good."

I perked up again. Kevin's voice was so soft and kind. He soothed the worries right out of my head.

"OK, don't forget to bring your booty-bag. We're staying at my place tonight."

He bent down and kissed me on my lips softly.

"Love ya, baby."

I rang my mother's doorbell and waited for someone to open the door. I took the time to psyche myself up into breaking the news about Carl.

"Look, these things happen. Yeah, that's it. I'll say, 'look, these things happen. I've been in love with Kevin, you know that…'"

Just then, the door opened and my grandmother was looking at me suspiciously. My mother must have told her something was up.

"Hi. How are you?" I said as if nothing was wrong.

"I can't complain. Come on in here."

Oooh, you're in trouble.

I followed her in, and shut the door behind me. She led me to the living room where my mother sat in an armchair, arms folded.

"Hey, Ma," I said.

I walked over and gave her a hug and kissed her on both cheeks.

"Channa, spill it. I call you and you're all happy, then I mention New Year's and you shut down. Something's going on with you."

I sat down on the sofa and sighed.

"Ma, I shut down because you mentioned Carl. We broke up last night."

"What?" my mother and grandmother said in unison.

My mother jerked forward in her seat and my grandmother sat down beside me. From the look on their faces, they were ready to comfort me. They probably felt like this was Andre all over again.

"OK, don't worry. I broke up with him because…well…because I'm in love with someone else and it just wasn't right to string him along."

"Is this that Kevin boy?" my grandmother said, still ready to comfort me.

"Well, yes. I didn't know you'd remember him."

"Child, you been talking about him for years."

"I know!" I was so relieved to hear she understood. "I have been in love with him for years, but he wasn't ready to commit to me. But, the other day, he told me he was."

"And just like that, you broke up with Carl?" my mother asked accusingly.

"Well, yeah. I explained the situation and he didn't take it well."

"Understandably."

"Yeah, but, these things happen. I love Carl, but I'm not in love with him. There's a difference."

"Mmm-hmmm."

My mother furrowed her brows, restraining herself from saying what she really wanted to say.

"That Carl sure is a nice boy," my grandmother chimed in. "He really loved you. He must be really hurt."

"Yes, Grandma."

"And," my mother broke in. "He has been there for you, Channa. He's such a good man."

"I know, Ma."

"Well, where was Kevin?"

"Ma, what are you saying? Where's this coming from?"

My mother seemed surprised at herself once I pointed it out.

"Well…I don't know, Channa. All I know is I did a lot of waiting around for a man I was in love with, and he was never there for me when I needed him."

"Ma, Kevin stayed the whole time I was paralyzed. That means a lot."

She looked away. She didn't like to remember those days. I suppose I didn't either.

"Well, all I'm saying is it's been a long time. If he was smart, he would have scooped you up years ago."

"Are we going to meet this boy?" Grandma piped in.

"Sure. Soon."

"Good."

"Ma? Are you going to be OK?"

She was looking off to the window and pumping her dangling foot over her crossed leg.

"I just want you to be happy. Are you sure about this man?"

There it goes again.

"I'm happy. You heard me this morning. He makes me happy."

"OK then."

I drove back home. I wanted to spend some time with Tango and call Arnelle. I knew how I could be. I was all tied up with my man. I was forgetting to return calls to my friends. But mostly, after the reaction my mother had over the whole thing, I needed someone who could understand. Arnelle definitely did.

I was in my den, snuggling with Tango, and I called her office line. Arnelle picked up after a couple of rings.

"Hey, girl."

"Channa? I've been trying to call you."

"Well, I've been busy…and guess what…I've been getting busy."

"What? With who?"

"With Kevin! He finally committed himself to me!"

"When did this happen?"

"The other night. I broke up with Carl last night. He didn't take it well."

"He's a man. He'll get over it."

Listen to Arnelle, girlfriend trying to be tough on men.

"Yeah, that's true. I still feel bad, though. He's a great guy."

"Oh, well then, you can give me his number."

We laughed over that.

"I dunno, Arnelle, you need some action and he's just not *there* if you know what I mean."

"Please, if he can get it up, that's all I need."

I didn't know if she was serious about getting Carl's number, so I just laughed it off. She was good for saying something surprising, but she had to be joking. Who wants sloppy seconds?

"Well, I wondered if the Marie Laveau stuff was working, I see it did."

"Yeah, Marie Laveau is definitely the one to go to."

"Oh! Look at the time. I have a meeting. Thanks for calling, Channa. Morgan is working me to death over the holidays. I gotta go, but we're going to have to go out again soon."

"OK, Arnelle. See ya."

We hung up and I marveled about how much she had changed since we first met.

As Baby New Year 2005 started to make way around the globe, Kevin and I decided to make our way around our families. It was our first holiday as a couple.

"Hey baby, you wanna hit Times Square tonight?" Kevin asked over yet another breakfast, this time in his apartment, this time his cooking.

"Puh-leeze Kev, I don't do Time Square. Stuck in between all those people...standing the whole time...and ugh, no easy access to a restroom. Been there, done that, I can watch it on TV."

Ever since the accident, I had to think some things through. I wasn't comfortable standing for long periods of time, and I didn't like being closed in by a crowd of people.

"My family wants me to go to church with them tonight anyway."

"What, no party?"

"Well, I used to party on New Year's Eve, but now I give that moment to God. It felt wonderful to celebrate all the blessings that God gave me in the past year, and to thank him for a new, future year. I have a lot to be thankful for. And Kev, you don't know how much power runs through the room. Everyone is praying as it turns midnight. You know what the Bible says: when more than two are together in His name, He is there. Church is packed on New Year's Eve."

"Hmmm…OK."

"OK?"

"OK, I'll go too."

"What?"

"What? That wasn't an invitation?"

"Oh, I was just telling you what I was doing, I didn't even think…Baby, I'm sorry. Would you like to join me for New Year's Eve?"

"Yes."

He got quiet. He looked to be in deep thought.

"Channa, I have a lot to be thankful for too. I just want to thank God for you."

Once again, Kevin Dean Walker left me speechless. My nose started burning and my vision blurred from tears. *Lord, it's been worth the wait just to hear him talk like this.*

"Um…OK…"

I shook my head, wiping my eyes. Kevin glanced up at me, but looked back into his pancakes and strawberries.

"So, it's church tonight. *We* have so much to be thankful for."

"And then tomorrow, we can go to my parents' house." Kevin stuffed a fork-load of pancakes into his mouth, probably to get out of speaking.

"Wha....wha...."

I wasn't stuttering over another loving boyfriend gesture. Honestly, I was slightly terrified of Kevin's mother. He just kept chewing, and I imagined the pancakes must have turned into mush. He was stalling. He was afraid of me meeting his mama too.

"OK, Mr. Walker. We will go meet your parents."

I used my "All Business Smile"—the kind that I put on at Morgan Pharmaceuticals when I knew one of those jerks was out to get me.

"Would you like to give me some insight on how to make this easy?"

Kevin finally swallowed with a loud gulp. His bottom lip twitched a little like he was fighting off the urge to puke up nasty, pancake mush.

"Well, we won't bring any food. Moms got her kitchen on lock, and if you try to bring a dish, that's just asking for trouble. Besides, you don't know how to make any Jamaican dishes, do you?"

I shook my head. I wasn't even sure what was a traditional Jamaican dish was. *Jerk chicken? Yeah, Jerk chicken. I can't make that.*

"Well, if you bring flowers, it'll look like you're trying too hard, and you don't want to do that either."

"Isn't it a little soon for me to bring your mother gifts anyway?"

"Yeah, that's true. Yeah."

Kevin's mind was racing. This meeting was important to him and he wanted it to go well.

"OK, I bring you, you dress nice but casual...no problem there...and I'll bring the gift. You know what? Just act like she's a potential client."

"What?"

"Smile a lot. Be polite. Compliment her cooking. And when she wants to know about you...or about you and me... sell your ass off. I'm sure you'll get the feel of her before you get that far."

Kevin stood up and took his plate to the sink.

"I need to handle some business. OK, baby? Do you want to stay here until I get home, or do you want me to take you home first?"

"What business do you have to do on New Year's Eve?"

"There's a game tomorrow night. I gotta get Tyshawn ready. A lot of people will be watching, and one of his commercials is running at half-time."

"Oh."

I don't know why I had to ask. I was more worried about his mama. Must've been a defense mechanism.

"I think I'll go home. Gotta cook some black-eyed peas for good luck for the new year."

"What? I never figured you would be into that mumbo jumbo." Kevin laughed as he came over and kissed my forehead, then my shoulder where the strap of my nightie had fallen.

"Hey, I just want to cover all my bases."

"OK, remind me to get you a rabbit's foot the next time someone's selling them on the street. I'm gonna take a shower."

Kevin had no idea about me and mumbo jumbo. If I even thought about it too much, I'd worry myself wondering how much of his love was coming from a spell and not from his heart. But I didn't have time to think about that. I had to get my mind ready for meeting his mother. And what about meeting his father? Kevin told me about his womanizing ways. I worried that I'd shake his hand and imagine it going from woman to woman and then back to his wife and I'd get sick in front of everybody. But I told myself, I needed to honor the people who gave birth to the man I loved. Anyone taking part in creating Kevin Dean Walker could not be all that bad, and what about when we have our own children? These people would be the grandparents. The Walkers were going to be a big part of my future, so I needed to clean the slate and embrace them like family. They'd be my family too. It was only a matter of time. And with family in mind, there was another pending situation—my mother and grandmother. I told Kevin he could come to church with us, but judging from my mother's reaction earlier, I didn't think the night would go too smoothly.

Chapter 5

"Hey, Sunshine."

I had called my mother to talk about our New Year's Eve plans.

"Your grandmother and I are going through our old clothes to take over to the Goodwill. If we get it over there before it closes, I can deduct the donation from my taxes. That, and it would just feel better to go into the New Year without so much junk. I mean, I know I'm never going to wear these cranberry slacks again."

I could practically see my mother standing in her huge closet with a mountain of silks and satins in vibrant colors on the floor.

"Well, I called to give you a little warning…I'm bringing Kevin to church and we'll be at your house around ten."

"Aw, Channa, why?"

"Ma, you know I love him, and at least with this one, you know we've been together so long that marriage and grandchildren are around the corner."

Well, I didn't really know that for sure, but what better way to warm my mother up to Kevin than to make her think he'll give her the grandbabies she was dying for?

"Fine, Channa. I can't promise I'll be nice to him right away, but I'll try."

"Thanks, Ma. See you at ten."

It was 9:55 p.m., and we were standing outside of my mother's door. Kevin had on a long, wool coat with slacks and a sweater underneath. He looked very handsome and comfortable. We held hands and waited for someone to answer the door.

"Sunshine!" my grandmother sang as she flung the door open.

She put out her arms for a warm embrace, and I obliged. Once done, she stepped back and took a sideways glance at Kevin, who had yet to cross the threshold.

"And, who is this fine, young man? Is this Kevin?"

"Yes, ma'am," he said, extending his hand. "Kevin Dean Walker."

My grandmother pushed his hand aside and gave him a warm hug.

"It's good to meet you, finally. Come on in, you'll catch cold."

We walked into the living room, where my mother stood up from the sofa to welcome us.

"Hello. You must be Kevin."

My mother sounded businesslike and extended her hand for Kevin. He took her cue and shook her hand.

"Well, are you ready to get going?"

"Yes, ma'am. And it's very nice to meet you. Channa thought it would be a good idea to take my truck so everyone can have lots of room."

"That would be nice. Traveling out of 2004 and into 2005 comfortably is definitely a good idea," my mother raised her eyebrow as she leaned closer to Kevin. "And may the rest of the year be just as comfortable."

Kevin got the message. My mother just said in her classy way, *Don't hurt my daughter.* He nodded his head and gestured to escort my mother to his car.

We arrived at the church during the social time when

everyone was getting in, finding seats, and mingling with people they probably hadn't seen since the last New Year's Mass. Auntie June and Treasure were sitting in a pew near the front, and various people made their way over to greet them.

"Hello, Auntie June. I want you to meet Kevin, my boyfriend."

It was the first time I called him my boyfriend out loud, and I was relieved at how natural it felt to say. Kevin smiled and seemed to like it as well.

"Is he Catholic?"

That's all my aunt said. She didn't say "Hello" or "Pleased to meet you." That wasn't like her.

"Yes, ma'am, I'm Catholic," Kevin smiled and assured her. "My name is Kevin Dean Walker, pleased to meet you."

Auntie June forced a smile and a nod, and turned away to look straight ahead. I turned to look at my mother, but my mother just raised her eyebrow.

My grandmother tugged on my arm, saying, "Come on, baby, let's get us a seat." She inched her way down the pew behind Auntie June.

Treasure greeted Kevin by shaking his hand and thanking him for coming. She gave me a look that said, "When did this happen?" And I opened my eyes wide, meaning, "I'll tell you later."

The service went well. I was moved once again, as so many of us prayed together past midnight. At one point, I felt a warmth come over me and than tears rolled down my cheeks. I was sure I was quiet, and didn't really feel as though I was crying. But somehow, Kevin knew. He placed his hand over mine and squeezed it, and he didn't let go until it was time to stand and wish everyone a Happy New Year.

"Happy New Year, Channa Renée Jones."

Kevin leaned over and wiped the tears away with his thumbs.

"I'd kiss you, but I think your mom will kill me."

I laughed. I just felt giddy all over. Like I could have been the big ball that dropped in Times Square. The man I loved was wiping away my happy tears. His long, strong fingers were entwined over, under, and around my ears and on through my hair. Every ounce of me wanted him to kiss me, and yet, his resistance to do so also added into the energy that was happening between us. I could feel the eyes of my mother and aunt watching, and I knew they were witnessing something beautiful. There was no way they could ever disapprove of him again.

"God, I love you, Channa Renée Jones."

Kevin drew me into his strong arms and hugged me. It was a pure gesture, one that came from within. That wasn't any magic that came from Marie Laveau's *juju* bag. It was real.

"I love you, Kevin Dean Walker."

My face was planted into his chest, and my words must have been muffled, but it didn't matter. I was speaking to his heart.

We stopped by Auntie June's house before taking my mother and grandmother home. We didn't plan on staying long, but Auntie June needed a man to walk through her house. I remember from many New Years before, there was the common belief that if a man were the first one to enter your house, good luck would be on your home for the year. A woman being first was bad luck. Uncle Jake, even Kyle, had been on duty over the years to be the first one to go through our respective doors.

Treasure and I stood behind Kevin as he turned her key in the door. Her keychain had a green rabbit's foot on it. Kevin held it up to me and laughed. He took the first step through the door and found the light switch on the wall. Then Treasure and I followed.

"Girl, what happened to Carl?" Treasure said in a low voice.

"It just wasn't going to work. I've been in love with Kevin

for years. The minute he was ready to step it up, I jumped on it. What would you do?"

"Well, let's just say it's a dilemma I wouldn't mind having."

Once Kevin finished his rounds, I said, "Well, maybe we should get going. It's late and everybody should get some rest."

Kevin repeated his good-luck patrol at my mother's house and then on to mine. He finished his tour in my bedroom.

"What about that kiss?"

Kevin weaved his way in and out of traffic on the Long Island Expressway like he was some kind of racecar driver. We were en route to Westport where his parents lived, and his nervousness didn't put me at ease. I fiddled with the radio station, adjusted my seat a few times, and cracked the window for a little air. Kevin's eyes remained on the road. The next thing I knew, we were pulling up in front of a very nice house: a brick split-level with a picture window. His mother opened the door before he could reach the doorbell. Mrs. Walker seemed happy to see Kevin, but she looked me up and down and reluctantly let me in.

The house was spotless; immaculate. The walls were white, but the drapery was vibrant in a peach and blue print. There were big, healthy plants that seemed to be every bit a fixture of the house as the ceiling fan or furniture. The furniture was covered in plastic, and it was good to see that plastic furniture covers crossed the cultural lines.

"Your plants are gorgeous, Mrs. Walker," I said.

It wasn't a fake attempt to win her over. *I honestly wished my plants could look as good as hers.*

"T'anks."

Her response was short and sharp.

"Ya cold?"

She held her hands out for my coat.

"Thanks, Mom," Kevin said, taking off his coat and piling it on top of mine in his mother's outstretched hands. "What smells so good?"

"Gwon n' wake you fadda. 'im en front de tee-vee, sleep."

Mrs. Walker was tall and thick. She looked like an older version of Kevin with a wig and pearl earrings. She wore a long, colorful dress with the ocean blue background dominating. Her feet were in simple black flats with a little bow on top, and her hands were big and strong. I could imagine her snapping the necks of chickens or snatching up misbehaving boys by their collars on old dirt roads. There was the essence of strength and grace in all she did.

With that strength and grace, she set her dining room table with dishes of food I figured took her days to make, but suspected she whipped up in a few hours. There was jerk chicken, curried goat, and saltfish. Something for everyone, and it all tasted so good that I forgot where I was and threw down. She had cooked fried dumplings, callaloo, rice and peas, and oxtails. There was sorrel, ginger beer, and rum to drink. And I didn't even mention the desserts. The whole time food rotated around the table, onto people's plates, and up into their mouths, I never saw Kevin's mother take a single bite. She took pride in making a big meal for her men and seeing them eat it joyfully.

"Oh, Mrs. Walker. This was a fabulous meal," I said, sitting back into my chair, "Can I help you clear the table? You deserve a break after all of that cooking."

"'ush, child. Me not a tad bit tired from cooking." She pulled away from the table. "But, you kin 'elp twant."

I stood up and began stacking the empty plates as Kevin and his father sat back, picking their teeth and loosening their belts. Somehow, Kevin looked like his father too. They had the same complexion, smile, mouth, and the same flirtatious eyes.

Kevin slid a plate closer to me and said, "Thank you,

baby."

Before I could reach for the stack of plates I made, Mrs. Walker scooped them up and disappeared. I turned to follow her to the kitchen that was just as bright and immaculate as the rest of her home. And though I could see she had a dishwasher, Kevin's mother was already at work, scrubbing away at the sink.

"Would you like for me to rinse or dry?"

"Me tell ya what, put dem containers in de icebox. Dem dere wit de red lids."

Mrs. Walker used her head to point me in the direction to the leftovers. She had them stored in plastic containers on the white-tiled, center island. I followed her directions. Closing the refrigerator door, I was prepared to ask for another chore, but I was interrupted.

"Hey, there you are. Are you ready to go?"

Kevin came in looking distracted and I couldn't imagine he'd be ready to leave after the day was going so well.

"I guess so, you OK?"

He looked like he was picked for jury duty.

"Yeah, I'm fine. Tyshawn gets nervous before big games and he's really freaking about this commercial being shown during half time. I'm going to go see him, and calm him down."

"Oh, what can I do?"

Or should I say, why do you need to hold this grown man's hand?

"Nothing, baby. I'm just really sorry I have to cut our day short. I'm going to drop you back home and I'll try to get back after the game."

Kevin pulled me in for a hug and pressed his lips to my forehead.

"I doubt it, though. I got a feeling it'll be a long night."

We said our "goodbyes" to his parents and left. Kevin looked just as distracted on the ride back home as he did before we got to his parents' home. His mind wasn't there and I didn't understand why. His job always seemed to be the kind of career most men would kill for. He got paid well to rub elbows with all-star players and play pick-up games with future all-stars. But I still didn't understand his close involvement with Tyshawn Morris. Kevin was a recruiter. He schmoozed these guys into playing for the Knicks, and then you'd think his job was done. But he kept holding their hands and continued to make them happy long after donning the jersey. Even so, Kevin stayed busy, but never appeared to be stressed. Until now. Tyshawn seemed to have a negative affect on him.

"Good luck tonight," I said as I got out of Kevin's vehicle. "I don't suppose I could interest you in a quickie."

I laughed and shut the door before he could even respond. I wanted him to have something else on his mind than whatever psychosis Tyshawn Morris was pulling. I planned to send him little love messages throughout the night.

Once inside the house, I decided to call Deja. I needed to give her the Kevin update, but my clothes felt uncomfortable. They were made for showing and not lounging, and after all of Mrs. Walker's food, I needed to lounge. I went upstairs and changed into the baggy sweat suit I often wore to physical therapy and flopped across my bed. Grabbing the phone, I dialed Deja.

"Hello?"

Deja sounded frustrated.

"Deja? What's wrong?"

"Channa? Gurrrllll, I thought you were one of those damn telemarketers. I just got three calls in a row from three separate companies. No, I don't want to refinance my home. No, I don't want to take a vacation. No, I don't want to change my long distance service."

"You still get calls from long distance companies?"

"No, it's just leftover frustration from when those fuckers used to call," Deja sighed, "So, Happy New Year, gurl. What's your resolution list looking like?"

"I gave up on New Year's resolutions...it's the only resolution I could keep."

"Gurl, you're silly. I'm supposed to stop cussin' so much, but these telemarketers bring it out of me. So, what's the deal? Did you give up Carl or are you still ho-ing around with your two men?"

"I broke up with Carl. He didn't take it well, but we're done."

"Did he cry? He seems like the type to cry."

"Well, his eyes were a little glassy, but he yelled at me. He never yelled at me before. He was so hurt, and I felt so bad. I cried myself to sleep."

"What, you broke up with him and *you* were the one crying?"

"Hahaha, you're right. Talk about a surprise. But then Kevin..."

"Kevin? What did he do, kick Carl's ass or something?"

"No, Deja, nothing like that. He just brought me some dinner and made me feel better. Deja, he loves me. He said it."

"Wuh?"

"And I just got back from his parent's house. He took me to meet his parents. Gurl, you better toss that bouquet to me at your wedding. Kev and I are next."

"Whoa, slow down, Channa. He had you chasing your own tail for ten years and suddenly he says he loves you and you're talking marriage? Think, Channa. Just take your time. Make him chase *you* for a change."

"Deja, I'm not going to play some game with the man I love. I'm done with games, and I'm very happy."

My voice was flat. I tried not to let her know how hurt I was by her words, but I wasn't doing a good job concealing it.

"I'm sorry, Channa. I just worry about you, and as much as I joke around, I've been a little mad that Kevin's been stringing you along all these years. I never was able to change your mind, so I'm just going to stop and wish you the best. Just please...please know...that you're my gurl and if he hurts you, I'm going to be here for you. And if he makes you happy, I'll be here for you too."

"Wow. Thanks, Deja. That means a lot. And the same goes for me."

"Good, cuz I'm wearing this corset thing under my dress, I may need you to do a ventriloquist act at the altar if I can't breathe in that thing."

I laughed as Deja made strained noises that sounded like she was saying "I do" through clenched teeth.

Chapter 4

Night lights stream behind me. I'm in warp speed, and yet time is standing still. I see stop signs and they see me. Flashes of red dance in my head—my shoes, my dress, my blood on a white tissue. I bite my lip, and don't feel it until it is too late. Like I was being hurt for months, and didn't feel it until it was too late. Like I saw the signs, but didn't read them until it was too late.

Red light, stop 1-2-3.
Channa.
Red light 1-2-3.
Don't turn the knob, Channa.
RED LIGHT, 1-2-3.
Don't go inside, Channa.

I sleepwalk through my dream world, not listening to the screaming voices, batting them away like buzzing mosquitoes. Batting away the buzzing mosquitoes never stops them from sucking the sweet blood from soft flesh, dampened from the humidity of a hot summer night. The buzzing blends with the sound from the traffic sign, indicating to walk, or don't walk. Walk, don't walk. Walk. Don't you dare walk into that room, Channa.

The college basketball season bounced along like the pro, and went into the final playoffs. I finally had the playoff disappointment of loving a man who was married to the game. He had late nights, and we didn't fight. I was awaiting his vacation. There'd be one week just for us, where the sun would shine just because we were together, and not just because we were on the beach. Cell phones would stay on the hotel dresser, and we'd only answer the call of our wild, burning desire. But it was with a lie.

I wanted to surprise him and model the handkerchief someone called a bikini in the office high above the blistering cold of the stubborn winter. I bought it for our Jamaican getaway, and I knew my man could use the preview after all the long hours he'd put in. It was April, and still felt like winter. I just wanted to wear the bikini and my pumps under my full-length coat, but I had to opt for a tight red dress too. *Click-click.* There went my heels as I slunk to the doorman. *You know me. I've slipped in after office hours before.* Before the elevator doors close, I can see him wondering what's under my coat. *I'd wink if you were watching my eyes, honey.*

His hushed voice whispered sweet nothings into the phone as I had to make something out of his words, because I'd gone from seeing him every night to only two or three nights a week. This had been the longest stretch, and his love juices had to have been overflowing just as mine were—ready for one volcanic eruption of cataclysmic proportions. *What happens when you stick your finger into a full bottle, baby?* The nectar was already flowing from my honey hive, and I wanted him to try to cork it—an impossible feat that would require multiple attempts. *Stick it in, say you missed me.*

Stick it in, say you love me.

St...st...stick it in and tell me you've been waiting for this for so long.

And...and...and...finally we've cum together.

Only, this wasn't the surprise I had planned.

Night swallowed the office, and red letters glowed over a doorway...E...X...I...T. I wasn't looking for a way out. I was there to get him in. The carpeting absorbed the blow of each step. There goes the Channa of four steps ago...the Channa of three steps ago...I could see the red letters of the emergency exit reflected in the shiny handle that could give me entrance. EXIT. I touched the knob and the reflection could no longer be seen. I slowly turned the cool metal and the door quietly unlatched. Quiet, keeping quiet, I slid my head into the opening door, trying to sneak a peek of my man's face when he first saw me. I was met by moans, groans, grunts, and hissing. What was I missing? What was I missing?

Bare feet, two sets, toes furled and curled used as leverage to keep the legs steady. All legs were dark and firm, a distant light outlining each muscular calf, and two sets. The legs I recognized were planted between the legs I didn't. The ass I'd seen a thousand times flexed and released, the grunts didn't cease. There was a pounding flapping noise, like someone was clapping, but I was the only one in the audience.

"Oh shit!" he said, "OH-OH SHIT!"

The unrecognizable grunting got muffled. And all I could see was him.

Kevin's back had stiffened, but often gave way to sudden spasms.

"Ahhh!" he said, "Ahh-ahhh!"

He reached his strong and dominant hand before him and violently grabbed what I would soon see was a handful of braids. Kevin's body jerking, the grunting un-muffled, he pulled back the head of the body he had overtaken, and released the creamy lava I thought he'd been storing for me, squirting hot doses onto someone's cheek.

Falling to his knees, just as my heart had fallen into the pit of my stomach, Kevin gasped for air and braced himself with one hand on a cushion of the white couch. I was watching a train wreck and couldn't turn away. Yet something told me I had seen this all before, or had I lived it? The realization poured over me like a bucket of blood from an old horror movie. *No.* I felt my mouth moving but no sound could come out. *Don't.* I felt my chest pounding, but I couldn't locate my heart. I knew what was coming next, and it would be the most revealing experience of my relationship with Kevin Dean Walker.

As he tried to steady his breathing, Kevin pulled back at the shoulder of his conquest. The shoulder was large and muscular.

No!

Kevin's hand went back to grab the handful of braids that braised along the thick neck, and with a forceful jerking, I saw the face that belonged to the body.

No!

Kevin leaned in for the kiss, and diverted to the cheek on which he'd left his mark.

No!

And then he licked at it with slow, short movements. He was savoring it. And then the moment was shared as Tyshawn Morris kissed and licked back at Kevin, collecting his creamy treat from Kevin's tongue.

No. No. No. This couldn't be happening. I recoiled through the door, slowly walking backwards, slowly mouthing what my soul was saying, without releasing sound. No-no-no. My head began shaking as my body was drifting backwards through the dark office. I found the elevator door with eyes that couldn't have belonged to me. Once on the elevator, the tears began to stream down my face with the force of Niagara Falls. I remembered leaning over that white couch, Kevin fucking me from behind, and then pulling me by my hair and cumming on my face. The kissing and licking were feelings so personal and passionate. It was like something that could only happen one time and only with me. I was attacked with so much, but the problem was threefold. First off, Kevin was cheating on me. Secondly, Kevin was sharing something that I thought was only between us, with someone else. And thirdly, that someone else was a fucking man!

Kevin was gay.

The elevator ride was the longest in history. I felt like I was descending into hell. I gripped the railing on the back wall and held on for dear life. All along, I was shown all the signs. I didn't listen. I didn't acknowledge what I saw. I ignored what was told to me, and was blinded by my arrogant desire to have Kevin Dean Walker. Now I was going to pay.

"Are ya sure, chile?" Marie Laveau's brash accent seemed to echo. "It's against the saints."

There were the words of wisdom from Deja, asking if I was sure, and even the gleeful squealing of Tyrone. He warned me in his own way that Kevin was on the down-low. Then, there was Kevin's voice, "Are you ready for all of me?" All of those warnings were lost on me. I thought everyone wanted me to stick with the good and safe Carl. Not once did I think the actual warning was about Kevin.

"Are ya sure, chile? Are ya sure dis da man you wan?"

Marie was pleading with me, and I saw her as some slightly crazy voodoo priestess I'd let pour a beer over my head. It could have been a hammer or a bowl of crushed ice. I wasn't hearing her, and it wasn't just the language barrier.

Did Kevin think that my accepting, "all of him," would include sharing him with a man? All of those times he'd gotten angry when I asked to meet Tyshawn...I should have known. The picture Kevin had on his desk of them together, smiling, Kevin's arm behind Tyshawn, Tyshawn's arm draped around Kevin's shoulders. The phone calls, "That was Tyshawn, he's worried about this, he's worried about that," and Kevin would take off running. It was all right there in front of my face. Kevin and Tyshawn Morris.

I clenched my fist so tight, my nails dug into my flesh. But the pain was no match for what I was feeling in my chest, my heart, my head. The very core of my soul hurt like hell.

This just isn't happening. I couldn't believe Kevin just took his dick out of a man's ass and licked the cum off the guy's face. It couldn't possibly be clean or safe. I felt as though my stomach caved in under the weight of some sumo wrestler's foot. Safe. I never used condoms with Kevin, and that included the time when I was on my period. And it was obvious that Kevin wasn't using a condom with Tyshawn either. How long had it been going on? And if I asked him, would he tell me the truth? Tyrone told me, he really did, and I just thought he was being catty because I was in love and happy.

But look at the life he had. Tyrone was HIV-positive, and he knew the science of brothers on the down-low. Kevin could have given me HIV, or any number of other diseases, and he didn't seem to care about my safety. And I opened myself up to it by not insisting on using a rubber. I was supposed to be an educator, a facilitator, an expert. I preached the importance of condoms and safe sex all the time and yet, I didn't practice what I preached. Even when I knew that Kevin had other women, I continued to have sex with him without a condom. And I had sex with others too.

I needed to get tested. I needed to take responsibility for my actions and find out if I was carrying the virus. The fact of the matter was I had been sick lately with a cold or flu that I couldn't seem to shake. As it was, I'd been on my third antibiotic, each one stronger than the last. Something was wrong. I never stayed sick like that. My mind raced with the faces of various men I'd been with over the last ten years. What if I'd been sick all along?

The sinking feeling had been going on only inside my body and mind. I'd forgotten to push the "G" button, and was still on Kevin's floor. I smacked the glowing circle with the heel of my hand, and sent the elevator down with my spirits and hopes. I rushed past the doorman, and made my way to my car where I locked myself in, turned up the radio, and screamed until my throat was raw.

Chapter 3

The last time I had sex with Kevin, before finding him and Tyshawn going at it like big Pit Bull, bald dogs, there had been a little discomfort. We were at Kevin's place, and he was sitting at his desk in his home office. I was standing above him, naked, and straddling his body as I let his tired eyes feast on his appetizer for a long evening of carnal indulgence. When I saw his flagpole, saluting through the opening in his boxer briefs, I eased down on it and let out a little hiss of pleasurable pain. At first, I didn't know if it was because we'd gone days without making love, but I felt sharp sensations deep inside my honey hive, like I was too dry and Kevin's flag pole had a splinter. You see, if Kevin put his mind to it, he could have put the KY Jelly people out of business. Just looking at him got me thoroughly lubricated. So, this dryness was an oddity.

Kevin had been working so hard, and I could sense his exhaustion. I didn't want to add insult to injury by letting him know sex wasn't as joyful as usual. I stood again, making sure to keep my eyes in a seductive gaze, and maneuvered myself so that I was kneeling on the floor between his legs, eyeing I-95 like it was an all-day-sucker and I'd been a very good girl. I licked at him like he was an ice cream cone, and I was in a hot desert. I worked up and down on the sides, always returning to that big mushroom, taking it all into my mouth. Kevin moaned with great relief, like I was just what the doctor ordered to cure all that ailed him. I stroked the shaft as I made his love sack dance on my tongue, and his legs started to shake uncontrollably. I went in for the kill and swallowed I-95 whole, and sucked on it like a starving baby until his milky potion erupted into the back of my throat, and Kevin hollered like he was in church getting saved.

Once he could gain control of himself, he hoisted me up on his desk and pulled my legs apart then devoured me like a death row inmate at his last dinner. The skin around my tunnel's opening felt sore, and I guided his head upwards, where he could focus on my rum drop. The dam to my honey hive broke in record time, and I left a puddle on his paperwork.

Kevin stood up and smiled with pride from his job well done, and went to the bathroom for a towel. I looked down at the puddle and saw tinges of creamy white and I shook my head. Yeast infection, again. It was the third one in two months, and it was frustrating. The treatments burned more than the infection itself, and worse, I had to wait a few days before I could have sex.

After I calmed down from my shocking experience in Kevin's office, I couldn't help but remember something that was written on the information provided with the yeast infection treatment I'd taken.

"Recurrent yeast infections could be a sign of HIV."

The day after peeking into the down-low with Kevin, I put on big sunglasses and wrapped my hair in a plain-looking silk scarf. I dug way back into my closet and found a coat I hadn't worn all season, a three-quarter length in heather gray. I felt I needed a disguise so no one would recognize me, Channa Renée Jones, going for an HIV test. The coat and glasses weren't enough, though. I needed to go to another town. I wanted total anonymity. I'll admit that a large part of me was afraid of running into one of the men from the GHC, who could only grasp for invisible pearl necklaces and feign utter shock. But, more than that, I believe I was trying to hide from myself. Maybe if I didn't look like me, I could imagine someone else was facing this devastating possibility.

I topped my ensemble off with a black cashmere scarf, but that was for my throat that was very sore from the cold I was fighting, and all of the screaming I'd done in the parking garage. I needed to keep warm.

I had lists of clinics from my volunteer work. The Gay Men's Health Center is affiliated with at least twenty other clinics in the New York/New Jersey area, and more outside of the two states. There were pamphlets with addresses listed in alphabetical order, and divided by region. I decided to head south and picked a clinic in Trenton that was a good hour drive away.

I drove past the building twice before I realized I had the right address. There wasn't a large sign designating it as a clinic. It may as well have been in a plain brown wrapper, like other things that needed discretion. I parked in a small lot on the side of the building, and walked in the front door. *Now, it looks like a clinic.* The floor was dingy, like no one mopped the white tiles, and now they were gray. There were about sixteen chairs with metal legs and rough blue material, half on one wall and half on the other. And of course, what clinic could be complete without a receptionist who never looks up when you spoke to her?

"Take a number."

She raised her caramel-cream-colored hand that was overloaded with gold rings and herringbone bracelets, and pointed an extra-long, orange fingernail at one of those number dispensers you see at the deli, never raising her eyes from the tabloid she was reading.

I took a number, as told, and turned to find a seat.

"Hold it," she grunted, her head still in her magazine making me believe she had great peripheral vision. "Fill this out."

She picked up a clipboard and slid it over the counter.

I took the clipboard to a chair and bent forward to find a comfortable position to fill out the paperwork. It took a while, but I did it, and returned to the woman who hadn't changed her position.

"Excuse me," I interrupted and tapped my fingertips on the counter to get her attention, "I'm finished with the paperwork, do I hold on to it or do you need to take it?"

She put her hand out, her long nails looking like orange claws with perfect, blunt edges. I took it to mean, "give it here" though she didn't say a damn thing. *So much for hospitality.*

But, I wasn't there for companionship. I walked across the small waiting room that was full of people from all walks of life. There were all races and all ages. I didn't know if all were there for HIV testing, but we could be a poster to showing the virus does not discriminate.

"Threeee-twen-ee-threeee!" the receptionist belched out my number and pointed to the closed door at the back of the waiting room.

I stood and went to the door where another woman in pink scrubs met me. She was heavy-set with huge thighs that rubbed together loudly. She escorted me down the tiny hallway as it stretched to circus mirror proportions. I felt nauseous thinking about the test. The nurse's thighs swished with every step, sounding like whispers from the souls who'd walked this same hall before me.

"Dead-man-walk-ing-dead-man-walk-ing."

Finally, I was shown into a small exam room where a small desk and chair were squeezed in with the examining table.

"Just have a seat."

The nurse was jovial. Dare I say, bubbly. I was so happy she led the way instead of the lady at the desk.

"Thank you."

My nerves were getting increasingly tense by the second, and when the nurse was gone, I was left to my overactive thoughts.

My life is over. In a few minutes, I'll know for sure that tainted blood is pumping through my veins, breaking down my immune system and working to take me out all together. And I'll have to take medication every day, eat right, exercise...and all for what? So I can look at men I can never have? So I can prolong the inevitable? I can't believe this is happening to me.

Just then I coughed. *Cough-cough! Cough!* Suddenly, the reality of what the virus was, got very real. I had been sad, and damn sure mad at Kevin. I felt used and I was lied to. But, the initial shock of something always has a very surreal effect that keeps you just above the situation. Just as I wore a disguise to distance myself, my emotions also used a defense mechanism to keep me an arm's length away from reality. Being in the exam room, awaiting the HIV test that would tell me my fate, brought that wall of protection down like a demolition crew. *Kevin put my life at risk. My life is at risk. I could actually die because he lied to me, he kept secrets from me, and he had sex with me, and who knows how many other men and women without protection.* I thought about the men I had counseled on their death beds; their eyes sunken, their skin clinging to bones, the emotional strain on their faces, like they'd been pleading with God to have mercy and release them from the physical prison they were trapped in. It had to have felt like being stuck on a railroad track and seeing the train coming, the light getting bigger and brighter, then after hysterically trying to escape, resigning yourself for impact.

I suddenly felt so tired, and I'd barely taken the first step of my uphill battle.

A few minutes later, a short white man with blue eyes and dark, curly hair walked into the room.

"Hello, my name is Robert Ross, and I'm a nurse practitioner."

He leaned back against the examining table and looked at a folder that probably had the paperwork I filled out in it.

"So, you're here today for an HIV test. That we can do. But first, there are some things we need to talk about."

He folded one arm over the other and looked at me sympathetically, and then he began to counsel me about HIV and what HIV was, the ways it was transferred, its symptoms, and the possibilities for a long, productive life. I'd heard it all before, because I'd given a similar speech to hundreds of people over the years.

"Now, why do you think you need to be tested?"

"Well, I thought I was in a straight and monogamous relationship, but I caught my boyfriend having unprotected sex with a man."

I flashed back to the image of Kevin pulling Tyshawn by the hair, then ejaculating on his face.

"I see. And do you use condoms with him?"

I felt the shame of what I was about to say, but I couldn't lie, Kevin pulled my hair and came on my face too.

"No."

"What about drug use? Anything else?"

"No, Mr. Ross, I don't do drugs and as far as I know, my boyfriend doesn't either, but I've learned a lot of new things about him now haven't I? Look, I have to know if he has given me the virus. He's been as healthy as a horse, but I can't shake this cold and I have another yeast infection."

"A yeast infection?"

"Yes. For the third time, and I remember reading on the box of treatment about recurrent yeast infections having something to do with HIV."

"Well, that or diabetes, or a number of things. But I understand."

"So, can we get it over with?" I pressed rudely.

"Yes. What I have is the Rapid Test. I only have to swab your mouth and you can have results in about 20 minutes. It is all confidential, see?"

He showed me a sheet of paper with the same, long number repeating itself on peel-and-stick labels. All except for one.

"This is your number. One label identifies your chart. I swab inside your cheeks and stick it in this vial."

He picked up a test tube.

"We put your number on it and another will go on your call-back card."

I nodded. I understood all of that but I wasn't there for a lesson.

"Let's do it."

He swabbed my cheeks and put my sample in the vial.

"Well, then, that was painless. See ya in about twenty minutes."

Wow, just twenty minutes! It used to take two weeks before you'd know the results. Of course, when you figure it only takes a second to catch the virus, twenty minutes sounds like a long time.

The place smelled sterile, like a Lysol fairy "poofed" the walls, doors, and floors with disinfectant fairy dust. Considering the fear associated with HIV and AIDS, I felt like I was amongst the ranks of the plague, walking around with people pulling their children out of my way and washing everything that I had come in contact with. You never know how important the human touch is until you're no longer touchable. I had to remind myself of the hugs I'd given Tyrone, and various other infected men at the GMHC. There was no harm in touching, and it actually made them feel better. I tried to shake the nonsense out of my head as I found an empty seat in the crowded waiting room.

The twenty minutes wore on me like a decade, as the last decade played in my mind. Meeting Kevin at the password party, he acted as if I was the only person in the room. Or was that just an illusion? While I turned my back to show off my booty in my tight, white shorts, was he checking the room for a man he'd leave with? When I went to his messy, basement apartment, were there any signs of it being a gay love nest? Fast-forward to years later, when Kevin upgraded himself to one of the most coveted places of real estate in New York, did the nods and smiles from the doorman acknowledge that I was the special lady Kevin brought home? Or did he know that I was the ONLY lady, and he'd been holding the door for Kevin's boy-toys since the day he moved in?

My stomach did a somersault as I remembered the night I had sex with Kevin in his office and I was on my period. The memory of that night used to excite me—the raw passion made me feel like the most desirable woman in the world. I felt like my stuff was so good, Kevin couldn't wait, and was going to get what he wanted. That moment, when we shared his creamy treat felt like some sacred ritual our souls relived. It was messy and sensual, and I felt like we were one. But he shared that same intimacy with Tyshawn Morris and how many other people? My blood, his semen, and the bodily juices of countless others had been marinating in my body for months, possibly killing me from the inside out. *Damn you, Kevin! Damn you!* I shuddered, feeling the utmost betrayal. Then I shuddered again. My twenty minutes were up.

"Well, have you thought about your future based on the possible outcomes from the test you've taken?"

Robert Ross was leaning up against the examining table again, his arms folded with my file dangling from the bottom hand.

"If not, I can give you a list of counselors. We have a couple that come here four evenings a week."

"I've been thinking."

And the thoughts I was having were scaring the hell out of me.

"Well," he finally opened the file and glanced over the results, "it seems as though the results are inconclusive. It's not a positive or a negative. I know if seems pretty strange, but it happens all the time."

It wasn't strange to me, but I knew all about indeterminate test results. It was quite common. He went on to tell me what I already knew.

"When this happens, we need to retest you, but we need to wait at least 90 days. This happens sometimes if there are other medical conditions involved, so you may want to see your doctor about diabetes or Grave's disease. Some antibiotics can affect the test as well, and you said you've been fighting yeast infections lately. Of course, we have to be realistic here. People often have inconclusive test results when they're furlough converting. That means you could very well have the HIV virus and it is in its early stages. I'm sorry."

I dropped my eyes to his feet and nodded. I understood from the second he said "inconclusive" but a part of me wanted it to mean something else, anything else.

"Look, you're going to have to treat this like you have the virus for the next three months. You have to take care of yourself and you need to be safe."

He leaned over backwards and reached for a big, glass jar full of condoms that sat on a shelf.

"If you *have to* have sex, please use these."

He pulled a sleeve of condoms out of the jar and handed them to me.

"Of course, abstinence is the safest."

"Oh, you don't have to worry about me. I'm done with sex."

He patronized me with a nod.

"Also, you're really going to have to notify the sexual partners you've had since the time you figure you may have been infected. We can't chance them infecting someone else. If you want, you can give us a list and we'll make the calls, of course, it would be better coming from you."

List? What are you trying to say? I nodded again and got up to leave. I didn't have a laundry list of lovers, but the one name I worried about the most was Carl's. I'd done so much to hurt him already, how was I going to break this news to him?

The closer I got to home, the stronger I felt about calling Carl. I told myself that I could do it, like when I broke up with him. It was to save him for a bigger hurt down the road. I pulled into my garage, and pushed the button to close the door behind me. I turned off the car, and flipped open my cell phone, but first, a little prayer.

Dear Lord, please give me the strength to intrude on this man's life. Let him be open to the information so he can get the testing done. I accept the anger and pain I've caused him, and I just ask that you give me the strength to hear it come from him once again. Dear Lord, I've asked for many miracles, and I've been blessed time and again. But if there is one thing I can request that you would not deny me, it is that Carl be safe from HIV.

I crossed myself and gave my "amen." I dialed Carl's number and felt the chill when he answered apprehensively.

"Hello?"

I was direct, my tone even. "Carl? It's Channa."

"Yes, Channa. I'm surprised you've called. What do you want?"

His voice was soft but I could tell I unsettled him.

"Carl, I know I've brought you nothing but pain...there's something I have to tell you. You're not going to like it, but you need to hear it from me."

Carl's breathing came through the phone. I could tell he was there, but he wouldn't say anything.

"Carl?"

"I'm listening, Channa. Say what you gotta say. I have someplace to be."

"Oh, well, I guess there is no right time for this. I was recently tested for the HIV virus, and the results were inconclusive. I could be fine, or the virus could be building. Either way, I need to tell you to get tested. We weren't exactly safe and I wasn't faithful."

"Channa..." Carl trailed off.

He stayed silent for a few seconds.

"Channa, this is really messed up. I don't know what I should say to you...I'm just going to hang up before I say something I regret."

"OK, I understand. It isn't the best time to tell you that I still care about you, since I keep messing up your life. But I do."

"Um, whatever. Bye."

Carl hung up.

Before I put my cell phone back in my purse, I noticed that I had a message waiting. I scrolled through my phone's options and selected "listen" under the highlighted message.

"Channa Renée Jones!"

It was Kevin. This time his seductive pronunciation of my name disgusted me.

"I know you went shopping for our getaway, are you going to come model that bikini for me?"

I threw my phone into my bag and put my head down on the steering wheel. I was there to model the bikini for him last night. I was so excited about going away for an entire week after years of romantic interludes where I had to share him with his job, and leave before enjoying a tropical sunrise. *Well, this Sunshine has set on your triflin' ass.*

For the next month, I kept moving. I felt like a shark; if I stopped moving, I'd die. I went from one room to the next in my home; dusting, vacuuming, organizing to the brink of an obsessive-compulsive disorder. Magazines were separated by publication and stacked in accordance to date. Canned food was alphabetized and broken up into categories: fruit, vegetable, other. Socks and panties were neatly folded and color-coded. But that was only the first week. Calls from Kevin, my mother, and Deja flooded my answering machine. The GMHC had called to check on me. I'd missed my volunteer slot and they wanted to know if I was OK and if I would be in the next week. I couldn't face them—I felt as though I failed them. I couldn't bring myself to answer any calls. Instead, I wiped down my phones with alcohol swabs and poked at dirt that accumulated in the crevices of the receiver until each phone looked as new and sterile as it did when taken out of the box.

I bundled up everything that reminded me of Kevin and filled my trunk with one garbage bag after the other. All of the bed linens, sexy lingerie, and expensive outfits I purchased to impress him were shoved into a black garbage bag. Simple things like his favorite brand of bottled spring water and a throw pillow he'd rested his head on had to be removed. But no matter how Kevin-free my house became, nothing erased the image of Kevin and Tyshawn sharing that messy kiss, or the date marked on my calendar to get retested.

I started to take trips. I visited museums, aquariums, and historical landmarks in New York, Connecticut, and New Jersey. Every day I took off in a different direction, hoping to escape the term. I sent my mother and grandmother a postcard from every gift shop. I imagined they had to be worried, but after all we'd gone through, I couldn't put this burden on them.

My mother and grandmother weren't the only people worried about me. After a month of field trips, I returned home from the Philadelphia Museum of Art. I tackled the famous Rocky steps, but didn't feel any stronger. I just wanted to go home and rest. I was exhausted. I went into the kitchen, and pushed the play button on my answering machine for the messages.

"Baby, it's me." *Hmpf, Kevin.* "Where have you been? I haven't been able to get a hold of you and it's been a month. I've driven by your house and you're never there. I even knocked on your mother's door today, and she showed me some postcards you've been sending her. What's going on?

Is it something I said? Something I did? Call me, I'm worried."

"Sunshine? Are you there?" *My mother.* "Pick up if you are. I can't believe you can send me postcards but you can't pick up the telephone. And now, Kevin comes by and tells me *he* hasn't seen you in a month either? This isn't like you. If you don't call me by six o'clock tonight, I'm calling the police and filling out a missing person's report. Do you hear me? Are you there?"

"Gurrrlll! Your mama just called me on the phone to see if you were in D.C." *Deja.* "She said Kevin even knocked on her door looking for you and ain't nobody seen you in weeks. I don't know what's going on, but if you don't call me, I'm going to be on your doorstep before the end of the night. I told you, no matter what I'm here for you. Just call me, gurl."

"This is your grandmother. You know I hate these machines. But everybody is worried! Your mother will call the police. I don't like these machines. Can you hear me?"

My grandmother never realized that you could speak into the telephone with your regular volume and the answering machine would still hear you.

"Channa, what's going on?" *Oh my God, it's Kyle.* "Everybody is calling me, asking me if I've seen you, saying no one has seen you for a month. My answering machine is full because everybody from our family has called me except for you. You really need to call Ma so she can calm down. I'm about to go out, and you know my cell."

Someone got Kyle's head out of his own ass? Oh this has escalated enough.

I snatched the cordless phone off of the wall. I was angry at first that my mother would call my brother and Deja to find me. Why couldn't she just respect that I needed space? I sent her postcards to let her know I was OK.

"Hello, Ma?" I snapped at the phone.

I looked up to the wall clock and figured I'd caught her in time before the police would be over.

"Channa Renée Jones. Watch your tone! You have me

worried to death and you're *hello, ma*-ing me?"

"You called Kyle and Deja? What am I? Twelve?"

"Well, when you stop returning phone calls and start sending postcards from around the Tri-State area, you sure seem like you're twelve. How was I supposed to know that some lunatic didn't kidnap you and sent me postcards to keep me off the trail?"

"Oh, well. I'm home. I'm OK. I just needed some space."

"Is it Kevin? Are you running from him? Did he put his hands on you or something?"

"Ma. Stop. Kevin didn't hit me. I just saw him doing something I didn't approve of, and needed to be by myself. I'll tell him it's over later. I just gotta make sure he's out of my system first."

That was a lie. There was no way I could go back to Kevin after seeing what I saw, and I never wanted to talk to him again.

"Look, I gotta call Deja so she doesn't wind up on my doorstep tonight with two suitcases and a switchblade. Thank you for worrying, but you didn't have to. We'll talk about this when I'm ready. Right now just isn't the time."

"OK, tell Deja I'm sorry for worrying her too. I just thought you may have gone to see her since you seemed to be driving all over God's green earth."

"Bye, Ma."

I hung up.

I dialed Deja and told her that I was OK but I would have a lot to talk with her later. I just needed time to think.

"Channa? I don't like to hear you talk like this. What happened?"

I couldn't talk to her about Kevin then. She'd understand that Kevin was a cheater, but it was with *whom* he was cheating that I was still trying to wrap my mind around. Deja would ask a lot of questions, dredging up too much that I wasn't ready to deal with. And she had been trying to get me to see how dumb I was for years. Telling her about all of this would warrant an "I told you so." Only, there was one thing she never warned me about.

"I'll just say that you were right about some things, and then there were some things that even *you* missed. But I can't talk much more without breaking down. I'm gonna go for now and I'll definitely tell you everything…later."

I hung up with Deja and turned to see the kitchen trash. It was overflowing with dead and dying flowers. Kevin sent me a bouquet every day that week. His messages became more frequent, and sometimes he was angry.

"Channa, how are you going to just stop talking to me out of nowhere?"

He just started yelling into the phone without the slightest "hello." Other times, he was remorseful.

"Channa? It's Kevin. Are you there? Pick up. Well, can you at least tell me what it was I did? Can I make it up to you? Channa, please call me, you know I love you."

His sad messages only made me angry.

"Love isn't shoving your dick all over the place and bringing it back to me with a virus!" I yelled at my answering machine.

I was done with Kevin. He could send me flowers and leave me sweet messages, but I would never forget what I saw. Especially if it turned out I had HIV. My yeast infection wasn't clearing up, and I still couldn't shake my cold. I yanked the garbage bag out of the can, and took it to the curb for pick-up. If Kevin gave me the virus, I'd never be able to put it on the trash heap.

Chapter 2

Tango's barking woke me up from a decent night's sleep. He needed his early morning walk. I got up and slipped into my terry cloth bathrobe. We moped down the stairs together, taking each step with groggy hesitation. Some mornings are easy, but this wasn't one of those days.

My body wanted to go back to sleep so badly, it hurt all over. My chest felt sore as I breathed in the cold morning air that blew in as Tango ran out. I coughed. The cough ripped through my throat like barbed wire, and I doubled over. Once I managed to take a full breath, I straightened up and put on the teakettle. I'd been drinking hot tea with honey and lemon every morning to soothe the pain since the "eternal" cold started months before. Waiting for the kettle to whistle, I pulled out a bottle of cough medicine from the cabinet above the sink. The nasty-sweet syrup coated my throat, making it tingle. The coughing was heavier than it had ever been, and I wasn't getting any better. The nagging voice in the back of my mind kept saying, "*This is the virus.*" As I put away the brown medicine bottle, I tried to put away my thoughts.

Feeling too tired to climb the stairs, I decided to take my tea to the den. I'd watch a little TV, and curl up for a nap. I pulled the extra-large teacup to my lips to blow cool air over the steam, but I leaned in too hard. The cup banged just between my bottom lip and chin, and it felt like needles pricking into my gums.

"Tch! Ow!"

I grimaced and put the cup down on my coffee table. I went into the downstairs bathroom and pulled down my bottom lip, looking into the mirror to see what caused the pain. Three red blisters with little white heads sat in the crease that bound my inner lip to my gum. I'd had fever blisters before, but never more than one at a time. These three popped up overnight. Terror shot through my body.

"Ahhh! It's the virus!"

I dropped my head deep into the sink and threw up the little my stomach had to offer. The slimy goo was tinged with the syrupy redness of the cough medicine, but my first thought was that it was blood. I was frozen in place, my hands gripping at porcelain as I stared at the red in the sink until I couldn't see anymore. I was blinded by my hot tears, and deafened by my own cries.

There are five stages of grief. People don't only exhibit these stages for the death of a loved one. People grieve over getting divorced, getting fired—any life changing event that seems to signify the end of something. Even though everyone handles these things in their own way, psychologists have been able to make some common classifications.

I worried that I had the virus once I found out about Kevin being on the down-low, giving rides on I-95 like he was some kind of commuter bus driver. But with my worry, there was always an ounce of hope. It was just as possible that I didn't have HIV. Seeing all of those blisters in my mouth closed the door on what bit of hope I had. It happened two weeks after getting the second HIV test. Even though that test was negative, there was still a chance I was furlough converting the virus. I couldn't take the last test for two weeks and two months. However, the blisters and cold, and never-ending yeast infections were all the proof I needed. For sure, it was the end of my life as I knew it. I'd be chained to medications and fear. I'd be afraid of infecting others and afraid of getting sick. I couldn't ever be that fearless, headstrong Channa again. This was the end of me.

The first stage was **denial**.

I began to grieve.

I found myself in my closet. The time between throwing up in my downstairs bathroom and sorting through clothing in my bedroom closet was lost to me. I pushed through blouses and sweaters, talking to myself.

"Where is my purple sweater?"

I was standing there with nothing but a bra on.

"I know it's in here somewhere."

I finally found what I was looking for and shoved my hands into the sleeves and pulled the sweater over my head.

I grabbed the first skirt I saw, a red one with gray pinstripes. Stepping in, my mouth kept yammering about nothing.

"I'm going to be late. I hate to be late."

I zipped the skirt up, fastened it, and spun it around to my side. The sweater twisted with the skirt, but I didn't fix it. I slid my feet into the closest pair of shoes, my sneakers. My clean, white sneakers. I came out of my closet and went to the mirror. I picked up my lipstick, and spread it across my top lip in a thick, sloppy line and repeated the step for the bottom lip.

"Girl, there's nothing wrong with you. I don't even know why you're trippin'."

I pressed my lips together, and then puckered them.

"See, all you needed was a little lipstick. You're fine, Channa, you're OK."

I gave myself a wink in the mirror and left the room.

"One, two, three..."

I counted my steps down the stairs, but heard Tango barking outside before I reached the bottom.

"Tango! You made me lose count. I've got to start all over again."

I turned around and counted the steps back up.

"One, two, three..."

Tango barked again.

"Huh?"

I snapped out of the funk I was in and realized I was standing on my staircase looking like I escaped the fashion police. The morning's events started to play back, with the exception of how I got from the bathroom to my closet.

"Damn, I must really be stressed out. This just can't be happening to me. I've been through too much already. I'm still young, I'm not married, I don't have any kids...my whole life is ahead of me. This can't be happening to me right now. Hell, not ever."

I turned back around to go downstairs and let Tango into the house. I wasn't sure how much time had passed, but he was probably cold.

I picked him up and took him back upstairs so I could get out of the crazy outfit and take a shower.

"I'm fine. I'm just under stress."

Tango was licking my hand.

I stayed in the denial stage for a few days, keeping myself busy with shopping and reading. Sometimes I just watched old TV shows. A sickening feeling would wash over me every now and then, but I kept shrugging it off. Why should I worry, I was just fine, right? My conscious mind may have been in denial during that time, but subconsciously, I must have been a wreck. Waking up with dark circles under my eyes and a ransacked bed, I realized I had been tossing and turning all night.

Then one night, I learned what wouldn't let me sleep easily. I was having bad dreams. I remembered dozing off listening to the tranquil sounds of the new age CD I bought, that promised relaxation to all who listened. I concentrated on my breathing, and felt like weights were being removed from my chest with each exhale. The next thing I saw was my family standing around me in a hospital bed. A faceless nurse whispered to my grandmother, "All we can do is keep her comfortable."

I jerked myself awake, looking around my bedroom to make sure I was still home.

I started the CD back at track one, and took a deep breath, finding myself back in dreamland soon after. This time, I was walking across a meadow, until I came across a small crowd of people, but they all looked down. I pushed between two men in black suits and saw Carl lying in a coffin, sitting on wooden boards over an open grave.

"Carl? Is that you?" I said, reaching out and poking at his shoulder.

He opened yellow angry eyes, and yelled at me, "You killed me, you bitch!"

I jumped backwards and bumped into a guy with a tray of Styrofoam cups.

"Cup of Joe? Cup of Joe?"

He handed the cups to a few people standing around, and handed the last cup to Carl. He took a sip, gave it back, and leaned back into the coffin.

"Ahhh! Carl!" I woke up screaming, "What have I done?"

I looked around the room, expecting to find the crowd from the cemetery standing around, but I was alone in the dark.

I put my head back on my pillow and stared at the ceiling until my eyes accepted the dark. Carl just wanted to love me, and I spent many nights with him inside me, yet I pretended it was Kevin. I recalled one lovemaking session after another. When my mind turned off Carl's body and conjured up Kevin, I had no trouble coming to climax. But, was that really it? Physically, it was Carl's sensitive shaft, throbbing inside me, with his hurried strokes. Had I kept myself from getting aroused by him because I convinced myself that no one could love me like Kevin could? Were those pleasurable sexual experiences really happening between us all along? Plenty of men react to the ecstatic coos bursting forth from his lover. His confidence gets a boost, his thrusts fall into the rhythms her body is setting. His pelvis lurches down as hers rises. She tells him to go faster, go deeper. Her tone is different, letting him know that he's touched her primal being, and now she is the sexual animal he desired. Of course, he's going to comply. That's his pussy. He's going to drop his barriers, his fears, his worries of inadequacies and turn into a primal animal too.

Could Carl's shortcoming be an obstacle that I had created? Had Carl been giving me good loving all along?

I felt flushed at the thought of sex, then discomfort from knowing what it led to. Sickened by the thought of dismissing Carl all that time as I betrayed him, it really hit me that I possibly infected him. How could I do such a thing to such a wonderful person? How could I do that to myself? I had a tight grip on love and happiness, and threw it all away for Kevin's lie.

The second stage of grief was **anger**.

"Why would he lie to me? Why string me along and let me throw away a good man like Carl?"

There was no going back to sleep. The room felt like it had gotten larger and I was all alone in it. With HIV, it was likely I'd stay that way. Kevin took so much away from me, and I hated him for it. I got out of bed and went to the bathroom.

As I sat on the toilet, I banged my fist on the wall just above the toilet paper dispenser. *Bang-bang-bang!*

"Who'll want me now?"

Bang-bang-bang!

"He took away my hope, my future, MY LIFE!"

I stood up and went to the sink. Washing my hands, washing my face, I muttered to myself the whole time.

"He knew he was gay. Why did he do this to me? I want

everybody in New York to know that he's a lowdown brother on the down-low."

I dried my face, and looked in the mirror. My face was covered in dark lesions.

"Ahhh! No!"

I put my hands to my face, finding that my skin was smooth and damp.

"Huh?"

I looked back at the mirror and the lesions were gone.

"Damn you, Kevin! I hate you!"

I was screaming at my reflection and pounding on the mirror.

"You did this to me! I hate you!"

I lashed out at the mirror as if it was Kevin standing there, and I heard the first crack. Little jagged lines spread across the mirror, my fist flying, my head swung from side to side, tossing my hair into my face. I just kept screaming and punching.

"I hate you! I hate you!"

Shards of glass fell about the sink and landed into my hair. The edges of my hands were raw and bloody.

I woke up the next morning, curled up on my bathroom rug. My eyes were swollen from tears and sleep deprivation. My hands were cut up and crusted over with dry blood. I felt horrible, and I knew I wasn't ready for HIV. I couldn't go through many more nights like that.

The third stage of grief was **bargaining**.

"Lord, I know I'm not perfect. I made lots of mistakes and hurt a man who really loved me. I've learned my lesson, oh God, I learned my lesson. If you spare me from HIV, I promise I'll never do anything wrong again. The next man you send my way, I'll love only him. I won't look at another man. And I'll save myself for marriage. I'll be a born again virgin,

and I'll only hold hands and give kisses on the cheek."

I was sitting in my bathtub, soaking my body and my hands in hot water. I hoped my words would catch a ride on the steam and get to God faster.

I made a mess of things. I knew that, but I didn't deserve this, did I? I didn't want to have the virus. I didn't want some deadly virus racing through my veins. God had saved me before. Surely He had a better plan for me. He could save me from this too.

"I confess, that I let the desires of my flesh rule me. I went against the saints, lusted after a man who kept his sexuality a secret, and based our relationship on sex and lies. Please forgive me."

It was all sex, secrets, and lies. If he loved me, he wouldn't have held onto me, keeping me from finding happiness. He let me come back to him again and again, even when he knew I had another man waiting for me. And he screwed me and went back to Tyshawn. That wasn't love. He had all of me, and I had to share him with a man.

"God, haven't I suffered enough? I've lost everything once. And now, I think I've lost myself. If you can just forgive me and spare me, I'll do whatever it is you have planned for me. Just give me one more chance. I'm so sorry."

I spent the rest of the day talking to God, and promising all that I'd do for Him. I would go back to my volunteer work. I would warn teenaged girls about the need for condoms, and plead with teenaged boys to be honest with the people who gave their bodies to them. If God would only take away the fever blisters that burst and multiplied; if God would only cure my cold and yeast infection; if God would only take away my nightmares; if God would only make this last test return a negative, I would be the poster child for Christianity and do whatever I could to make the world safe from cheating brothers on the down-low.

I continued to bargain with God for over a week, but I found myself bargaining for other things, easier things.

"If You'll let this light turn green right now, I promise not to stop by the jewelry store and desire big diamonds," or, "If you'll just make this line go faster, I promise not to read the tabloids and laugh at the celebrities."

When I found myself making deals with God over the length of commercial breaks during my favorite TV shows, I knew I had to stop. *Sometimes, God just says, no.* Deja reminded me of my own words when I tried to rationalize my desires for Kevin. I got frustrated with her, but if I only I had listened to her advice...well, I didn't, did I? What use was it to play the "Shoulda, Woulda, Coulda Game" when there wasn't a damned thing I could do to change the outcome? Kevin would still be gay, and my heart would still be broken. Trying to figure out what I should have done was hopeless.

The fourth stage of grief was **depression**.

Depression is the overwhelming feeling of hopelessness.

I couldn't sleep and I didn't see the point in it. I didn't see the point in anything. I sat around and watched TV. Tango was the only thing to get me off my butt, and that was only to feed him and let him outside. When the temperature dropped at night, he would scratch at the door and bark, and I'd get up and let him in.

I rarely fixed any food, and if I did, it usually was dry cereal or some frozen leftover from months before. At first, the dirty dishes piled up in the sink. Tasty sauces stuck to the surface, dried, turned rancid, and finally molded over with green fur. But I didn't care. I dropped one dish on top of another until a mountain formed, and spilled over onto the counter. Finally, I stopped adding bowls with soup residue and plates smeared with strawberry jam to the disgrace and threw them away. Expensive dishes given to me by my mother when I moved out of her house and into this one, tossed away like Dixie cups. It was inevitable that I'd eventually run out of dishes, run out of food. It didn't make me snap out of my funk and shop. It freed me from the obligation to eat.

I didn't bathe much. I didn't brush my teeth. I didn't comb my hair. Every once in a while, my scalp would itch and I fought with matted hair to scratch the trouble spot. When the itching got to be too much, I'd take a bath, sinking beneath the water until I felt like my lungs would explode. Then I'd emerge, taking some pleasure in being able to feel anything at all, but it quickly subsided, and I'd blankly stare at the wall with renewed numbness. *I could make it so much easier if I just went back under the water and stayed there.*

One day, I sat in the tub, my shoulders weighed down by my worries. I, Channa Renée Jones, had no control over my life. I couldn't control the way Kevin loved me, or what he did without me. I couldn't control my own desires, and now I couldn't control what was going on inside of my body. My future wasn't certain, and I always liked to have a plan. I dipped under the water, closing my eyes and feeling the wet heat fill into my ears and up into my nose. The warmth was comforting. That was what I wanted. I felt the pressure build in my chest. My body struggled from the lack of oxygen. I jerked forward, breaking through the water, and gasped for air. Water dripped down my face from my wet hair, mixing in with my tears. *Why do I keep doing this to myself? This isn't the life I wanted, and I'll be damned if I go out in some hospital bed with tubes coming out of me, and strangers digging in me and at me with gloved fingers. No, I can take control of this one thing.*

I made up my mind to die under my own terms, grasping at one last string of dignity. I let the weight of my life push me down slowly. Kevin seduced me when I was on my period, not using a condom, and then the two of us sharing in the climatic cream like starving lovers. Then he did the same thing with Tyshawn Morris. He'd been taking juices from us, and served it back with his own blended cocktail. His cock's tale. I stacked the memory of Carl's face when I broke up with him on top of the Kevin drama and sunk further into the tub until the water was just under my lip. I heard the dejected tone of Carl's voice when he answered the phone the last time I spoke to him. Just knowing it was me on the other end sucked out his spirit. I hurt him once more telling him I could have infected him. I basically kicked him when he was down, and cloaked it in the guise of concern. He couldn't even talk to me after that. Imagining Carl's hatred for me pressed me further. The water was above my nose, and started to seep into the creases beneath my eyes. And then the phone rang.

I left a soggy trail of footprints from the bathtub to the telephone on my nightstand. I sat down on my unmade bed for the first time in over a week. I'd been sleeping and living on the couch in the den. The phone stopped ringing, so I sat and watched it, wondering who called but not exactly having the energy to find out.

I felt cold from the air in the room, in combination with my wet skin. I wanted to be back in the warm water, allowing it to cradle me as I'd fall into the deep sleep I longed for. Just as I made up my mind to go back to the tub, the phone rang again. I flinched as the shrill sound ripped through the peacefulness. I picked up the phone before it could ring again.

"Hello?"

My voice was raspy, and I couldn't remember the last time I spoke a word. I was consumed with an internal dialogue of despair.

"Channa? Gurl, why haven't you called me?"

It was Deja. Her voice was mixed with tones of worry,

anger, and relief.

"I was supposed to call you? I said that?"

A part of me felt like I recently spoke to her but I missed her terribly.

"When did we talk last?"

I'd lost track of date and time.

"Channa, I haven't spoken to you in weeks. You won't return my phone calls, and you told me you would tell me what was going on with you. I know it has something to do with Kevin, and I know you like to disappear for a while when you're dealing with shit, but still, this has gone on long enough."

"Oh, I didn't realize it's been that long. What day is this?"

"What? You don't know what day it is? You're scaring me."

"Tuesday?"

"Channa, it's Friday. You're way off. I'll be there in a few hours."

"It's Friday? OK, yeah, sure, it's Friday. Now, wait, what are you saying? What comes on in a few hours?"

"Gurl, you haven't understood anything I've said, have you? I've got to move some things around, but I'll be there in a few hours and I'll take care of you."

Deja rang my doorbell about four hours later. She had a suitcase and her cell phone in her hand. When I opened the door, she was dialing numbers and she looked worried.

"Deja? What are you doing here? I like your hair like that."

Her hair was in the micro-braids she told me so much about, and she had them pulled back into a French roll. She must have come from work.

Deja looked me up and down, her mouth fell open with surprise.

"Gurl, you really need to tell me what's going on."

I stepped back and let her in. I caught a glimpse of myself in the hallway mirror, and was immediately stricken with vanity. My hair was a matted, frazzled mess. I was as pale as I could get, with dark circles under my sunken eyes. My face was thin, and I pulled my bathrobe together with my bony fingers. I was emaciated. Someone could have started a "feed the hungry" campaign just for me.

"Uh, excuse the mess. I haven't been feeling well."

I let Deja follow me into the living room where I pushed aside the books and newspapers on the couch. I had filled my time with reading all different kind of journals.

"I, uh, I've been thinking of hiring a cleaning lady, but, uh, I don't know, what if she tried on my clothes and stole my jewelry?"

"Channa, just stop. Don't talk to me about cleaning ladies and jewelry. Tell me what happened."

Deja refused to sit down on the space I cleared for her. She stood with her hands on her hips and watched me until I responded.

Her eyes felt like they saw right through me. I felt so exposed, and at the same time, I wanted her to comfort me.

"I just can't, Deja. I'm too ashamed."

I dropped to the couch and put my hands over my face to hide from Deja's exploring eyes.

The fifth stage of grief was **acceptance**.

Deja knelt in front of me and took hold of my hands.

"Channa, I told you, I'm here for you. You can tell me anything."

Her eyes were warm and forgiving. I knew that I could tell her everything, and she would love me anyway. I needed her.

"Kevin was cheating on me. I walked in on him and...and a man."

Deja's jaw dropped again, but she quickly pulled it back and nodded like she understood and wasn't going anywhere.

"And, they weren't using a condom. I think I have HIV."

I had accepted it.

"Why didn't you tell me sooner?"

Deja put her arms around me and slid beside me so she could hold me close.

"You warned me about Kevin, and you warned me about using protection. I didn't listen to you, and now I'm probably going to die because of it. There isn't anything else I can do."

"Of all people, Channa, you know that having HIV isn't the death sentence it used to be. People are leading full, productive lives. *You* helped some of them do this. Your life isn't over."

Her arms were around my body, rocking and talking to me. She reminded me that I wasn't a quitter.

"Gurl, if anyone can wait ten years to get a commitment from a player like Kevin, she can hang in there with this virus. You have the knowledge, and you have the strength. You can handle this, Channa. I know you can. What's next?"

I pulled away so I could see her face.

"What do you mean, what's next?"

"Well, are you taking your medication? Are you eating right? Are you going to fight the drug companies for a cure? What?"

"Well, I have to wait to get my last test before I get a real treatment plan…"

"Your last test? What?"

"I have to wait until I test positive so I…"

"Wait! You didn't test positive yet?"

"No, the first test was inconclusive. I could be furlough converting and the antibodies won't show up until the next test."

"So, you mean to tell me there's just as good a chance that you're HIV negative?"

"There's a chance, but I doubt it. I've been sick and I have these blisters in my mouth and you know I never used condoms with Kevin."

"How do you know Kevin has HIV?"

"I don't, but he's just sticking his dick in any hole he can find, what do you think?"

"Well, I think he's a fucking asshole but still, that doesn't mean he has it and gave it to you. You've got yourself all stressed out. Look at you. You're skin and bones. Of course you're sick, when was the last time you ate anything?"

Deja ordered steamed vegetables from a Chinese food restaurant that delivered. She looked through the cabinet above my sink for a multivitamin, and tried to find a cup to put some water in. Deja never did anything half-assed, so she loaded the dishwasher with the dirty dishes from the sink, picking out the cleanest glass to wash by hand. She found the rest of my dishes in the garbage, and put them in the dishwasher too.

"I'm going to have to use a whole box of dishwasher detergent for that mess. Here, take this vitamin with some water. Then I want you to go get out of that nasty bathrobe and put on some clothes. And wrap that nest up in a scarf."

I did as I was told, and let Deja nurse my fragile mind and body back to health for the next two weeks, when I would go and get the test that would let me know one way or the other how my future would be. She told her boss that she had a family emergency and would take a few weeks off. Her fiancé knew she was worried about me, so he didn't even argue that she had to go. When the Book of Hebrews tells you about angels disguised as strangers, you best believe Deja had a halo under all those braids.

Chapter 1

I sat alone in the doctor's office. Outside, the day was sunny—like nothing would dare go wrong with such beautiful weather. But inside, the office was gray and gloomy. The walls were gray, and the chairs were gray. They were like rain clouds that were only over me, and no one else. This was the day I'd find out for sure if I had the virus.

Cough, cough.

The phlegm balled up in the back of my throat. I gagged on it and looked for a trashcan. Just then, the door opened and my doctor walked in, looking grim. I gulped. The slimy lump got caught and I gasped for air.

"Ms. Jones?"

"Here."

My doctor grabbed a white, plastic cup and a pitcher of water he had on a tray near his desk. He poured the water as I clutched my neck, my eyes pleading for his assistance. Finally, he handed me the cup, his eyes forcing calm over concern. He gave an awkward smile.

"Drink up."

I took to the water like someone who'd crossed a desert. The coolness trailed down and reminded me how cold I felt already. My doctor leaned against the edge of his desk, waiting for my full attention. I took my time meeting his apologetic gaze.

"Ms. Jones. Do you feel better now?"

"I'll let you know after you read the test results to me."

"Yes. Fine."

He opened a file and rummaged through some of the pages, but judging from his look coming in, he'd already known what was written.

"There is no easy way to tell you this..."

Oh no! Oh no!

"...I'm sorry to have to tell you..."

Oh no! No, no, no! I shut my eyes.

"...but...you've tested positive for HIV."

"NOOOOOOOO!!!" I screamed, "NO!"

Tears managed to escape through the tight squeeze of my eyelids.

"NO!"

"Channa? Channa!"

Deja called my name over and over again. I could feel her hands on my shoulders.

"Channa! Open your eyes!"

I opened my eyes, and Deja was there in her nightshirt with her hair wrapped up in a silk scarf. I wasn't in the doctor's office. I was in my bedroom.

"Deja?"

I looked around to be sure.

"Gurl, that must've been one helluva nightmare."

"Nightmare? I was dreaming?"

I looked at my alarm clock and it was 4:18. The sun hadn't even come up yet.

"Yeah. It's OK. It was just a dream. You've got yourself so stressed out. Do you want to tell me about it?"

"I was at the doctor's office, and I was HIV-positive."

"Oh Channa, we'll know for sure in a few hours. But you need to take your mind off of it until then, OK? Let's just get dressed, get some coffee and some breakfast, and talk. Tell me everything, even stuff I already know. You won't have to think about the test until you have to."

"Deja. Where? How do I begin?"

"And so, it's come full circle, I guess."

Deja and I were sitting on a park bench outside of my doctor's office. I'd just taken the Rapid Test and the truth would be ready in about twenty minutes. We'd been talking about everything that had happened in my life for the last ten years.

"I couldn't be with Andre because he was a cheater. But then I turn around and hook up with Kevin, the man who can't commit to one woman because he's gay. I hated Erica for sleeping with Andre when she knew he was engaged to me, and then I turn around and sleep with Kevin while I was with Carl. Meanwhile, I keep falling for these fake ass brothers who lead double lives. Andre supposedly has a thing for white girls, but can't bring one home to his family so that's where I came in. Kevin has a thing for men, but can't be openly gay in his career in sports, so he had me."

"Channa, you can't beat yourself up over this stuff anymore. You can't change a man. There was no way you could have known about either of them."

Deja rubbed my back.

"I guess you're right. But still, am I any better than Erica? I mean, I even called one of Kevin's women and told her that he was with me. And look at how I broke Carl's heart. I know how that feels. I am played the game like Andre and Kevin."

I had been no better.

"Stop, Channa. You're human, gurl. You're supposed to make mistakes. The thing is learning from them."

"I know. Well, Deja, I just want to thank you. You really saved me, no matter what they tell me. If I have HIV, I will do all that I can to lead a productive life and stay healthy. And if I don't have it, I'll do the same damn thing. I'm starting new."

I kept nodding my head like I was making sure I'd believe it too.

"Well, I'm glad to hear that. But, you've got some loose ends."

"What?"

I stopped my nodding and looked at her.

"Gurl, you need to talk to Kevin. He doesn't know what's going on with you, which means he's going to keep trying to find out. And if he gets back into your life…"

"No. I'm done with Kevin. I don't need to talk to him. When I cut people off, I don't want anything to do with them again."

"I know, and then you carry that stuff around and it isn't good. You need to tell him that he's hurt you, and that it's over so he won't need to come back. And you probably need to call a few other people who've done you wrong and get to the bottom of things."

"If you mean my so-called friends that bailed on me when I was paralyzed…"

"Channa, you really need to close some chapters, and yeah, you need to get everything out in the open with them too."

"Close some chapters? Deja, I'm trying to shut the book! I just want to start fresh. Today is my new chapter. It is chapter one."

I felt that Deja was right. I needed to confront a few people who'd done me wrong. I just didn't want to think about them while someone held the test result that could change my future. I did know that regardless of the results, I would be different. Having Kevin pop up in the picture wouldn't be good at all.

We got up from the bench and ventured back into the building. Deja held my hand on the elevator ride, and neither one of us spoke a word. For Deja not to rattle on about something, she had to be just as scared as I was. Suddenly, I felt like I needed to comfort her in some way. Someone needed to be the rock.

"Do you think I should get my hair braided?"

"With that big head? If it took two days for me, it's gonna take a month for you!"

We laughed and the elevator door opened.

"Gurl, I'll be right there in the waiting room. Just holler if you need me. I swear I'll break down a door to get to you."

She hugged me and we walked in.

The nurse took me to the doctor's office, and I sat on the other side of the desk waiting for him to come in. Since Deja had come to take care of me, I managed to shake the cold and my throat felt much better. One last fever blister was healing, and the yeast infection was gone. I didn't know if it meant anything. There were tons of healthy people walking around with HIV. So, I wouldn't say that I was hopeful.

The doctor came in and sat in his chair across from me.

"Ms. Jones, how have you been feeling?"

"I've been feeling much better. But, I won't be happy until I know what that paper says." I pointed at the folder that sat in front of him.

"Yes. That is what you're here for, isn't it?"

He opened the folder and scanned the page inside.

"A-ha. A-ha."

He put the folder back on the desk.

"It's good news, Ms. Jones. You've tested negative. You're in the clear."

"Oh thank God!"

I leaned forward and put my head in my hands.

"Yes, Ms. Jones. You are HIV negative, and you're going to keep it that way. Right? No more unprotected sex, and I'm sure you won't take up intravenous drugs, right?"

"Right."

I stood up and shook his hand, and went out to Deja who could tell I was fine just from the look on my face. I gave her a big hug right there in the waiting room.

When we pulled away, Deja laughed and wiped the tears out of her eyes.

"Gurl, let's get out of here before these people think we're horny-ass lesbians and tell us to get a room."

We drove back to my house and Deja packed her things to return home.

"Deja, I don't know what I would have done if you hadn't

been here."

"You'd probably be fine. You've got to give yourself more credit, Channa. You're stronger than you think."

Deja hugged me, and then got into the driver's seat.

"Well, I'll see you in a few weeks. You better get back to your fiancé before he thinks you're leaving him at the altar. I can't wait for the wedding."

Deja's wedding day was just a little over a month away. I waved as she drove off. I missed her already.

Deja was right, as usual. I needed to have a talk with Kevin. The relief I felt from the negative test result only heightened the fact that I'd been carrying around a lot of anger and stress because of his lies. I shouldn't have carried it all by myself. And more so, I needed some payback.

I sat at my kitchen table with the phone. I tried to manage my breathing so I could remain cool when I made the call. *Breathe in, Channa. Breathe out. Relax.* When I felt I was ready, I dialed.

"Hello, Kevin? This is Channa."

"Channa! What's going on? You haven't you haven't returned my calls. I've been worried sick."

"Well, come over so we can talk, and I'll end your worries."

I didn't think my voice gave anything away. I wanted to take him by surprise, just like he took me by surprise.

"Channa? What's going on? Everything was going fine and then you disappear. I haven't talked to you in months. Can't you tell me something right now?"

"No. See you when you get here."

I hung up.

I didn't get up from the table. Instead, I sat there and outlined all of the things I wanted to say to Kevin. I was going to put him on blast about screwing Tyshawn and about his lies. I would let him know what a dangerous game he's playing with all of his unprotected sex, and I was going to let him know that we were through. His sweet-talking no longer affected me, because I'd see him swapping spit and spunk with a man every time I thought about him. He could say my full name until he was blue in the face, but he'd never get any of my GP again. I knew it, and it was about time he knew it too.

By the time Kevin pulled up in my driveway, I was livid. I was at the door before he reached the top step. He had roses, a bottle of champagne, and a seductive smile. It was obvious what he was coming for, but the honey hive was closed, and his business was no longer wanted.

"Channa! Thank God you're OK."

Kevin leaned in for a kiss and I slapped the charm right off his face. *WHACK!*

He stumbled back a couple of steps, rubbing his cheek.

"Uh-uh, I'm not having it, Kevin. I haven't talked to you for months for a reason, and I'm not about to act like nothing is wrong."

Kevin stepped inside hesitantly.

"I figured something was wrong. But did you have to slap me? Really, Channa, it can't be that bad."

"Look Kevin, I saw you. I went to your office to surprise you with my bikini and when I walked in, you were with Tyshawn Morris."

"I'm always with Tyshawn Morris, or some other player, in my office. So what?"

"You were screwing him, Kevin! Don't play me. How long have you been gay?"

"What? I'm not gay. I don't know what you're talking about."

I shook my head and put my finger up giving the "wait a minute" gesture.

"Uh-uh, Kev, I told you, I saw you, so you don't have to lie like every other cheater when he gets busted. My question to you was how long have you been gay?"

"I'm not gay, Channa. And anything you've seen was probably just us blowing off steam. The last time I talked to you was during the play offs and I was stressed out."

"Stress had made happen for you to cheat on me with a man? No. Kev that doesn't just happen. You and Tyshawn must have been at it for more than just one night. That wasn't blowing off steam. You came in his face! Sound familiar? You licked the cum off his face, and kissed him just like you did to me! That wasn't just blowing off steam! You're gay."

Kevin didn't say anything.

"What's wrong Kev? Don't you want to deny it again? You told me you loved me and that you were going to cut all your little friends loose...I gave up Carl for you! Why would you do that to me when you knew good and well you're gay? You messed up my life!"

"Channa, this is why you haven't returned my calls? You think I'm gay? Look, I may have messed up, but that stuff with Tyshawn was nothing. I do love you. You know that. I gave up a lot for you too. Then you just disappear. What was I supposed to think?"

Kevin was trying to turn things around to be my fault, and he was doing a bad job at that.

"Hold up. No you didn't! You are NOT trying to say this is my fault! You can't tell me that you're not gay, because I saw you pull your dick out of his ass. You tongued him down, just slobbering all over him with all that cum between the two of you. How long have you been having sex with men?"

"Since always!"

I hit a nerve and Kevin raised his voice.

"Well then, why Kev? Why would you lead me on for years and years and not tell me that you were fucking men too?"

"Because you never asked."

Kevin said it with disgust. Like I disgusted him. I lost it.

"I never asked?"

I lunged toward him and smacked him again. SMACK!

"I hate you!"

I reached out to hit him again and he grabbed my hand.

"Don't hit me again, Channa. You act like this is all about me. What about you? It didn't matter that I was seeing anyone else, as long as I brought my dick around your way once in a while. All the times you had it in your mouth, did you ever once ask me where it's been?"

He was glaring at me, and it was clear that I didn't really know this man at all.

I pulled out of his grip and backed away from him.

"I loved you! I told myself I didn't care about the other women, but this is different."

"Why? It's just sex. You're the one I loved. Did I take anyone else to all of those VIP events you'd practically burst out of your panties for? Did I bring home anyone else to meet my mother? No! When I was ready to be with one woman, you're the one I chose. You could have it all with me. And you know it. You wanna trip over some shit you saw one night? Please, I've seen you at some pretty low points in your life and I NEVER bounced on you. You know that."

I couldn't believe he wanted to equate my paralysis with his gay fling. I reached for the crystal vase of flowers Deja put on my kitchen table to brighten my spirits, and threw it at Kevin's head. He put his hand up just in time, and connected with the vase that fell to the floor and shattered.

"Fuck you, Kevin! I was in a wheelchair. There's a difference. I had no choice in the matter. You don't *have* to stick your dick in men's asses and then come stick it in me. Do you know how dangerous that is?"

"What, will I get hit with another vase?" he sneered.

"What about HIV, Kev? Did you ever once think about me when you were screwing around? Did you ever once think that you could have brought back some disease that had the potential to kill me?"

"Channa, what are you talking about? I don't have any disease."

"Yeah, well, how do you know? We never used condoms,

and from what I saw, you weren't using one with him either. I don't know what that man has, or who else he's fucking, and I bet you don't either. I loved you, Kevin. I opened my heart to you and I trusted you. I would have done anything for you. Anything! And you put me in danger."

I started to lose my edge and the tears started to come. I sat down at the table.

"You know what? Just forget it. Go home Kevin, I don't want to see you anymore."

Kevin didn't move. He watched me for a while and then he sat at the table across from me.

"Channa, why did you wait so long to tell me about this? What's really wrong?"

"What, you being a fucking faggot and lying to me isn't enough?"

"I know you. You would have come to me when you first found out. Something kept you away. Look, I know I can't make it up to you, but if you want me to, I'll try. But, I really do love you and it was never my intention to hurt you."

I didn't say anything. I was a little surprised with this soft side showing up when he was just being so hateful moments before. Kevin stared at the bruise on his hand, the one I hit with the vase.

"Channa, you wanted to know why. Well, I don't consider myself to be gay. I love women and lately, it's just been you. The stuff with Ty has all just been something I can't quite explain. I don't want to be in a relationship with a man. It's just for recreation. It's like going out to a strip club or a boys' night out to Atlantic City. I don't remember where sex came into play, but to me, it isn't this great big betrayal you make it out to be. I guess, I knew that I had to hide it from everybody though. No team would want a recruiter who had sex with men. And you know for damn sure my parents wouldn't understand. But, I don't have to do it. I can stop. OK?"

"I can't act like it never happened, Kevin, and I can't trust that you won't do it again. And, I'll never feel safe with you again."

"Where have you been, Channa? Have you been hiding right here all along?"

"I was sick. I had a cold and an infection that wouldn't go away. The guys at the GMHC told me all about the down-low, and when I saw you and him, I just put it all together. I thought I had HIV and that you gave it to me."

Kevin's eyes almost popped out of his head.

"OK. Well?"

"The first test was inconclusive. I had to be retested, and had to wait three months. The coughing just got worse, and then I started getting these blisters in my mouth. Oh, and then there were the nightmares, and the time when I hallucinated lesions all over my face. I was sure I was furlough converting. I've been in living hell."

"What's the verdict, Channa?"

Kevin couldn't bring himself to look at me. I realized he was scared. If I had the virus, he knew he had it too.

"Kevin, I don't want to tell you what my test result was. I want you to go get tested and for you to feel what I felt. I want you to sit on your bathroom floor covered in broken glass and beg God to be spared. I want the weight of worry and hopelessness to sit on your shoulders and make you want to end it all."

"Channa, no, you didn't..."

"Try to kill myself? Well, all you need to know is that I'm still here today, and I've never been angrier at you, or felt more hurt by you in all the years I've known you. Take the way I look right now; the bags under my eyes, the clothes falling off from all the weight I lost, and how disgusted and defeated I appear, and put it on your trophy shelf. You've earned this prize, and I hope you remember me every day as you wait for your test results to come back. Now, I'd like for you to leave. I'm tired."

Telling him that I was HIV negative would have been too easy. He wouldn't learn anything, and he'd still be irresponsible until he really did get the virus and spread it around. And, quite frankly, I was still pissed.

"You know what, Kevin? You're really a joke. You act like hot shit with your big car, and your big dick, and your big job that's supposed to pick up the tab for everything in your life. And then you hide your little boyfriends behind a woman, hoping no one will find out and knock down your sandcastle. Man, you think you're a player. You're just playing yourself. Get out! Lose my number. Go figure out what you really want in your life."

Kevin looked shocked, like I'd reached across the table and slapped the shit out of him again.

"Channa, I know you're mad, I'm sorry. I didn't mean for any of this to happen. I hope you're OK and when you calm down, you'll give me a call."

I leaped up out of my seat.

"Call YOU? What for? A movie premiere? The opening of a new club? Uh, save it for your boyfriend. I'm done with you!"

Kevin got up and headed for the door.

"Well, I guess this is it. Ten years and I'm out just like that Channa? I'm not even going to argue. I'm going to wish you the best of luck and leave. If you need me, you know where to find me."

"Uh huh, all up in Tyshawn's ass!"

I slammed the door as soon as he stepped out. Another major weight was lifted. I was finally free from Kevin's reign. I was happy, but I was lonely, and he had nothing to do with it.

I noticed that he left the bottle of champagne on my kitchen counter. There was only one person with whom I wanted to drink it. I picked up the phone and dialed the familiar number.

"Hello?"

The voice was apprehensive, but the sweetness behind it couldn't be hidden.

"Carl? It's Channa."

My heart started to race in my chest. He probably hated me.

"Yes, Channa, I know it's you."

"Um, yeah. Ha-ha, of course you do. Carl, I bet you don't want to hear from me again, and you have every reason, I know. I just wanted to let you know that I tested negative. I didn't know if you were waiting and worrying like I was."

"No, I tested negative. But thank you for letting me know. Bye."

Carl was about to hang up the phone.

"NO! Carl! Carl?"

"Yes?"

"Oh, I thought you were hanging up. Um, Carl, do you remember telling me that if you love someone to let them go and if they come back they're yours?"

Carl sucked his teeth. I figured he didn't want to be reminded of that night.

"Yeah, I said something like that."

"Well, you let me go, and now I want to come back."

My voice started to shake, I was so nervous, but I had to give it a shot.

"I'm ready to love you, Carl. Is there still a chance?"

Carl got silent, but I could hear him breathing.

"Carl?"

Carl let out a long, hard sigh.

Epilogue

I stand naked before the full-length mirror as a woman, a perfect woman. Perfect in my fearlessness about looking upon my naked form. Perfect in my ability to stand still and move confidently through rose colored glass and glass which is not tainted. Perfect in every flaw and scar that others see as faults, but I see as a story. Perfect. I am amazed that I can stand here naked and know perfection when I see it.

My hair reveals ten strands of gray mixed in with my long, brown locks which fall seductively on my bare shoulders. One gray hair for each of the ten years of earth-shaking ecstasy and unforgettable disruptive disappointments. I won't dye them. They are my medals, testifying that I loved, I lost, and I survived.

My eyes aren't only rain-soaked windows from my soul; they are witnesses of loving people and ugly lies presented by fair-weather friends and lovers. My lush lids blink for the lessons my eyes have learned, and though I may not see what the lettered chart wants, I know these eyes are too perfect to risk having surgery. Though unnoticed by most, tiny lines fan out from around my eyes, and I can read the laughter and excruciating pain of the body, and of the heart, that placed them there. I am thankful that joy is always restored. Just like in Sunshine, I can always see through the rain.

My full lips raise mountains because I can smile, even though things have happened in my life that would leave-most in unfathomable despair. I can speak fiercely, kindly, intelligently, and spiritually without fail.

Perfect are my strong arms that have pulled me through a battle zone in my homeland. I have wrapped them around lovers and loved ones, and used them to cuddle little lost ones that needed to feel security. When faced with the bottomless pit of despair, God gave me arms and hands of strength to hold on. I take them and slide them down through the crevice of my breasts, and over my flat stomach, and onto my full hips. My soft skin is sensitive to the touch and I am reminded that I am alive; I can feel the sensation where there once was numbness. These hips remain my symbols of womanhood, as they've enticed and participated in such pleasure, never losing firmness through the pain and feelings of everything and nothing at all. I can make them sway to the memory of beats heard long ago, and they can find the rhythm of passion-filled nights with transforming thoughts that take me back. It is truly a miracle that I can move them, and I choose to move them in miraculous ways! Thank God!

Life puts you through trials and tribulations for a reason. You are supposed to learn and grow from them. I had to learn that what I wanted wasn't always what I needed. I also needed to be thankful for what I had, and what I have, or I'll lose it. So I'm not 22 anymore, I'm older and wiser. I know that designer labels, cars, and an occupation mean nothing at the end of the day when I am alone and naked, and all there is to see is "me." How many people can truly face themselves? I had to, and I didn't always like what I saw. But when I consider the inner strength that brought me through, I'm proud of me, and that's a beautiful thing.

So, say what you will, but I know I'm perfect. Perfect the way God wants me to be, naked before this mirror. My body once swollen and bruised sentenced to slumping without any hope of walking, now stands on two feet. I have traversed many miles, some without ever touching the ground. And before I slide them into new pumps with two-inched heels and kiss my skin with fine fabrics, I turn to my side just like I used to. I straighten my back with a new found pride and I give thanks for another day.

Book Club Discussion

1. Why is Channa in love with a man that has not offered her a "true" commitment?

2. Why was Channa drawn to Kevin Dean Walker and not to Carl?

3. What are your thoughts on the effects of women not having both parents within their homes during childhood?

4. Why do women often look at "safe-sex" as something that is done with a new man vs. practicing "safe-sex" when having sex in general? Is there such a thing as "safe" sex partner? If so, share your thoughts with the book club group.

5. Was Arnelle a good influence on Channa when they were in New Orleans? Do you blame Arnelle for Channa's mistake in tricking Kevin into a relationship? Certainly you know a woman or women who have "tricked" a man into a commitment. Share your thoughts on these women and if they have had long-lasting relationships with the men they have "tricked."

6. Why are nice guys always finishing last, and the bad guys are always first? Do you feel that women like to be mistreated?

7. Do you believe that magic can really make a person do something that they would not naturally do on their own? Have you ever experienced anyone or yourself being a victim of magic? How did you deal with the discovery?

How to contact the Author

Email: Queenbeeoffiction@ImperiousPublishing.com

Sherrance Henderson, a.k.a Queenbee of Fiction™
1539 Merritt Blvd. Box 110, Baltimore, MD 21222

Please feel free to send Sherrance Henderson your thoughts, suggestions, and any feedback. All emails and all letters will be answered.

Q & A with Sherrance Henderson

Q. The Ten Year Date is a tale of a woman's rocky and tenuous relationship with a man for ten years. What made you choose this topic?
A. *The Ten Year Date* is the second part of a trilogy. My first novel was *Sunshine Has Rain*. In *The Ten Year Date*, our protagonist, Channa Renée Jones, has been in a relationship with one man for ten years without a commitment. This is not a new, or unusual occurrence among women. I felt that this story would prick the conscience of women everywhere who have, or are experiencing a "Ten Year Date;" a long, dead-end relationship that is going nowhere. It's a message for women to move on if your man doesn't want to commit, or if he doesn't want to get married. This is a wake-up call for women everywhere who are suffering from the inertia of the perpetual "date."

Q. Did you have a ten year date and use this experience as the basis for your novel?
A. Not personally, no. But I do have a multitude of girlfriends who are experiencing The Ten Year Date, now, and it's very serious. It is so serious, so disheartening, that I felt it had to be addressed.

Q. Channa Renée Jones is a woman who is living with a Spinal Cord Injury, like yourself. Why did you choose a woman with a disability to be your protagonist?
A. I wanted to show readers that women are not picture perfect. Life just doesn't work that way. Perfect is not the norm. There aren't too many books out there that deal with a protagonist or a heroine that has a physical disability, but lives a full and rewarding life. Heck, Channa has two men in this book. It just goes to show you that she's not missing out on anything. She is a reflection of a typical woman, and lives the life of a typical woman. She just walks a little slower.

Q. Is there a little bit of Channa Renée Jones in you?
A. There's a little bit of Channa Renée Jones in all of us. I think a lot of Authors who write fiction sprinkle a dash of reality into their pages. This is how you create three dimensional characters and characterizations. I think how Channa would react in specific situation, is how a lot of us would react if we were in the same place. There's a little bit of Channa Renée Jones in all of us.

Q. In The Ten Year Date, Channa discovers that her love of ten years is a down - low homosexual that might be HIV positive. Why is this a big issue within the African -American Community?

A. The issue of men creeping on the down-low is not limited just to the African-American community. This is an issue that affects every community, regardless of color, race, or ethnicity. It just so happens that the media spotlight is on the African American citizenry. The down-low phenomenon is without prejudice, every group can relate to it. However, since the majority of reported, new HIV cases pertain to Black women, I will tailor my response to this issue. Our community is imperiled with many societal ills: men in and out of the prison system, men growing up without fathers, women raising "boys," illegal drug usage, undisclosed homosexual relations between men, the list is long.

In a nutshell, women, no matter who they are, need to choose their partners carefully. Being college educated, looking good, and having a great job is not going to be enough. It should not be a prerequisite for women to disregard "safe-sex." Women have to be their own advocates, protect themselves, and investigate the man they are going to be intimate with. Proper judgment and good common sense can work wonders, JUST GET THE MAN TESTED! Regardless, do not feel empowered to have unprotected sex until you can say for sure that your man is not sleeping with anyone else.

Q. Why did you choose to self publish?

A. Well, I wouldn't describe myself as a "self-publisher." I am an Author under Imperious. I own my own publishing company with several authors and several books in the Imperious Publishing catalogue. So am I still considered a self-publisher, even if I publish the work of other Authors? After *The Ten Year Date*, I will only publish one more book under my name. It will be the last book under the Sunshine Has Rain trilogy. After this, I will focus solely on publishing the work of other Authors.

Q. Has it been difficult placing your titles in mainstream retail locations?

A. It has been difficult placing my books in Black-owned retail locations. I thought that would have been the simplest of tasks, but apparently, it isn't. I don't know why. Maybe they are inundated with a lot of African-American titles, I just don't know. Oddly enough, I have had many successes getting my titles placed in mainstream locations.

Q. Where are your books currently sold?

A. Wal-Mart, Barnes and Noble, Waldenbooks, Borders, and wherever else books are sold.

Order Form

Sunshine Has Rain **Qty.** _____ **Price each:** $14.90 **Total:**__________

The Ten Year Date **Qty.** _____ **Price each:** $15.25 **Total:**_________

Subtotal:__________

+ 4.05 (S/H)

Total: ________

Ship To:
Name: ____
Address:______________________________________
____
City: ____
State: ______ **Zip:** ___________
Email: (optional) ____________________________

****CORRECTIONAL INSTITUTIONS ONLY****

Sunshine Has Rain **Qty.** _____ **Price each:** $10.00 **Total:**__________

The Ten Year Date **Qty.** _____ **Price each:** $10.00 **Total:**_________

Subtotal:__________

+ 4.05 (S/H)

Total: ________

Ship To:
Inmate #: _______________________
Inmate Name: _________________________________
Address:______________________________________
____
City: ____
State: ______ **Zip:** ___________

Also available wherever books are sold.

Send Checks or Money Orders (made payable to Imperious Publishing) to:

Imperious Publishing
174 Washington Street, Suite 3,
Jersey City, NJ 07302

Pay by Credit Card:
Name on Card: ____________________________________
Billing Address: __________________________________
Phone: ____
Card Type (check one): MC___VISA___DISC___AMEX___
Card Number: _____________________________________
Expiration Date: _______/_______
Security Code: _______________

IMPERIOUS
PUBLISHING